TARNISHED

RILEY EDWARDS

1

"Motherfucker!"

The low, aggravated rumble slipped out before I could stop it.

"You wanna tell her or should I?"

I dropped my binos and looked at Matt. His pissed-off scowl was a far better sight than watching King Douchebag snort a line of coke off a whore's double Ds on the balcony of a hotel room like he was the star in a bad Eighties action flick. And the whore was a whore in the sense he'd paid for the prostitute's services which apparently included blow as well as blowjobs.

The "her" was Lauren Saunders. Sweet, shy, sexy Lauren.

The "motherfucker" was her boyfriend, Guy Stevens. The dude was a tool. Lauren was way too good for the jackass and that was before Matt and I caught him with his face in a pair of tits that were most certainly not Lauren's.

"I'll tell her."

"Logan, she's not gonna appreciate learning her man's stepping out on her. Combine that with him snorting coke and her head might explode."

"She can't get more pissed at me," I reminded Matt.

My jaw clenched as the memories of my last interaction with Lauren assailed me. She was right pissed-off when she stomped away after calling me an asshole for the hundredth time.

"Yeah, well, her being pissed and what she's gonna feel when she learns what Guy's been up to are two vastly different things. She's gonna be hurt and embarrassed and you better believe she's gonna shoot the messenger. Which, now that I'm thinking on it, maybe no one should tell her while she's on Triple Canopy property and close to an arsenal of heavy artillery."

What *had* Guy been up to?

That was the million-dollar question, literally. What the hell was the moron doing in Atlanta four hours away from where he lived? At the same hotel as the drug dealer we were tracking was staying, in the same city where a million-dollar deal was going to go down? Using a whore bought from another scumbag we were tracking?

I ignored Matt's comment—though I thought it was smart to keep Lauren away from all weapons; for a shy little thing, she had an explosive temper. Unfortunately for me, seeing her pissed and ranting was a serious turn-on. Lauren might be reserved but she was no pushover. The woman wasn't light, she was *fire*. And when she caught, her blaze scorched. And I must've turned into a masochist because I needled her whenever I could to watch her burn knowing she'd never be mine. I did whatever I could do to get two minutes of her attention.

"Long drive to get a blowjob," I noted.

"Quite the coincidence that blowy's coming from one of Frank's girls."

Seriously? *Blowy*? I shook my head in disgust.

"Brother, if you ever say the word 'blowy' again I'm kicking you in the nuts."

Matt's smile told me he was wholly unaffected by my threat. His laugh punctuated it. And the wave of his hand dismissed it.

"Frank's known to give freebies to his associates. A perk of doing business with a pimp. He's also known for having the highest-priced ass in Georgia. Guy *supposedly* works in computer networking. No way in hell he's got five-grand an hour to blow on a hooker."

It was the *supposedly* that had my gut churning.

"Anyone run a background check on him?" I asked, knowing I hadn't.

"Not that I know of."

That was a mistake. We had the resources; someone should've run the asshole when he started dating Lauren. She worked at Triple Canopy. She was one of us and there wasn't a single employee of TC that liked Guy.

The men thought he was a tool and I heard some of the women complain he gave them the creeps. Yet no one but me had said a word to Lauren about not liking the douche. Anytime I'd voiced my opinion in the last few months it had started an argument. The last one being a month ago at Liberty and Drake's wedding.

"Do you have what you need?" I asked Matt, gesturing at the digital camera.

"Yep."

"Then let's get out of here and get back to the warehouse."

"Listen, Logan, let me tell Lauren."

"She already hates me." The veracity of that statement coated my tongue with a layer of grit, making it hard to swallow. "It's better coming from me so she can turn to the rest of you when she falls apart."

"The last thing she feels for you is hate, you stubborn asshole."

I needed Lauren to hate me. I needed her to despise the very sight of me. I needed her to cast her beautiful eyes at me in disgust. I needed her strong because when she was near me, I was weak.

"Then me telling her that her man's stepping out on her should do the trick."

"You're not—"

"Leave it, Matt," I warned.

"Stubborn asshole," he muttered.

Better a stubborn asshole than a wife-beating moth-erfucker.

2

My body ached. Top to toe, every muscle screamed. I needed a hot bath, BENGAY, and a shot of vodka to dull the pain. Unfortunately, I didn't have vodka.

I slammed my front door and limped across my small living room, barely making it to my couch before I collapsed. My phone rang and I used what little strength I had left to dig it out of my purse still strapped over my shoulder.

The caller ID flashed Quinn Walker's name and I groaned before I connected.

"The answer is no," I said as my greeting.

"I'm guessing Addy didn't take it easy on you."

"Your sister's the Devil."

"I told you to tell her no," Quinn huffed.

My mind filled with Adalynn's sparkling green eyes as she demanded another mile on the exercise bike. She'd called it a "cool down". I called it torture. Never again was I agreeing to work out with her.

Never.

Every part of me hurt.

"Lesson learned. From now on my answer is no, to everyone."

"Well, that sucks. I guess I'll have to give my extra ticket to Firefly to Sawyer."

Funny how the mention of my favorite music festival made the muscle ache subside. And I didn't know who this Sawyer person was, but they were shit out of luck.

"How'd you get tickets? They sold out the first day."

"My dad knows the guy running security for the event."

Of course, Jasper Walker knew a guy; he knew everyone in Georgia and the surrounding states.

"Take me, please."

"Don't be a dork, I'm taking you. The festival's this weekend," she reminded me. "You think you'll be up for walking around all day?"

I had two days to recover and even if the concert was tonight I could rally.

"Um, yes!"

"Is Guy still away on business? I only have two tickets."

Quinn was the only person who acknowledged I had a boyfriend. The men I worked with made it no secret they didn't like Guy. Everyone except Logan was polite about it. But then, Logan was rarely polite about anything. In the beginning, my friends were supportive. Delaney, Addy, Liberty, Hadley, and Quinn all understood I needed to move past my ridiculous crush on Logan. But right after Liberty and Drake's wedding, something changed. None of them said anything, however, at times it felt like they were disappointed I'd given up on Logan.

So now Quinn was the only person who uttered my boyfriend's name while the rest of the women avoided all mention of him. I had to admit, that stung. I didn't think Guy was the man I'd end up spending the rest of my life with, but I enjoyed his company and he didn't pressure me into sleeping with him. Something that after three months of dating would've been the next step in a committed relationship. Something I'd put the brakes on but couldn't put my finger on why—and I refused to acknowledge that Logan could've been the reason I was holding back. It wasn't fair to Guy and I'd promised myself I'd work through my feelings while he was on his business trip. He'd be home in a few days and I still didn't have answers. Hell, I wasn't even sure what questions I had. But something just felt off.

"Yeah, he's in California through the weekend. His flight doesn't get in until Monday night."

"Then you won't object to brunch with the girls on Sunday."

I loved brunch with the girls. But this time when Quinn mentioned it my tummy clenched thinking about the awkwardness.

"Yeah, that sounds great, too," I semi-lied.

On one hand, it sounded wonderful spending time with my friends. On the other, it almost felt like an ambush. I knew one or all of them had something to say about Guy but they were trying to be gentle with me. Everyone who worked at Triple Canopy handled me like I needed a fluffy bed of cotton to cushion any falls I might take.

There was a knock at my door and I groaned at the thought of having to get up.

"I gotta go, someone's at the door."

"Check the peephole," Quinn unnecessarily reminded me.

"Yes, mother," I chirped.

"You won't be so sassy when you check your peephole one day and are happy you didn't open your door to a serial killer."

"And I'd know he was a serial killer because..."

"They wear shirts that say, I kill and mutilate stupid women who don't check their peepholes."

"Right. Did your dad teach you that?"

"Nope. My mom. My dad taught me how to turn the tables and be the one mutilating and dismembering."

There was another knock, this one impatient.

"Lauren," Quinn's voice warned.

"Yes. I'll check the peephole."

"Bye, see you tomorrow."

Quinn disconnected and I tossed my phone on the coffee table, groaning as I pushed myself to standing. My abs and thighs protested and as I slowly made my way to the door my calves cramped.

I took a deep breath and fought back the curse that was dying to spill out. I stopped at the door and leaned in to check the peephole.

My insides froze, then they burned.

"Go away!"

"I need to talk to you, Ren," Logan called back.

No, now my insides burned. Logan was the only one who called me Ren. The stupid nickname was not a shortening of my name. It was born from him catching me working at the TC gym wearing a Ren and Stimpy tee.

I loved that he called me Ren just as much as I hated it.

"Go. Away."

"Open the door or I'll open it."

"Why are you such an asshole?"

Logan didn't answer. The doorknob twisted and the

door crept open. As quickly as my protesting muscles would allow I moved back before the door hit me.

"Get out and go away, Logan. I'm not in the mood for your bullshit."

I hobbled back to the couch and whimpered as I sat back down.

After some deep breathing and a good mental scolding on my stupidity, I chanced a look at the most irritatingly handsome man I'd ever laid eyes on. He wasn't leaving. No, not Logan. He didn't do anything I asked. It was his way or the highway. He controlled every interaction. Every damn thing was on his terms on his timeframe.

So. Annoying.

"What happened?"

"I don't know what happened, you tell me. You're the one who barged in here saying you needed to talk."

His stupid, beautiful, hazel eyes narrowed as he stalked closer.

"Why are you limping, what happened?"

"Addy happened. Now, why are *you* here?"

"Addy?"

"Yes, Logan. Addy. You know, Adalynn Walker. Our boss's sister. Hadley's evil twin. The sadist who talked me into working out with her."

The stiffness in his shoulders fled and he visibly relaxed. What a joke. Logan Haines didn't give the first two shits about me.

"We need to talk about Guy Stevens," he announced.

My spine went straight and my back cramped at the same time, making me wince.

"You're totally dehydrated, Ren. Did you drink any water today before you worked out?"

"Get out!"

I wasn't talking to him about my water intake, mostly because I hated water so I knew he was right. I also needed to get up and get an Aleve before the pain got worse. But more importantly, I was not talking to him about Guy.

No freaking way.

"I need you to listen to me. He's not a good guy—"

Not this shit again.

"Stop." I got to my feet, and with the anger now pumping in my veins, the pain barely registered. "I'm not listening to this shit again. I don't care why you don't like him but he's a good man. He treats me with kindness and respect. There's nothing you're gonna say to me that's gonna make me change my mind."

"Where is he?"

"None of your business."

"Tell me, Ren, where'd he tell you he was going? Because if it's not Atlanta then he fucking lied."

Atlanta?

Logan, Matt, Brady, and Trey were just in Atlanta. I know because I booked their hotel rooms.

"Guy's not in Atlanta, he's in California."

"He sure as fuck is not in California. He's in Atlanta staying at the Imperial."

That didn't make any sense. I talked to Guy early this afternoon. It was morning for him and he was getting ready to go into meetings all day so he called to say hello before he got busy. See? Totally thoughtful. And yesterday he called me as I was getting into bed to say goodnight before he had a late dinner. We talked for thirty minutes about how horrible the traffic was and how he couldn't wait to get back to the Georgia humidity because it was better than the Southern California smog.

"You're a liar. I want you to leave."

Everything about Logan softened.

Every. Thing.

I'd never seen his eyes so gentle. This new look made him look a little less predatory. My heart rate picked up and instinct told me to brace. I didn't like anything about the way he was looking at me—almost guilty, sad, empathetic.

"Ren, babe, I'm not lying to you. Matt and I saw Guy at the Imperial last night."

"That's impossible."

"Guts me to tell you this but he wasn't alone."

Wasn't alone?

"What do you mean he—"

"He was with a woman."

Time stood still.

Logan's eyes latched onto mine and I was right—empathy, clear as day.

No. I had to be reading him wrong. Guy wouldn't cheat on me. No way, not when he was the one making all the effort. He was the one who called me more than I called him. He put the work in and had hounded me until I agreed on a date. Maybe hounded wasn't right, but he'd chased me. Told me I was beautiful and funny and he loved spending time with me. He was always pushing for more dates. Hell, it was his idea to be exclusive. I wasn't stupid; I knew he'd suggested it so I'd know he was serious about being with me to get me into bed sooner rather than later. I also knew men cheated but why would Guy chase me if he wanted to screw other women?

But I haven't slept with him and it's been months. Was that why he was okay to wait? He had women on the side to take care of his needs?

"What woman?"

"Let's sit down and talk about—"

"No, Logan. Just say what you have to say."

He flinched—actually flinched like he was uncomfortable.

What in the hell?

"Okay, Ren. As you know, the team was in Atlanta setting up surveillance on a warehouse. Matt and I tracked a car leaving to the Imperial. We didn't know who was driving until we saw Guy valet the car."

"That doesn't make sense. You were there because you got a lead on Lucky. Lucky sells drugs. Guy doesn't do drugs. I know this because one time we were leaving a movie and there was a group of teenagers smoking pot in the parking lot and he walked us the long way to his car because he gets drug tested for work and can't take any chances."

Logan's jaw clenched and the corners of his eyes crinkled. Empathy was turning into impatience and I didn't give a rat's ass if he was getting pissed. I was sick and tired of this game.

"Matt was right, he should've told you," Logan mumbled. "It never occurred to me you wouldn't believe me. I figured you'd be pissed at whoever told you and since you already don't like me..." Logan let that last sentence dangle in the air.

But that was the problem. As frustrating as Logan was, as pig-headed, as bossy, as arrogant, as many times as he'd pushed me away I couldn't hate him. I wanted to. I'd tried. Yet the stupid part of me saw something inside of him— pain, darkness, despair—and I wanted to fix him. I wanted to make him smile. I wanted to make him happy. I wanted to make him fall in love with me the way I'd fallen in love with him.

I can't fix him.

Right before my eyes, Logan transformed back to his

normal dickish self. Gone were any vestiges of gentleness and kindness. He was back to hard and cynical.

"I didn't want to do it this way. I wanted to soften this for you so it sucks I gotta lay it out for you. Bottom line is your man was with a prostitute. Not only was he with her he was snorting coke with her. We didn't have time to watch the whole show. We got what we needed and we left. You need proof." Logan held up his phone and shook it. "You wanna see your man getting a blowjob from a pro I got the pictures. I don't know if he fucked her after that but at five grand an hour I'd say he didn't waste the fifty minutes he had left on chitchat."

I recoiled from Logan's venomous words but it was too late—they'd already seeped into my skin. My calves hit the couch and I plopped down feeling sick to my stomach. And confused. So confused.

"I wanna see the pictures," I told him.

"Fuck, Ren, seriously? You think I'd lie to you?"

Actually, no, I didn't think he'd make up a story as elaborate as this. And when I wasn't pissed at Logan I could admit he'd never lied to me. He was always honest even when the truth scalded my heart. From the beginning, he'd told me love wasn't real and only a fool believed otherwise. It didn't matter that his friends had found it, that they loved deeply, that they were happy. Logan still didn't believe. That was his excuse for pushing me away. Twice I'd gathered the courage to proposition him. Twice he'd told me he would never touch me. I'd gone as far as telling him I wasn't looking for anything other than sex. He'd scowled and snarled at me when he told me I was too good for a quick fuck and a shove out the door. Logan was right; normally I had more self-respect but when it came to him I was desperate.

Now, after this—Guy cheating on me after he'd

convinced me I meant something to him—I was beginning to think Logan was right about a lot of this. Love was a fool's game. Not that I loved Guy, but I thought that was what we'd been working toward.

"I just need to see for myself."

"Why?"

Great question.

"I don't know why, Logan. I just do. Give me the damn phone."

After a long scathing perusal of my face, he finally closed the distance and handed me his phone. I looked down at the locked screen then back up at him.

"You sure?"

Was I sure I wanted to see the man I'd been dating for months with his dick in another woman's mouth? No, I wasn't sure I wanted to see that. But I needed to.

"Yes."

"Zero-eight-two-four."

Holy shit, Logan gave me the code to unlock his phone.

With surprisingly steady hands I tapped the numbers on the screen.

"Top row, last app is a red square. Hit that." I did as I was told and when the application opened I needed another password. "Zero-six-one-zero."

File folders appeared, the first one labeled 'Guy Stevens.' I tapped on his name and didn't have to wait long.

Guy on what looked like a balcony, sitting in a chair, his head tipped back, no shirt on, and a naked woman on her knees in front of him. I didn't have to see the act to know what she was doing.

My stomach clenched and I swiped the screen.

Another image. Guy had his hand in her hair like he was guiding her mouth. I swiped again and the couple had changed positions. The woman was lying naked on a lounger. One of Guy's hands was between the woman's legs, the other held a bill rolled up to use like a straw, white powder on the prostitute's massive boob.

My brain revolted but I swiped again. The makeshift straw was gone, Guy's hand was still between her legs, and he was licking her breast where the powder had been.

I closed the app. I saw everything I needed to see.

Fucking liar.

Piece of shit.

My heart stuttered then it hardened and after that, I built a wall. It would take time to fortify it. Maybe days or months or years before it turned to stone. But that was what I needed to do, what I was going to do.

I held up Logan's phone but he didn't take it.

"Ren, honey—"

Fuck him.

"Take it, Logan. Then tell me you told me so and get the fuck out."

"I told you so?"

He sounded puzzled and I couldn't imagine why.

"Love's bullshit, right? It's not real and only an idiot would think it was. You were right, about *everything*. Happy now?"

"Fuck no, I'm not happy. I never wanted you to get hurt."

"Yeah, see, I'm not hurt. I didn't love him. That's the blessing in this; I found out he was an asshole before I could give myself to him and I saved myself a trip to the clinic to get an STD test. Blessing number two I suppose. But really the good news about all of this is it showed me you have the right idea. No attachments. It's safer that way. Be the user before you can get used."

"Ren—"

"Stop calling me that stupid pet name. I'm not your lover, I'm not even your friend. We work together and that's all. My name's Lauren. Not Ren or babe or honey."

"I'm not your friend?"

God, why did he have to look so damn hurt when I knew he didn't care?

I couldn't take another minute of this. I needed him to leave. I surged to my feet, forcing Logan to take a step back or risk me touching him and I was intimately aware he *never* wanted me to touch him.

"Take it!" I tossed the phone, leaving him no choice but to catch it. "Now go."

"Ren, please, honey, talk to me."

Fire lit in my chest and singed my windpipe as I exhaled and charred my lungs with every breath.

I couldn't break down in front of him. I couldn't let him see how affected I was.

I hated it was Logan who saw Guy cheat. I hated he knew my humiliation. I hated he'd been right all along. I hated that no matter how hard I tried I couldn't stop thinking about all the things he'd never give me.

"I have nothing to say to you, Logan."

If he wasn't leaving I was. I turned and as calmly as I could even though I wanted to sprint to my bedroom, I walked. I gently closed the door, turned the meager lock he could pick in two seconds flat, and made my way across my room.

Not until I was behind another locked door, in the shower with icy cold water pounding on my back, did I let the first tear fall.

The worst part was I wasn't crying because Guy Stevens was a slimy piece of dog shit. I wasn't even crying because I was sad. My tears were frustrated, angry, and pitiful. Like a two-year-old, I cried over what I'd never have. The one man I wanted didn't want me—not even physically. And after Guy's shit-tastic lesson that was all I had left to offer.

I was thirty-four years old—and my heart was closed for business.

3

"Yo," Matt greeted from the doorway. "Are you coming?"

I looked at my friend's smiling face and I wondered what had him so happy. The last week had been shit. No, the last three months since Lauren had started dating The Weasel had been fucking torture. Watching her smile at her phone while she texted that bastard had given me heartburn. Hearing her make plans with the fucker had made my blood boil. And the few times I'd seen them together had me plotting murder.

I knew she'd ended it with Guy and without me having to say anything to her, she didn't give him the real reason. Lauren was smart, she'd worked at TC longer than me, she understood operational security. From what I'd heard from Brady, my friend and co-worker, who'd heard it from his wife Hadley, Guy was still texting Lauren asking what he could do to change her mind. The creep had another few days, then he'd be getting a visit from me to convey just how done Lauren was with his lying, cheating ass.

What had not happened in the last nine days had me getting more and more irritated by the hour. Lauren refused to speak to me. She did her job, she gave one-word answers when I asked her work-related questions, but walked away if I tried to ask something personal. But that wasn't the worst of it. She was different. The shy, happy receptionist with a quick smile and quicker comeback was gone. I wouldn't call her sullen because she wasn't sulking. But the old Lauren was gone.

I fucking hated it almost as much as I'd hated hearing her say that I'd been right and love wasn't real. Or perhaps I hated her telling me I wasn't her friend more than anything else she'd said that night.

"Hello, earth to Logan," Matt said and snapped his fingers.

"What time are you going?"

"Now."

I glanced at the right corner of my laptop and damn if it wasn't already close to seven. Two hours after I normally left work.

"I'm gonna finish this up and I'll meet you there. Balls, right?"

Matt's mouth quirked like the juvenile idiot he was and nodded.

"The owner missed a golden opportunity, shoulda named it Balls Deep."

"It's a pool hall, not a porn set," I reminded him.

"So? Think of all the marketing opportunities," he said and shook his head.

"I think you should buy it then. Rename it Balls Deep and market to your heart's content."

"You know what?" Matt started with a swift jerk of his chin. "That's a good idea. I just might."

God knows Matt Kessler could afford to buy Balls and still have more money than he'd know what to do with. The guy didn't need to work—he was loaded with a capital L. Too bad his friends didn't suffer from the same predicament, forcing Matt to keep his job if for no other reason but to stave off boredom.

"Go on, Money Bags, leave so I can finish up."

I waited for Matt to push off the doorframe and head out but he didn't. And he was no longer smiling. As a matter of fact, his serious-as-a-heart-attack look told me I wasn't going to like what he had to say.

"Your mom and sisters are coming next week."

Jesus. I didn't want to think about my mother's upcoming visit. I really didn't want to think about the reason why she was coming down to Georgia from Michigan. And I had zero interest in playing nice with my mother's boyfriend. The only part of the visit I was looking forward to was sizing the asshole up.

"Yep."

"That's it? Just *yep*?"

"What, do you want their itinerary?"

"Don't be a dick," Matt sighed.

"Then drop the subject. I don't want to talk about it."

Matt eyed me skeptically and I knew it was a pipedream he'd actually do as I asked when he stepped farther into my office.

"I'm gonna say one thing then I'll leave," he announced. "You know not all men hit women, Logan. You fucking *know* Luke would never touch Shiloh in anger. Drake would never hit Liberty. Brady would never beat Hadley. Trey would die before he let anything ever hurt Addy again. Brice would—"

"Christ. I get it." I cut Matt off before he could list every man I'd served with or my current co-workers.

"Do you? Because sometimes I think you're waiting for one of them to snap and prove your theory correct—that all men are abusers. Which I hafta tell you is goddamn insulting, you think I'd smack a woman around."

For fuck's sake, is that what he thought?

"I don't think any of you would ever hit a woman."

"So, what? You think it's just your mom and sisters and any men they'd be with would hit them? Like it's their fault and they'd bring it on themselves? Or do you just think it's you? That deep down you're hiding the wife-beater within."

I'm hiding all right. How could I not, I share DNA with that fucker.

"What the hell are you talking about?" I asked and shoved out of my chair. "My mother's not to blame for my father beating her."

"No shit, Sherlock. It's your father's fault. He's to blame. Yet you've got this chip on your shoulder like all men are filth and will turn out to be monsters. You haven't even met her boyfriend, yet you already hate him. And in the past, I don't know how many years have I known you? Fifteen? Sixteen? Any guy your sisters have dated you've vehemently despised. Then there's you."

I fought the urge to rub the scar on my stomach. The scar my father's blade left. The reason my mother killed her husband.

"First, they're my sisters and the twins shouldn't be dating at all, they should be concentrating on their futures. And Lucy's gay so there's never been a guy to hate. Besides, I love her wife; they're perfect for each other. Secondly, my mother spent half her life with a man who beat the holy fuck out of her and her children. Why would she want to chance finding another man who beat her?"

"Jill and Jackie are twenty-six, brother. They've graduated college, they both have careers. They are dating and that's them concentrating on their futures. The last time I saw them they both talked about wanting families. And the only reason why you like Lucy's wife is because she's a *woman*. If Lucy wasn't gay I doubt she would've made it down the aisle without you tackling her or tying up the groom so he couldn't walk down the aisle."

Okay. So, Matt had a point. I adored Lucy's wife and yes, part of that was because she was a beautiful, petite woman. But it was mostly because she believed Lucy walked on water.

"Your mom wants to be happy," Matt said softly. "Don't you think after everything she went through—that your family went through—she deserves to be happy?"

Yes, my mother deserved to be happy. I wanted her to be happy. I just wished she'd do it without a man.

"You know I love my mom."

"Then give this guy a chance."

I remained quiet, preferring not to lie whenever possible.

"Christ, you're gonna be a dick to him."

Again, I said nothing.

"Think on that, Logan. The only person you'll be hurting is your mom."

With that, Matt left.

I sat back down and stared at the wall. I'd moved into this new office months ago after Triple Canopy expanded the office, yet I hadn't hung a single thing on the walls. I hadn't even picked out the furniture. I'd left that to Lauren. I glanced around noting everything she'd picked was exactly right. It was what I would've picked out for myself. The black steel frame of the U-shaped executive desk with distressed walnut drawer fronts and top and the matching bookshelves were cool as hell.

I hadn't given her any direction when she'd ordered the

furniture. Hell, I couldn't even remember if I'd thanked her after it was delivered. I'd spent so much time trying to avoid the woman when I first met her it was surprising it had taken her so long to loathe the sight of me.

The problem was I didn't *want* to avoid her. From the first time I saw her shy smile, I was hooked. But when she didn't hide that she was interested in me, ice crystals formed around my heart and the poison that pumped through my veins started to bubble, reminding me I had my father in me.

I was protecting Lauren.

I had to stay away from her to keep her safe.

But now that she wouldn't look at me, the parts of her that I allowed myself to have, I missed so damn bad it hurt. I hadn't heard her laugh in months, not since before Liberty and Drake's wedding. She hadn't aimed a single smile in my direction in a long time. She hadn't gone out of her way to poke fun at me, tease me, annoy me, be in the gym when she knew I was in there. Nothing. Complete avoidance. The worst part about that was she did it better than I had.

My evasion had been half-hearted. I'd still sought her out on occasion. I'd lingered in the gym until she made her appearance then pretended I hadn't been waiting to catch sight of her in her tight-ass workout gear that showcased her rockin' figure. I found reasons to walk by her desk in the reception area just to get a sniff of her perfume.

Lauren made no such attempts. I walked into a room, she walked out.

I'm not your lover, I'm not even your friend.

Fuck.

Unable to concentrate on work I closed out the intel report Dylan, Triple Canopy's resident NSA-trained intelligence specialist, had sent earlier detailing Guy Stevens'

travel history from the last year. The dude traveled a lot.
Though according to his taxes, he was a self-employed
network engineer so travel wasn't out of the question. And
just like last week when he used his real name to check into
the Imperial, all of the hotel rooms and rental cars were
charged to him personally. He wasn't hiding, he was
deducting the expenses on his taxes. Everything looked to
be on the up-and-up. Only it wasn't. Matt and I didn't
imagine him getting a blowjob from a prostitute he couldn't
afford. And I didn't believe it was a coincidence that the
hooker belonged to a well-known pimp named Frank who
had strong ties to the man Lucky we were investigating. In a
city where a major drug deal had gone down.

When Matt interrupted, I was in the process of cross-
referencing the cities where the DEA believed Lucky did
business and where Guy had visited on or around the time
the deals had happened. So far I'd found two. I knew I'd
find more. Then the question would be where Guy fell into
Lucky's operation.

I finished closing down my computer, grabbed my cell
and keys off my desk, and left my office. I walked down the
dimly lit hallway acutely aware I was the last one in the
building. With the exception of me, Matt, Dylan, and
Lauren all of the other employees were happily attached.
And most had families.

Jason Walker's wife Mercy gave birth to their first child, a
daughter Cecile, a few weeks ago and he was still out on
leave. Nick Clark hit the door at five sharp to get home to his
wife Meadow and their two children. Carter Lenox was
never far behind to get to his pregnant wife Delaney and
their daughter. Brady Walker only stayed late if his wife
Hadley had something going on at the library where she
worked. Same with Drake Hayes pulling OT only if his wife

Liberty was deployed. But if she was home, Drake's ass was out the door ten minutes before five. Trey Durum wasn't as crazy as the rest but that might've had something to do with his fiancée Adalynn Walker being a physical therapist and using TC's facilities to see her clients. And up until recently, Luke would stay late with me, but now that he had Shiloh Kent—a badass SWAT operator—he left work as promptly as the rest, never knowing if Shiloh would get a callout and have to rush back to work.

Dropping like flies.

Matt and I were the only two still single from our SEAL element. Carter, Drake, Trey, Matt, Luke, and I were closest out of our platoon. The six of us had been a finely-tuned team until Carter didn't reenlist. Then there were the five of us. And after a shitshow of a rescue mission, we all left. But not before Drake took a dishonorable discharge to protect his wife, Lieutenant Liberty-then-McCoy's commission. Luke and Trey had been injured and were facing medical discharge. And since I couldn't bear the thought of my brothers leaving me behind I left the Navy and followed them to Triple Canopy.

Something I didn't regret, but now I realized TC couldn't offer me the one thing the Navy could. Deployments. Life-or-death missions that numbed my past. It was hard to dwell on beatings and the sounds of your mother and sisters sobbing when you were facing down unfriendlies waiting to deal death and destruction.

Now I got nothing but time. And time was not my friend.

Like the asshole I was, I paused at Lauren's desk when I got to the reception area and inhaled. No scent of the spicy perfume Lauren wore. No beautiful woman sitting in the chair. No sound of her soft voice asking me what I needed.

Nothing.

Empty.

Like my soul.

Yeah, I had way too much damn time on my hands.

I walked into Balls and the smell of stale beer assaulted me. *Maybe Matt* should *buy the joint and spruce it up a bit.* The pool hall was outdated by a decade. My gaze went to the bar and all thoughts vanished as I drank in the sight of Lauren standing there. Then my jaw clenched and my gut recoiled at the attention she garnered from every asshole with a functioning dick. She'd changed from the skirt and sweater she'd worn to work today into a pair of dark-wash denim jeans that cupped her ass to perfection. Long legs were highlighted by the high heel sandals she had on her feet. A slouchy white shirt hung off one of her shoulders. No bra strap in sight. Though I hoped to fuck she was wearing one; there were only so many times a man could see nipples before he lost his mind. And I was a man on the verge of losing it. Every damn time I saw Lauren in those sports bras she wore when she worked out with her pebbled nipples I couldn't stop myself from wondering what she tasted like. Spicy like her perfume? Sweet like candy? Fresh like the soap she used?

Jesus.

With a shake of my head, I dislodged the errant thoughts and looked around. Shiloh and Quinn were at the bar. Which meant Luke and Brice would be close. And sure enough there they were at the pool table closest to their women. Matt and Dylan were with them.

Not until I got to the table did I realize that I hadn't even scanned the pool hall for available women. It had been months since I'd bothered.

What the hell is wrong with me?

I didn't want Lauren. She no longer wanted me.

Time to get back to regularly scheduled programming and find someone to occupy my time.

My stomach revolted and my dick shriveled.

That was a big fucking problem; my dick was no longer cooperating. *Rat bastard.*

"You showed." I cut my eyes to Matt and he held up his hands in defense before he continued, "Said what I had to say. We good?"

"Sure, if the subject's dropped and closed for good," I returned.

Out of the corner of my eye, I caught Luke staring at me. He didn't need Matt nor I to elaborate—he knew what subject I was referring to. It wasn't long ago over whiskey that he and I had a similar conversation that had ended much the same way the talk with Matt had. They talked, I responded, we didn't agree on the topics discussed, then the chat ended.

"Did you go over the report I sent?" Dylan asked, effectively changing the topic.

"Yeah. I found a few connections. I'm going in tomorrow to finish."

"Yo! It's Friday night. No shop talk," Luke interjected.

A pretty redhead holding a tray stopped at the table, beaming an artificially whitened smile. No one's teeth were naturally that bright. I was a sucker for redheads, especially tall ones, with extra attitude and ample curves. And by the saucy smile, this woman was right up my alley. Yet, I felt nothing. Not even a stir.

What the fuck?

"What can I get you?"

A new dick. One that took notice of a pair of tits that were pushed together and mostly exposed for my viewing pleasure.

"Rolling Rock and a shot of Jack, please." I answered her with my drink order and ignored her cleavage that was doing its best to escape the confines of her tight black V-neck tee.

"Sure thing, darlin'." She nodded politely and glanced around at the guys. "Anyone need a refill?"

With drink orders given, she turned to leave and I saw Dylan's eyes drop to the redhead's ass, a smirk firmly in place.

"You know her?" I asked, and Dylan's smirk curved into a wide smile. "You know her," I concluded.

"Long time ago," he unnecessarily confirmed.

"Damn. Maybe if I keep working out with Addy I can lose twenty pounds and look like her." Lauren giggled from behind me.

What the fuck? Lose twenty pounds?

My body stiffened hearing her sweet voice so carefree. I hadn't heard her sound like that in months.

"Girl, if you lost twenty pounds you'd disappear," Quinn told her.

"Ten pounds and boob job," Lauren continued, and white-hot irritation slithered over my skin.

Lauren was perfect the way she was. There was no need for her to ruin her figure by losing *any* weight. And fake tits? What the fuck?

"Girl, you'd topple over if your boobs were any bigger."

"You're shorter than I am and you have bigger boobs," Lauren went on.

For fuck's sake, was this the shit women talked about when they were alone?

"I think your boobs are perfect and you don't need to lose weight. I'd pay good money to have a booty like yours," Shiloh put in. "And I love the new blonde streaks in your hair. I think it suits you better than the auburn color."

I agreed with Shiloh. Not that Lauren hadn't looked good when she'd dyed her hair, but her natural color was beautiful and the blonde highlights looked sexy.

"Who's winning?" Lauren asked, still not noticing me.

Or pretending she didn't. Either of those options pissed me off.

"Dylan," I snapped.

It was a guess, but an educated one. Dylan always won against Matt.

Lauren's back went straight and the hand holding her beer started to shake.

Interesting. She hadn't noticed me, but now that she had she was stiff and waves of hostility were aimed my way. Which only spurred me on.

"Wanna play a round when they're done?"

"No."

"Aw, what's wrong, Ren? Scared you're gonna lose?"

"Sure, Logan." Her sarcasm wasn't lost on me. "You caught me, I'm scared to lose. So scared that I think I'll take my beer and go hide in the corner."

What the fuck?

"Hey!" Some tall, skinny fuck stopped by Lauren's side. "You left before I could ask you to play a game. You up for it?"

"The better question is, are *you* up for it?" Lauren flirted.

She fucking flirted with some goddamn dullard right in front of me.

"Logan," Matt rumbled from across the table.

The guy lifted his hand, Lauren took it, and off they went.

"Fuck," Dylan murmured.

"You two finish your game." I heard Luke say but my gaze was still trained on the departing couple. "Logan and I have the table next."

The redhead approached with her pearly whites and cleavage on display and suddenly I didn't give a shit if my dick had protested the thought of touching a woman that was not Lauren. I didn't give a shit that Dylan had enjoyed the waitress. It wasn't like I was going to keep her. My dick was going to have to learn he wasn't in charge. He was never going to get Lauren. He'd get whatever I gave him.

Goddamn. I'm losing my mind talking about my dick like it's gonna argue back.

"Anything else?" she asked, setting my beer and shot on the high-top table next to me.

"Another shot when you get a minute," Luke answered before I could ask the woman what she was doing after work.

"Be back."

"Don't even think about it," Luke warned.

"Think about what?"

"You wanna take a woman home, go for it. But not from here."

"What's wrong with taking a woman home from here?"

"First, this is where we *all* come to have a good time. You, Matt, and Dylan don't need to leave a trail of disgruntled, pissed-off women so we can't enjoy a beer without dirty looks and attitude. Secondly, even with this little tiff you and Lauren got going on I know you wouldn't lay the hurt on her. And you taking that waitress home to fuck right in front of Lauren would burn."

Wait. What?

"Did you not just see *Lauren* flirt with that prick right in front of me then leave with him? And wasn't it Lauren who paraded *her* goddamn boyfriend in front of me for months?"

Luke got closer and dropped his voice when he said, "We all know she never fucked that tool, Guy. We knew she was never going to, same as the dude she's playing pool with is gonna go home alone. You though; you walk out of here with a woman..."

Luke left the rest unsaid.

If he only knew how long it'd been since I'd fucked a woman he'd be surprised. Hell, I could barely believe it myself. My dick was well and truly broken. Except when Lauren was around.

"I got no call to say shit about who she takes..." Christ, I had to swallow the bile down.

"Yeah, you keep telling yourself that when you can't even say the words."

Asshole.

"You're up," Dylan interrupted before I could make more of a fool out of myself.

Over the next hour, I played pool, I drank, I engaged in conversation, and I stewed. Lauren came and went. Stopping at the table Quinn and Shiloh were sitting at to laugh with her girlfriends before she went back to the bar to talk to the guy she'd played pool with. Brice and Luke had gone between the women and the pool table, enjoying their women's company between games.

I was biding my time until I could duck out without looking like an asshole. I was also waiting for my chance to get Lauren alone. And as luck would have it, I'd finished my last beer as Lauren went down the hallway to the bathrooms.

I slid off my stool to follow. I didn't miss the panicked look on Shiloh's face, and Luke tucking his woman close so she couldn't run to her friend's rescue.

I was done playing games.

This had to end once and for all.

4

What am I doing? I silently asked myself while staring at my reflection in the mirror.

I had no answer. But I did have a headache and was ready to leave. I turned off the faucet and gave my hands a good shake over the sink before I glanced around the bathroom for a paper towel dispenser. Spying the environmentally friendly hand dryer, I used my elbow to turn the damn thing on wondering which was better in the grand scheme of conservation—the electricity used to blow hot air or the tree cut down to make the paper towels. Then I remembered the plastic trash bag the towel got thrown into and fuel the garbage truck used to haul the trash and the landfill it drove to and I figured the use of electricity won out.

Those were my thoughts. Instead of thinking about how much my life had changed in a week. How humiliated I was. How stupid I felt. How cool my friends were being and not rubbing it in that they all sensed something was off with my boyfriend yet I hadn't listened.

Instead of thinking about the nice guy waiting for me at the bar and how I was using him to piss off Logan, and how wrong it was, but every time I'd caught Logan staring at me my blood boiled. He'd made it painfully, abundantly clear he had no interest in me yet he was staring at me like he was the wounded party.

I reckon Nice Guy Wayne had figured out during our second game of pool I wasn't interested despite my flirty banter. He'd gone from hopeful to friendly. Pre-Logan, I might've given Wayne a shot. But Post-Guy Stevens that was never going to happen. Nice guys are really assholes lying in wait. And assholes are just assholes. Logan taught me that last part.

So what the hell was I doing still sitting with Wayne at the bar?

Pissing Logan off.

Going home was my best course of action.

I needed to do that pronto.

With my hands as dry as they were going to get from the hot air blowing on them I hitched my purse strap higher on my shoulder and turned to leave the bathroom.

I'll say goodbye to Shiloh and Quinn, then...

I was viciously pulled from my thoughts when the dryer shut off, plunging the bathroom into silence, but that wasn't what had me frozen. That wasn't what had my heart galloping and my breath coming out in shallow pants. The tall, imposing man that I hadn't heard enter over the damn hand dryer, scowling at me was what had my feet rooted and my pulse pounding.

"You scared the shit out of me."

Logan said nothing but his frown deepened.

"This is the women's bathroom," I reminded him.

He responded by turning the lock on the door.

"What are you..."

"You're done," he told me.

Why did I have to love his deep, growly voice?

"Done with what?"

"Whatever game you're playing."

"What are you talking about?"

It was a dumb question. I was fairly certain he knew what I was doing with Wayne.

"The game where you avoid me."

Oh.

That wasn't what I'd expected. Logan made an art form out of evading. He'd mastered the skill of leaving a room minutes after I'd entered. Since I'd met him he'd controlled every interaction, keeping them short and to the point. And now he was accusing me of avoiding *him*?

Was he crazy?

"Just playing by your rules."

"Those rules have changed."

It was a statement that sounded like a warning.

"Oh, no, you don't get to change the rules halfway through the game. You set the board, Logan. You drew the lines. You made it clear you wanted nothing to do with me. We stay this course. You in your corner, me in mine."

All it took was two long strides and he was in my personal space.

Danger. Danger. Danger.

Logan's woodsy cologne perfumed the air around me, a scent I loved way too much. A scent I'd wished he left behind on my sheets after he rolled out of my bed. A wish I'd wished way too many times over the months.

Self-preservation told me to step away.

Self-respect told me to stand my ground.

Survival won out. I backed up until I hit the cold tile wall. Mistake. Big, huge, honking mistake. I should've rushed past him and escaped. Instead, I'd retreated like a scared animal.

Logan's eyes blazed with a predatory glow as he stalked forward. Again, he invaded my personal space. This time, however, he didn't stop when he was close. His left hand went to the wall next to my head, his right went lower near my hip, effectively boxing me in. And if that didn't scramble my brain enough, he leaned in until his torso was touching mine.

"New game. New rules." The rasp of his voice grated my skin and I was acutely aware of his presence.

Logan filled up all the space. With each breath he inhaled he stole the oxygen in the room leaving me desperate to escape. His proximity wasn't dangerous, it was hazardous. Logan was a threat—not only to my peace of mind but to my very existence.

"I like the old game," I fibbed.

Liar!

I'd hated it from the beginning. Hated I'd do anything to get his attention. Hated he ignored me. Hated that he made me restless and needy. Hated that Logan Haines and his troubled soul was the man who was meant to be mine. I loathed the day I met him and my stupid heart leaped to life.

I didn't want to want Logan.

"Bullshit, Ren. You hated it just as much as I did."

"If you hated it then why'd you play it?"

Logan's forehead dropped to mine. What he didn't do was answer. He never fucking answered.

"That's what I thought. Same game. Same rules."

I felt the rise and fall of his chest, and with each expansion, I was rethinking my choice of this evening's bra. The thin material of my bandeau did nothing to stop hard muscles from rubbing against my sensitive nipples. *Who the hell am I kidding?* I wasn't thinking about my bra, I was thinking about how good it would feel if there was nothing between us.

Stupid me.

Logan's forehead lifted off of mine and before I could contemplate his next move his mouth was on mine. His tongue swept my lips. My surprised gasp provided Logan the opportunity, my moan provided the encouragement— Logan didn't waste either and his tongue surged between my parted lips. He didn't start slow and tease—he raided. He didn't coax—he demanded. Logan kissed like he did everything else—aggressively, insistently, commanding. And I willfully followed every glide, every stroke, every brush, until I was lost in sensation.

He robbed me of my thoughts, stole my good sense. Logan managed to deepen an already deep kiss and his groan rumbled down my throat. The sound was strangely sinister, a warning, a precursor, an ominous hint that I was in way over my head. But I was too far gone to heed caution.

I wanted more. My panties were soaked, my breasts felt heavy, my nipples tingled, my legs were weak, and my head was swimming with need. Never had I been so turned on by a kiss. Never had I needed an orgasm so badly I'd been willing to beg. But there I was, kissing Logan, my pussy empty, clenching at nothing, waiting for him to fill me.

Then I did something I'd never done, not with any partner, ever. I instigated more. My hands went to Logan's chest. The hard wall of muscle I encountered spurred me on—I had to know what his skin felt like. With zero finesse, I yanked up his shirt and my hands went under the material —finding hot, smooth flesh over hard ridges.

Oh, God.

My hands continued to explore, my nails raked over the dips and valleys, my thumbs swept over his nipples. Throughout this, Logan kissed me. He didn't stop my wandering hands until I went for the button on his pants. He did this nonverbally by biting my bottom lip and griding his erection against my stomach. Then finally, freaking *finally*, he touched me. His right hand resting on the wall near my hip went to my bottom and I moaned my approval as that hand traveled down to the back of my thigh and Logan lifted it. Instinct took over and I wrapped my leg around his waist. After that, Logan boosted me the rest of the way, and my other leg wrapped around him.

Logan broke the kiss and rumbled, "Tighter, baby."

I clasped my legs and locked my ankles at the small of his back like he asked, bringing my core tighter against his erection. Oh, yeah, that was better.

"Arms over my shoulders."

I did that, too.

Logan thrust his hips, the hard outline of his dick rubbing right where I needed it.

Amazing.

"Gonna take the edge off then you're gonna get your sweet ass in your car and I'm following you home."

"Logan—"

"New rules, baby."

Baby?

Before I could tell him I was forfeiting the game Logan dropped his mouth to my neck. His lips brushed the sensitive skin below my jaw and he rocked his hips again, making me forget how bad of an idea this was. And when he engaged his tongue, licking across my throat down to my shoulder, I was ready for anything. Here against the wall, in the back seat of my car, in my bed, in his. I didn't care as long as he didn't stop.

"Fuck, you taste better than I knew you would. Move with me, Ren. I need you to get there fast, baby."

Move with him? I was pinned to the wall, his hard chest pressed against mine. His grip on my ass was so strong I'd have marks from his fingers. *At least I hope I will.*

As if understanding my dilemma he explained, "Use your arms around my neck for leverage."

It was then I appreciated the brilliance of Logan wanting my legs tight and my arms around him. With every thrust of his hips, I ground down, causing the most delicious, amazing, astonishing friction.

My limbs tensed and the air around us turned humid, thick, oppressive. It was hard to draw in enough oxygen. Or was I holding my breath? My orgasm was building with shocking speed. Me, the woman who never climaxed during sex, was going to come apart from grinding against Logan. Fully clothed.

I couldn't begin to process what that meant. I couldn't stop my body from taking what it needed. My hands fisted Logan's hair and I didn't have the presence of mind to conserve the memory—how soft it was, how good it felt. In his arms, I was living a dream I couldn't fully comprehend because all of my attention was on what was going on between my legs. The magic Logan had cast. My body was in charge and it was screaming for relief.

So close.

"Logan," I panted his name.

His head lifted out of my neck, his eyes came to mine, and I exploded.

Hot chased cold. Goose bumps raced up my arms and sweat trickled down my back. My pussy clenched and convulsed at nothing but weirdly I'd never felt a more powerful orgasm. Full body, top-to-toe, I felt it burn through me. I shook and bucked and cried out in pleasure.

"Jesus Christ, beautiful," Logan groaned and continued to pump his hips.

Logan's mouth dropped to mine and in stark contrast to the violent climax still ricocheting through me, he kissed me sweetly. Slow brushes of his tongue against mine, gentle swipes across my bottom lip, and teasing nibbles. This kiss was everything the first one wasn't—heartbreaking. A bleak reminder of what I couldn't have. Logan didn't believe love was real and I'd learned the harsh lesson that he was right. Love sucked. It hurt. It tore you up inside. It left you sliced and diced and bleeding.

That depressing thought plunged me back into reality. Only because I'd already been stupid I gave myself another few moments to enjoy being in Logan's arms, feeling his body against mine, tasting him, pretending that I actually meant something to the man I'd never have.

So stupid.

Logan broke the kiss and even that was done gently.

Kill me now.

Regret washed over me and my eyes closed as I locked my emotions back into the vault I never should've opened, not even for a moment to pretend. It had taken me many painful months to accept that Logan was untouchable, a bossy jerk who wanted to be left alone.

"Don't," Logan whispered.

The quiet word was louder than a gunshot and my eyes snapped open at his tone.

Pain and hunger mingled in his eyes.

The sound of Logan's voice coupled with the way he was looking at me pissed me right the hell off.

"Don't what?"

"Pull away from me."

Pull away from him? He was The King of Pulling Away. He had the whole detached, cold demeanor down to a science.

"Let me down."

I squirmed but Logan was stronger and he easily held me in place.

"Not until we get a few things straight."

I wiggled again, the movement reminding me his dick was still hard and pressed against my center.

"Oh, I see. This is the new game," I huffed.

"You don't see shit, Ren."

"Right. So you fuck me in a—"

"I didn't fuck, baby. I didn't even initiate that play—you did. And if you think back I told you what was going to happen after I took the edge off. No way in hell I'd fuck you in some dirty bathroom."

"Close enough," I argued, not ready to concede Logan was indeed correct.

I was the one who let my hormones get the best of me and he hadn't actually fucked me.

"Not even close," he corrected. "Trust me, Ren—when I fuck you, there will be no doubt I fucked you. And it won't be in a bathroom like some barfly."

My face heated. Logan might not have fucked me but I'd humped him like a bitch in heat in a bathroom like a slut. It would've been hilariously sad if I wasn't so embarrassed.

"I have no interest—"

"You grinding on my dick, flying apart, and moaning my name says otherwise. Let's not start lying to each other now."

God, he was an asshole.

"Let me down."

"Not until we get a few things straight." Hearing his denial, my teeth clenched and my body turned to stone. "Lauren?"

"You're an asshole, Logan."

"Baby—"

"Stop calling me that!"

I unlocked my legs and shoved against his chest, not caring if he dropped me on my ass. I couldn't take another second of being in his arms. As soon as my feet touched the floor I wrenched out of his reach.

"You know," I whispered. "You know and still you followed me in here. You know and you still kissed me. You fucking *know*, you asshole. Why can't you leave me alone?"

"I know what?"

God, why'd he have to sound so curious? Why couldn't he grunt and growl and snarl like he normally did? Why now? Why when I was finally, mostly—okay, only slightly— over him did he act like he cared?

"You know everything. You know how I felt about you. You made it clear you didn't feel the same. I tried to move on and you knew that wasn't working. And you know how that relationship ended. You know he fucked around on me with a hooker because I wouldn't fuck him because I couldn't stop thinking about you.

"So what, now that I acknowledge that love and relationships aren't for me, you thought I'd be up for what, being your fuck toy?"

There wasn't enough time for the humiliation from admitting the reason why I'd never had sex with Guy to set in. Logan had my back against the wall and both of his hands threaded in my hair, tugging it back so my head was tilted and we were eye-to-eye.

"My *fuck toy*?" There was the snarly Logan I knew. "Listen real closely, Lauren. I'm gonna *toy* with every inch of your body. I'm gonna *fuck* you with my tongue, my fingers, my cock, and, baby, I'm gonna do that until neither of us can walk." He leaned in closer so when he spoke again his words fanned across my cheek. "And after all of that you still won't be my fuck toy, you'll just plain be *mine*."

I shivered at his proximity, then I shivered again when his hand slid out of my hair and he let me go. Logan was at the door when he craned his neck and looked at me over his shoulder.

"I'll be at your house in thirty minutes."

And with that threat, he walked out of the bathroom, leaving me alone in my shame.

What just happened?

How did that happen?

But the bigger question was—would I open the door when Logan showed up at my house?

My heart screamed *no!* My body shouted *yes!*

5

"You're an ass," Luke mumbled when I got back to the pool table.

His assessment was spot-on; I was an ass. I was also the motherfucker who was going to take what he wanted, damn the consequences.

Lauren was smart, she knew there was no future with me. Besides, she needed this as much as I did. The tension between us needed to be eased. We'd fuck, get our fill, then in a week, a month, however long it took, we could move on. Lauren could find a nice guy, get married like she'd said she wanted, have some kids, live the white-picket-fence dream and I could go back to my life alone. There would be no wife or kids in my future. I wasn't safe. The bastard's beast lived inside of me and I'd never take the chance of it roaring to life.

"Oh, hell," Matt put in from across the table, his gaze on something behind me.

I didn't have to turn to know he was looking at Lauren. Yet, I did turn to look, for no other reason than to see her.

Lauren was a naturally pretty woman. It didn't matter

what color she dyed or bleached her hair, if she was wearing her work clothes, workout gear, or jeans and a tee. What little makeup she wore to work was unnecessary—she was prettier without it. Some days she had her nails painted, others she didn't. Heels, tennis shoes, sandals, it didn't matter.

Tonight in the bathroom, with her legs wrapped around me, grinding on my dick, she wasn't pretty—she was sexy as hell. And when she came apart she'd never looked more beautiful. Face flushed, eyes glossy and hazy, no barrier between us. No mask. No bullshit. No lies.

Now, though, Lauren strutting her tight ass across the room, face still flushed, eyes blazing with fire, hair messy, she looked hot as fuck. And knowing her hair was no longer perfectly in place because my hands had fisted it, and the blush on her cheeks was from an orgasm I gave her ratcheted up the sexy, hot look she was sporting and took her straight to stunning.

Lauren leaned down and whispered something to Quinn. Then without saying anything to the rest of her friends she marched to the bar and my gut tightened when Lauren put her hand on the guy's shoulder she'd been playing pool with.

What the fuck?

"Don't even think about it," Matt rumbled.

Too late; jealousy had sparked my temper and I was thinking about ripping the dude's eyeballs from his head the longer he stared at Lauren.

A better man would sit Lauren down, calmly explain all the reasons why we'd never work out, why I couldn't be trusted with a woman. Then step aside and let the untarnished, nice guy at the bar who was clearly interested in

Lauren have his shot. Unfortunately for Lauren, I wasn't a better man. I was a selfish son-of-a-bastard.

"What'd you do to her?" Luke asked.

I kissed her, then she rubbed herself to orgasm, damn near taking me with her. Then I told her I would fuck her until neither of us could walk. Which reminds me, I need to leave so I can pick up a box of condoms before I hit Lauren's.

I could have said that, but instead what came out was, "I don't remember meddling in your relationship, how about you don't meddle in mine?"

"Relationship?"

Well, fuck me running.

"Mind your business."

"Kinda hard to when I know you and I know her. Which means I know the two of you don't mix. You wanna dip your dick—"

"Don't finish that."

Luke's eyes narrowed and he leaned in closer. Too damn close. "She's looking for something you refuse to give a woman."

"Lauren's smart. She knows the score."

"Does she really? How sure are you about that? Because not even six months ago she was so hung up on you she couldn't hide it. Now suddenly she's okay with being fuck buddies with you? No feelings. No attachments. No promises. That's not Lauren and you damn well know it."

Luke was right, that wasn't Lauren. She was looking for love. But that was before Guy fucked her over. She said it herself; love was bullshit.

But it isn't bullshit, is it? Luke's found it with Shiloh.

This was where the better man would've conceded and disregarded his plans to take what he wanted.

My daddy didn't raise a man, he raised an asshole.

"You don't need to worry about Lauren—"

"Actually," Luke cut me off. "I'm worried about you."

"Me?"

"This is gonna get messy."

Yeah, it was going to get plenty messy as soon I got Lauren naked and on a bed.

I glanced back at the bar and caught sight of Lauren walking to the exit.

Time to leave.

"Catch you Monday."

"I hope you know what you're doing, Logan."

I knew exactly what I was doing. Further, I knew it was wrong. I was tangling myself with a woman who deserved better than I could ever give. But fuck if I could deny the pull of her. Just once in my miserable life, I wanted a taste of something good and clean and right.

Just fucking once I wanted to forget.

"Later."

I called out my goodbyes and hightailed my ass out of the bar.

Thirty minutes later I was pulling into Lauren's driveway with three boxes of condoms on the passenger seat wondering what the fuck I was doing.

I didn't do messy.

I didn't do complicated and tangled.

I didn't fuck shy, quiet women who were looking for husbands and happily-ever-afters.

But Lauren isn't looking for that anymore, right?

This wasn't right. I shouldn't've been there. But now that I was, I owed Lauren an apology. I'd give her what I should've given her from the beginning—an explanation—then I'd leave. Ignoring the condoms and wondering if my dick would ever work again, giving me a chance to use them,

I got out of my car. I ignored the painful throbbing between my legs that had yet to subside since I'd had Lauren against the bathroom wall.

Bathroom wall! Christ, I was an asshole. Another reason to steer clear of sweet Lauren. I lost my mind when she was near and my control went with it. Thank God, I'd had a shred of decency in me and hadn't fucked her. Who the hell was I kidding? If I'd had protection her jeans would've been around her ankles and I would've been balls deep and she would've been screaming my name louder than she had been. I was no better than a fucking animal.

Before I could knock on the door Lauren had it open and I nearly swallowed my tongue. Gone were the jeans that hid her tanned legs and in their place was a pair of *short* sleep shorts that I was positive would show ass cheek if she turned around. The loose-fitting shirt was replaced with a tight-fitting tank top and she'd lost the bra.

Fucking hell.

How in the actual hell was it possible that Lauren was dressed for bed, not seduction, yet she was sexier than any woman I'd ever laid eyes on?

Kill. Me. Now.

"Took you long enough," she clipped.

Say what?

Lauren stepped away from the door and with a sweep of her hand she invited me in. As soon as I cleared the threshold she shut and locked the door.

"I've been thinking," Lauren started.

"We need to talk," I said at the same time.

Our words clashed and Lauren's eyes went squinty like they always did right before she said something that pissed me off.

"Oh, no. Time for talking is over, Logan. You wanted a

new game, here we are. We're playing it. But I set the rules this time. No talking. No calling me Ren, baby, babe, or any other pet name. I'm Lauren. And if you can't remember that, just grunt—you're good at that. No dates. No phone calls. No texting. No mixing pleasure with work. No sharing personal information. No asking questions. No expectations. No dinners, lunches, drinks, or breakfasts. We fuck, that's it. Period. You don't like the rules, leave."

Yep, I should've gotten in there and said what I had to say before she had a chance because now I was pissed. No, I was *red-hot* pissed.

"Damn, woman, can we at least be friends?"

"Is that a requirement for you to fuck a woman?"

Oh, yeah, my blood was boiling.

"I guess that depends. If I'm looking for a quick fuck with a Frog Hog that wants nothing more than my dick so she can brag the next day she bagged a SEAL, no. If I'm looking for a blowjob in my car, that's also a negative. If I'm looking to bang a woman a few times, yeah I'd at least like to respect the woman taking my dick."

I was being an asshole, taking jabs at Lauren, and I knew I hit my mark when her face screwed up into a grimace.

"You're disgusting."

"I'm disgusting? Baby, I walked in here and the first thing you did was laid out some fucked-up set rules. Check this, Ren—you wanna fuck, I'm down. I'll fuck you any which way you want, anywhere you want it, as many times as you want it. But tell me this; how am I supposed to know when you want me over to play if we're not calling or texting or talking? You gonna send a message by carrier pigeon?"

"Don't be—"

"Fuck the rules, Ren."

"Logan!"

"Straight up, baby, I'm not following the rules."

Her hands went to her hips, her elbows cocked wide, and her shoulders went back. Her posture indicated she was pissed. It also had the unintended consequence of stretching that damn tank top tight across her chest, showcasing her pebbled nipples.

"But I have to follow yours."

She wasn't asking but I answered anyway, "Only got one rule. You stop ignoring me."

I knew my demand contradicted how I'd behaved pretty much the whole time I'd known her. Further, I knew it made me a dick that over the last few months she'd given me a taste of my own medicine and I found I hated the way it tasted, thus I was putting an end to it whether she liked it or not.

"You're unbelievable," she seethed.

No, I'm an asshole.

"Normally, women don't call me that until at least their third orgasm. Seeing as I've only given you one, I'd say we're starting this..." *What, relationship? I don't do relationships. Were we making a deal?* "...Arrangement off on the right foot."

"God, you're a..." Lauren shook her head and let that hang.

"I'm a what?"

Three feet separated us. Three strides and I'd be in her space. Three paces and I could kiss that dirty look off her face and hear her panting my name. I took a step toward her and she held her ground but her eyes darted around the room. I took another, and then another, not stopping at a polite distance. I got deep into her space. And since I was so close, I dropped my lips to her neck. When I did everything else fell away. The conversation I'd planned on having with her, the bickering that perversely turned me the fuck on, the sadness I'd seen in her eyes over the last month, the anger she couldn't hide, my past, and all of the reasons why this was wrong.

It was me and her.

Her warm, soft skin under my lips. The pounding of her heart thumping against the thundering of mine. Our bodies touching. My tongue tasting. Her breath in my ear.

"You taste good," I murmured against her soft skin.

Lauren's head tilted to the side, giving me better access, and I happily took what she offered—sucking and biting my way up to her ear. "Wanna taste other parts of you, baby."

She shivered and brought her hands to my chest—not to push me away but to slide her palms up to my shoulders and curl her fingers until her nails dug in. I didn't dare touch her with more than my mouth; what little control I had was slipping. My hands went to Lauren's hips, around then down into her sleep shorts, until I had two handfuls of her bare ass.

"Bed or couch?" I asked.

"Huh?"

"In two seconds you're gonna be on your back with my mouth on your pussy. You want that on your bed or couch?"

"Bed."

That was a shame; the couch was closer.

I gave her neck one last kiss, pulled back, and said, "Lead the way."

"Logan," she breathed.

Sweet Christ.

"Right here, baby."

"I'm..." She trailed off.

Shit, had she always been this cute when her brows pinched together and she bit her bottom lip?

"You're what?"

"Never mind."

Her teeth sank deeper into her bottom lip

"Ren." My hand went to her face to rescue the abused flesh. But before I could pull her lip free she dipped her chin and planted her forehead on my chest.

"No talking," she mumbled.

Any other woman said that to me it would be music to my ears. Coming from Lauren, it sent my teeth on edge.

"This only works if we talk."

Where the fuck did that come from?

Lauren lifted her head and she had that look, the one that was full of attitude. Seeing as I was smart and the last time she squinted at me she spewed a list of fucked-up rules that pissed me right the fuck off, I decided it was smart to cut her off.

"I might be an asshole, Lauren, but I'm not some dick that's gonna fuck you then walk out the door. Like it or not there will be conversation. And I'm not the sorta man that takes without giving. There's a lot your body will tell me, but I'm not into forcing women to do shit they don't like."

When she still didn't tell me what was on her mind I prompted, "What's going on in your head, Ren?"

"I'm nervous," she blurted out. "I'm not..."

"You're not what?"

"I'm not like that waitress at the bar."

"Well, thank fuck for that."

Her eyes got narrower and lines crinkled around their edges—clear indicators she didn't believe me.

"I'm trying to tell you I'm not skinny."

"I got eyes, baby, and I've spent a fair few hours over the last year staring at your ass thinking about how good it looked, how good it would feel in my hands, and dreaming about you bent over taking my dick from behind. And now that I've had my hands on your ass twice, I can confirm it feels as good as it looks. That weight you were talking to Quinn about shifts off your body, I'm gonna be seriously unhappy. You're perfect exactly the way you are."

Some of the tension in her face left but it was clear she thought I was blowing sunshine. I wasn't fucking a woman with less body fat than me. That had never been appealing. I like ass and tits and thighs.

"Trust me?"

Jesus fuck, did I seriously just ask her that?

Never, not once in my life, had I ever asked a woman to trust me.

"Actually, I do trust you."

Fucking shit.

My blood heated and my skin crawled.

No woman should ever trust me. I had too much darkness inside of me, too much pain waiting to get out, too much anger simmering under the surface.

But it was too late to take back my question and unhear her answer.

Lauren trusting me terrified the shit out of me. The kind of fear that went straight to my soul and sliced my heart because it felt so fucking good when I knew it was wrong.

Dangerous and wrong.

Soft hazel eyes stared at me. And there, just behind the nervousness, I saw the trust she proclaimed to have. Instead of doing the right thing and ending this before any damage could be done, I did the opposite and kissed her.

Closed mouth and soft. A slow brush of my lips. A silent vow to myself that no matter what I would walk away before I could inflict any harm.

I broke the kiss and ordered, "Go to your room and wait for me. I need to go out to my car."

"Car?"

"Condoms."

"Right."

I waited and watched Lauren walk across her living room and disappear down the hall before I moved to the front door.

I pushed aside all thoughts about why it felt so good to know Lauren trusted me. I shoved all the memories of my violent childhood back into the box where they lived, and I jogged out to my car.

You're one stupid sonofabastard if you think you're coming away from this unscathed. When she wises up and kicks your sorry ass to the curb you're going to be the one in pain.

I shoved that thought away, too, and I got the three boxes of condoms.

6

I was staring out my bedroom window into my plain, ugly backyard, wondering why I'd lived in this house for five years when I didn't like it. I didn't have to turn around and look at my bedroom furniture to know it was cheap and ugly. At the time of its purchase, I bought what I could afford, and since it was still in good shape, even though I could afford better I'd never replaced it.

That was my life in a nutshell. I got by on mediocre. I lived my life the way I'd furnished my house, taking what I could get and never getting better.

Over the last week, I'd thought a lot about why I wasted time spinning my wheels. Why I didn't allow myself to replace the ugly and get what I wanted.

And that was what I'd been thinking about on the drive home from Balls. How in the world that had turned into me giving myself permission to have sex with Logan I will never know. I mean, in what universe did I think that I could have no-strings sex with the man I'd been lusting after for the better part of a year?

Guy Stevens!

And there it was—the reason. The last boyfriend in a list —a short one but still a list—of men who had screwed me over. I was sick to death of being lied to, cheated on, and dumped. I was tired of my heart being trampled on.

I could totally do this. I could have great sex with a man who wanted nothing from me in return. He wouldn't lie to me because no promises would be made to be broken. He wouldn't cancel dates because there would be no dates. He couldn't cheat on me because there would be no relationship. He wouldn't beg me to be exclusive, tell me things I wanted to hear to get me into bed then turn around and screw a hooker.

Logan was upfront and honest. He wanted sex and nothing more. Perfect. That was what I needed—honest sex. Easy. No relationship. No hearts on the line, no bullshit avowals of love. Logan's way was so much better. Love was not in the cards for me and once I'd come to terms with how the rest of my life was going to play out it was almost a relief. No more dating games. No more putting myself out there. When Logan and I were done, we'd move on, no hard feelings. No broken hearts. No relationship postmortem where I relentlessly went over every detail wondering what I'd done wrong.

Shit, I forgot to shave my legs. When I got home from the bar I'd had just enough time for a quick shower to wash all the important parts but not enough time to shave.

I bet they're prickly.

I reached down and at the same time brought my leg up and rubbed from ankle to knee. Sure enough, they were cactus-like.

"What are you doing?" Logan asked from behind me.

Damn.

I dropped my leg but didn't turn around.

"Nothing."

There was no way in hell I was going to explain to Mr. Hot Guy with his perfectly sculpted arms, six-pack abs, and hard pecs I was checking how hairy my legs were. I'd already ruined the moment once with my insecurity. No way in hell was I doing it again.

Logan was here for sex. I doubted he cared my legs weren't perfectly smooth.

I heard something drop on my dresser but I still wasn't ready to face him.

That is gonna be a problem, sister, when it comes to getting down and dirty.

I felt Logan's hands on my hips right before he fitted his chest to my back.

"Baby?"

My eyes drifted closed as his endearment made its rounds, slicing me as it bounced around my insides. God, I needed him to stop calling me that.

"Huh?"

"This is the part where I need you to talk. We can take this as slow or as fast as you want."

Fast. I needed fast. I needed out of my head before I did what I always did and denied myself something I wanted because I was too damn scared to take a chance.

"Fast," I told him.

"Ren, baby—"

"Fast, Logan. I need fast. I need you to kiss me."

His hands tightened on my hips and he dropped his mouth on my neck and then touched his tongue there.

"You want me to kiss you here?" Logan brushed his lips down to the strap of my tank top.

"Yes."

Logan's left hand left my hip and traveled up my stomach until he cupped my breast.

"You want me to kiss you here?" he asked as his thumb grazed my nipple.

"Yes."

His mouth continued licking and kissing my neck but his right hand was now on the move—across my stomach then down under my shorts and into my panties. His fingertips skimmed over my clit and my body electrified.

"And here?" Logan dipped his finger inside of me. "You want me to kiss you here, Lauren?"

"Yes," I hissed as he pulled his finger out and pushed back in two.

His hand on my breast skimmed down to my stomach. Cool air hit my belly as he lifted my tank top, and before I could think better of it my hands were moving to help yank the material over my head.

Once the shirt was tossed aside Logan's mouth was once again on my neck and his hand was back on my breast—my *bare* breast, and damn if that wasn't better. His rough hands against my skin sent a thrill through me. And this time he wasn't grazing my nipple, he was rolling it while his long, thick fingers pushed in and out faster.

That was all it took for my brain to click off.

That was all it took for my body to come alive.

But I needed more.

My head fell back against Logan's chest. My hands reached back and found his waist, and my fingers dug in.

"Gonna take this part slow, Ren," he said, kissing the side of my throat.

"Fast," I reminded him.

Logan landed another kiss, this one on my cheek.

"Baby, when I get you on that bed naked and spread for

me you'll learn a new meaning of fast. But, right now, I wanna savor."

Top-to-toe, I tingled.

"Logan."

"Love it when you say my name like that, Ren. Love it more when you moan it. Lift your left arm and hold on to the back of my neck."

I did as I was told with a slight variation and slid my hand from Logan's neck into his hair, scraping my nails over his scalp.

My new position arched my back; thrusting my chest out and my booty back. Logan's stiff erection dug into my lower back, his hand cupping my breast massaged, and his fingers tugged my nipple.

All of it felt good. But his fingers toying between my legs felt better. And his palm sliding against my clit felt amazing. However, it was the soft kisses to the corner of my mouth, my cheek, and my jaw that felt sweet.

Too sweet.

Dangerously, mixed-signal sweet.

"Faster," I pleaded and pushed back, forcing his fingers deeper.

Thankfully, Logan stopped kissing me and brought his lips to my ear.

"You're gonna take what I give you, Lauren."

His growled, bossy statement made my insides clench, but it was the deep, deliberate rhythm of his fingers that built my climax. The pinch and roll on my sensitive nipple was the icing on a spectacular five-layer chocolate cake.

"Logan," I panted.

"Fuck, I can't wait to taste you."

Yes. You should do that right now.

"Honey, *please*," I begged and rocked my hips.

I was so close, so lost in the sensations Logan was creat-ing, but I still couldn't miss it when his body locked.

"Logan?"

"Tell me, Ren, what do you want?"

"More."

"More what?"

"Of you," I groaned.

"In a few minutes, you're gonna have all of me. But right now, tell me what you want more of?"

I was beyond being embarrassed, beyond caring he was asking me to open up in a way I'd never done. I didn't have the first clue how to ask for what I wanted but the promise of getting all of him spurred me on.

"I want to come. I want your mouth between my legs. I want your hands on my breasts. I want to pull your hair and moan your name."

Logan growled his approval and withdrew his fingers, skimmed them up to my clit, taking with them my arousal, and started swirling. Then as fast as he'd pulled out his fingers he slid them back inside.

"Ride my fingers, baby, and come for me."

My body obeyed and ground down on his fingers, rocked my pelvis against his palm, and the climax that had been simmering exploded.

"Lo..."

I started to moan his name but got no further when Logan's hand left my breast, went across my chest, and all the air whooshed out of my lungs from his tight hold.

"Beautiful," he whispered and slowed his fingers. "You hear me, Lauren? Every inch of you is beautiful."

I knew it was wrong, I should've blocked out his decree, I should've shoved it away and pretended I hadn't heard. But I stupidly allowed his compliment to wash over me; and if that wasn't dumb enough I let it settle in and warm my already overheated skin.

"I wanna touch you, Logan."

"Soon, baby. Get on the bed."

I let go of his hair and dropped my arm. A chill raced down my spine when Logan let me and stepped back. Suddenly very aware I was nearly naked and Logan was still fully dressed I lifted my hands to cover myself.

"Don't," he rasped and I glanced over my shoulder. "I want to see all of you when you climb on your bed for me."

I stood frozen and watched Logan remove his shirt and toss it on the floor. Next, he undid his pants and pushed them down his legs. My gaze dropped and the frozen I was melted as fire ignited low in my belly when his cock came into view. Long and thick and leaking.

Sweet Jesus.

Logan's right hand fisted his cock, his left cupped his heavy balls, and I couldn't stop the groan from slipping out when he started stroking.

"Pull off your shorts, Ren."

With my eyes focused on Logan jerking himself, I didn't hesitate to do as he commanded. With zero coordination and jerky movements, I ripped my shorts down and kicked them away.

"Christ, that ass," he growled and pumped faster. "Crawl on the bed, but don't stop watching what I'm doing."

It was like the orgasm he'd given me only minutes before had never happened. I was so turned on, my body so hungry for his, every part of me needing Logan so badly I trembled as I walked to my bed. I stumbled over an article of clothing, righted myself, and kept going, the whole time watching his big hand slide up and down his shaft.

My knees hit the bed and I bent to crawl on when Logan halted me.

"Stay just like that."

Logan reached beside him and grabbed a box of condoms off my dresser. One-handed, he tore open the box and tossed the packets on the bed next to where my hands rested on the mattress.

"Logan," I whispered urgently.

His gaze came to mine and hazel-green eyes glimmered with so much desire I shivered and looked away.

"Look at me, Ren." His voice sounded rusty and rough demanding my attention. When I lifted my eyes he went on. "Lots of nights I've gotten into bed, my dick hard and aching from thinking about you."

Logan made his way to the bed and I craned my neck the best I could, but he stepped behind me. I lost sight of his cock but still held his stare.

"So many times I wondered what you'd sound like, what'd it be like to have you touch me. Feel your skin under my palms." His hand went to my hip, then his fingertips danced across my lower back, leaving a trail of goose bumps. "So many times I've fucked my fist wishing it was you I was pumping into while you were bent over, just like you are right now." Logan listed forward, his heavy cock nestled between the cheeks of my ass. His hips mimicked his words and he thrust forward then slowly dragged back. "Gonna go fast now, Lauren, you ready?"

Between his dirty talk, his cock now resting on my ass, his hand roaming my back, I was more than ready for fast. I wanted catch-your-hair-on-fire supersonic.

"Yes."

"You need me to slow down, you tell me."

That wouldn't happen.

"Hurry, honey."

And just like a switch flipped.

Logan dropped to his knees behind me. His hand went to my thighs and he roughly spread my legs, then his mouth was on me. Direct hit. No coaxing or teasing or warning. He ate me like he meant it with his tongue spearing inside me and his hands on my ass holding me steady. He lapped and sucked and flicked and nibbled. He did all of this with such precision I didn't have time to enjoy it. My arms gave out and I went down on my elbows. My body quaked, my thighs trembled, and my lungs burned.

It was too much. Too fast. I had no control over what was happening.

"Oh my God," I slurred as my climax took over.

I lost Logan's mouth. His hands went from my hips, up my back, and separated—one wrapped my hair around his fist and the other planted on the bed next to my face. And before I could catch my breath he slammed inside of me.

My hips bucked and my orgasm went nuclear. Everything burned. Inside and out I was on fire as he slammed into me. Hard, pounding thrusts. I felt every inch of his cock as my pussy clenched and spasmed around him.

"Fuck!" Logan's roar was animalistic. "Can you take more?"

My head shook no but I said, "Yes."

Logan's forehead went between my shoulder blades. He kissed my back, then gave me more. So much more my throat was raw from panting. Sex sounds filled the room. Logan's grunts, my moans, skin slapping together. He filled me perfectly; I was stretched to the point of pain that felt so good I reared back, matching his thrusts.

Nothing had ever felt this good.

"I want one more, baby."

"One more what?" I slurred, prepared to give him a hundred more of whatever he wanted if he didn't stop.

"I wanna feel you come around my dick one more time."

"I don't..."

Before I could deny him Logan lift his weight off my back, hitched my right leg up, and shoved it forward so my knee was resting on the corner of the mattress, and drove deeper.

"Holy shit, Logan!"

"Beautiful," he grunted.

Logan's pace didn't slow as he slid his hand around and down, found my clit, and rolled.

I fisted the sheets and fought to hold on or hold back or stop myself from shattering into a million pieces and float away.

"Love your ass, Lauren." And to punctuate his exclamation, his fingers dug into the muscle of my behind. "Come for me, baby."

I shook my head but it was more of a thrashing seeing as I was floating, or maybe I was drowning. His fingers rolled and twitched and finally, he pinched my clit and I gave him what he wanted in a fiery blast that shattered my soul.

I chanted his name. I called to God. I cried out as pleasure consumed me.

"Christ," he grunted, drove in, and planted himself deep. I felt his cock swell and twitch then I heard a tortured whisper, "Lauren, baby. Fuck."

I didn't need to be in my right mind to know I'd never recover, even in a sex-induced fog of euphoria I knew I was ruined.

There was no coming back from Logan. When he left me I'd be broken. When he walked away—and he would—I'd never in my life feel anything as magnificent as Logan.

7

Once the room came back into focus Lauren's ass filled my vision. Correction: her fine, round ass with marks my fingers left on her skin filled my vision. I slowly dragged my still hard dick out and went solid.

Bare.

Fucking hell.

My eyes darted to the pile of unused condoms then went back to my wet dick.

I never lost control. I always, *always* used protection. I'd never in my life fucked a woman ungloved.

But the proof I'd lost my mind was glistening on my dick. The sight shifted something inside me, brought to life a feeling of proprietorship, a possessiveness I had no right to feel.

I'd marked her inside and out, the crudeness of it made my dick throb. Seeing the evidence of her excitement and my come leaking down the inside of Lauren's thighs brought one word to the forefront of my mind: mine.

Unable to stop myself, I reached out and tracked the dripping liquid.

The only thing I'd ever seen sexier than watching my come roll down Lauren's thigh was watching her come apart while I was buried inside of her.

"Baby?"

"Dead," she drunkenly mumbled.

"Don't move. I'll be right back."

"Dead," she repeated.

I walked to the bathroom and quickly completed the unfortunate task of cleaning her off my dick, found a wash-cloth, and wet it with warm water, and was back before Lauren had found the energy to open her eyes.

She's gonna find the energy to murder you when you tell her you fucked her without protection, dumbass.

I knelt behind Lauren and she jerked as soon as the cloth touched her leg.

"I can—"

"Stay still and let me," I cut Lauren off.

Never having done it—first, because I'd never come inside of a woman without protection, and secondly, I'd never cared enough to clean someone—I muddled my way through.

Halfway through my ministrations, she relaxed, and when I pressed the washcloth against her pussy she mewed.

"Sore?"

"Empty and achy."

Jesus.

My dick liked the sound of that and was more than ready for another round but my conscience had taken over. I'd put off telling her as long as I could.

"Didn't use a condom, Ren."

She jolted, turned to stone, then a few beats later she picked up a handful of condoms and shook her hand while she spoke.

"They were right here," she unnecessarily told me.

"Yep. No excuses. I lost my mind and wasn't thinking. I'm clean and that was a first for me."

"What was a first?"

"Never had sex without protection. Not with anyone, not ever."

Her body sagged in relief and I didn't blame her.

"I have an IUD so birth control is covered. And I'm clean."

Awareness hit so hard I felt like I'd been sucker-punched in the gut.

Birth control.

Not once in my observations of the raw, primitive, covetous feelings that had surfaced had I thought about pregnancy.

What the hell?

I should've been freaking out. Knocking her up should've been the first worry that popped into my mind.

What now?

This was the part where I normally got dressed and left.

"I should...um...take a shower," Lauren muttered, uncertainty creeping into her tone.

I stood and in a flash, Lauren yanked the comforter up and covered herself as she sat up.

This pissed me off.

I reached down and cupped her cheek, using just enough force to tilt her head back until she was looking at me.

Her normal pretty was fucking stunning after three orgasms.

"Don't hide from me."

"Logan—"

Squinty eyes. I knew what that meant and I was too mellow to spar with her.

"Ren, I've had my tongue in your mouth and in your pussy. You've come on my cock, on my fingers, and in my—"

"I get it," she cut me off.

The rosy glow on her cheeks turned bright red and I liked that when I had her worked up she got off on my filthy mouth and I could even get her to talk a little dirty to me. But when my hands weren't on her, edging her toward the pleasure her body wanted, she was shy.

"I don't think you do, Ren. I don't want you to hide from me—not your body, not your thoughts, not your desire. I want all of you."

"That's not smart," she rightly returned.

"I don't give a shit what's smart. No bullshit rules."

"Seriously, Logan."

I'm not sure what the fuck my problem was. The more Lauren fought her corner—that being the right corner, the smart one, the safe one, the place I should've been with her thanking God she understood—the more I wanted to pull her from it.

This was the moment where I should've gotten dressed, kissed her goodbye, and left. But I couldn't do it. I couldn't get my feet to work or my brain to function.

"Seriously, Lauren." I hauled her to her feet. My over-the-top maneuver earned me wide eyes and a scowl. "I'm telling you it means something to me. I want this honest. No hiding."

"Honest?"

"Can't get any more honest, baby, than us standing here having this conversation with my come inside you."

"That's—"

"How's this for honest? Pulling out, seeing my bare dick

wet with you, wet with *us*, was so goddamn sexy I wanna toss you on the bed and fuck you just so I can watch it drip out of you again."

Lauren's eyelids went half-mast and her eye color changed to more green than brown. Knowing what that look meant my dick stirred.

"We're gonna take a shower," I told her.

"We are?"

"Yeah, baby, we are. And while we're in there you'll get on your knees 'cause I want your mouth on my dick. Then I'm bringing you back to bed and we're gonna play some more."

I saw the hesitation and waited for her rebuttal but when none came I prompted, "Honest."

"I don't know how."

Her face tinged a deep red and my heart slammed into my ribs. I was weirdly humbled by her candor.

"Change of plans," I said, and just because I could I lowered my mouth to hers and kissed her.

It took all of my control to keep the kiss from turning wild—keep it a tangle of tongues rather than a duel. A kiss to savor rather than ignite. Slow and wet and gentle. A kiss like no other I've ever had.

I broke the kiss but didn't have it in me to pull away so I murmured against her lips, "Shower, then bed. If you're up for it, I'll teach you."

I didn't miss the shiver. I also didn't miss the whistle of air as she sucked in a breath.

Thirty minutes later, showered and in bed, I learned the meaning of the seventh circle of hell. Our shower had been torture. A soapy, wet Lauren was a temptation. Her hands on me washing me after I'd washed her was the beginning stages of the hellish inferno I was caught in.

When Lauren had said she didn't know how to give head, she meant she'd never done it before. That didn't mean she wasn't a natural.

My dick in her mouth was heaven. She used just the right amount of suction and speed. She'd licked my shaft from root to tip. She'd swirled her tongue over the tip and traced around my engorged head, digging her tongue in as she went. Now she was experimenting, playing, taking her time, learning every inch of my dick, and assessing my response to each new trick she tried.

"Ren, baby, I'm gonna come," I warned.

She must've said something. But with a mouthful of dick it was all vibration and my eyes nearly rolled to the back of my head.

"Last warning," I groaned. "Pull off now and jerk me off if you don't want me coming in your mouth."

Lauren's answer was to bob and suck.

"You sure?" I asked one last time knowing it was a fruitless question because I couldn't hold off any longer.

Watching my dick disappear into Lauren's wet warm mouth was too fucking much. Couple that with her enthusiasm and talent and I was a goner. My muscles tensed and pleasure ripped through me. My vision blurred and I fought from thrusting deeper into her mouth. My orgasm ebbed and I blinked the haze away and for a second time that night, I froze solid.

Stunning hazel eyes full of wonder stared up at me and my heart felt like it was going to burst from my chest.

With one last swirl of her tongue, Lauren's mouth pulled off my dick with a pop. My gaze went to her mouth, a drop of come at the corner, and fuck me there was that feeling again. Possessive, raw, primitive, and this time I could add barbaric to the list.

She wiped her mouth with the back of her hand. The ploy to clean me off her face was unladylike and so damn sexy I couldn't hold back my groan of approval.

Careful, asshole. Remember yourself.

Ignoring the rational part of my brain I ordered, "Come here, baby."

Lauren crawled up from between my legs and when she was close enough I helped her settle on my lap. This was one of those times where she was too turned on to care she was naked. I took my time taking her in, fully exposed and not hiding a single inch of her perfect body.

Needing her closer, I tugged her hand until she fell forward and her head rested on my chest.

"You're good at that," I told her.

"I am?"

"You just swallowed a mouthful. Not sure why you'd ask that."

"Has anyone ever told you you're vulgar?"

I smiled into her hair and told her the truth.

"I've been called a lot of things but vulgar isn't one of them."

"Seriously? With your dirty mouth, no one's called you that? What about crass?"

"Nope."

"I don't believe you."

"You should."

Lauren lifted her head and looked me square in the eye.

"You're telling the truth."

I was. No one had ever called me vulgar or crass.

"How honest do you want it?" I asked.

Lauren's lips curved up into a smile that stole my breath and I was rethinking how honest *I* wanted to be. Distance might've been in order.

"Well, as you so sweetly put it, you've already come inside of me and now I've swallowed you, so I'm not sure if we can get more honest than that."

We could, and if she'd let me, I'd introduce her to a new place I could...*fuck*...I shook the thought of taking her ass out of my head. Now was not the time, but later might be.

"Never shared a bed with a woman long enough for her to comment on my dirty mouth."

Understanding flickered in her eyes right before the shutters on her feelings slammed shut.

"Oh."

"You're hiding from me."

"No, I'm not. There's just nothing to say to that."

Sure there was. She could call me out on being an asshole but she'd closed down.

Did I want her to call me out on my bullshit and accuse me of being a grade-A douchebag? Strangely, I did. I wanted all of her thoughts, all of her feelings. I wanted her to say whatever was on her mind as soon as it popped into her brain.

"I'll give you that play even though we both know you got a lot to say."

Lauren never disappointed, and when her eyes narrowed, a tinge of excitement crawled up my spine.

"You'll give me that play?" she asked and started to push off of me.

I rolled, yanked the covers from under us, and condoms scattered. I pulled the sheet over us and pinned Lauren under me.

I pressed close and dropped my mouth to her ear and whispered, "All my life I've been a certain way. I take what I want and give just enough not to be a royal dick. I do not stay and chat when I'm done. I don't shower with women. I don't kiss and cuddle. I keep myself to myself so no one ever gets the wrong idea. That is not how I am with you. That is not us. It might not be smart but, Ren, for once in my life I'm taking more than my share. I'm taking clean and honest. I will not fuck you over in the process. I will not ever lie to you. I will not make you promises I cannot or do not intend to keep. You might call it vulgar or crass but I swear I will tell you exactly what I'm thinking.

"Now. I've come twice in the last hour, given you three, plus one at the bar. I'm beat and need some sleep, but if you need more I can rally and give you another."

I felt Lauren shift her legs and rub her thighs together.

"You want another," I growled.

"Not if you're too tired."

"Never too tired to fill you up, baby."

"Logan?"

"Right here."

"This time, can I be on top?"

Jesus fuck.

I rolled to my back taking Lauren with me. I lifted my arms and tucked my hands under my head.

"By all means, baby, take whatever you want. Condoms are somewhere on the floor."

Lauren took. First with her mouth then with her pussy. She didn't stop to get a condom. That meant when she was done I got to clean her up again with the added pleasure of seeing us mixed together and leaking out of her.

Maybe one day I'd give headspace to why seeing that stirred something deep inside of me. Not that I cared too much about the why, but the feeling I didn't understand was worth investigating.

However, with Lauren tucked close as I drifted to sleep I thought of nothing else but how good she felt in my arms.

8
_____

"I'll be back," Logan said as he entered the kitchen freshly showered.

Back?

It was Sunday afternoon. Logan hadn't left my house since Friday night. Two nights and one and a half days. That was a lot of hours for a man who proclaimed he didn't stick around to chat, kiss and cuddle, or shower. He hadn't said expressly but one could assume if he didn't stick around after sex to chat he didn't sleep with his flavor du jour.

This was confounding. And the four times I'd tried to kick him out yesterday were thwarted when Logan found a variety of ways to distract me. While his methods might've been different from how he'd started the proceedings each of them had ended the same—me screaming his name while in the throes of ecstasy.

I'd had so many orgasms in the last forty-eight or so hours I was afraid I'd need to seek medical attention if Logan didn't leave and stay gone. I needed a warm bath and some IcyHot. Correction: IcyHot on the vagina didn't sound like a good idea. An ice pack. Yes, I needed a bag of frozen peas on my nether region.

"Ren?"

Shit. Right. Logan said he'd be back.

"Why are you coming back? I'll see you at work tomorrow."

"I'm taking you to dinner tonight."

Um. No, he wasn't. No dates.

"Logan," I started and shook my head. "That's not gonna happen."

"I'll be here at five." He ignored my protest.

"No way am I going out with you."

In three strides he was in my space and his big, talented hands that could dispense immense pleasure went to my neck. His thumbs coasted from my jaw to my collarbone while his fingertips pressed into the nape of my neck and his gaze locked onto mine.

"Yesterday you made breakfast, lunch, and dinner. This morning you made breakfast. I'm repaying the favor."

"By taking me to dinner?"

"Trust me, it's a better option than me cooking for you."

"I think dinner's a bad idea."

Logan tipped my chin up and lowered his face but before he kissed me he muttered, "It's a brilliant idea."

His mouth brushed mine and his tongue touched my bottom lip and Logan kissed me.

This was what I'd trained him to do. I argued—he kissed me. I told him it was time for him to go home—he kissed me. I reminded him we needed rules in place—he kissed me.

And since I'd turned into a spineless, orgasm-hungry, moronic woman he knew all he needed to do was kiss me and that would lead to other things and once his hands were on me I'd lose my mind and give him what he wanted so he'd give me what I needed.

This was not good.

I never thought I'd be one of those women who'd give in to a man just because he was hot and good in bed. Though, I had no idea how good sex could be. I had no idea that it wasn't so much the act of sex but the intimacy behind it. When Logan and I were naked all emotional barriers were gone. It was me and him and a sea of sensation and lust. It was wild abandon. It was savage. It was dirty and beautiful and honest.

If this was a real relationship, I wouldn't fight it. I'd let him take me wherever he wanted to go. But it wasn't real, it was temporary. We were scratching an itch and I needed to remember that.

With a smooth slide of his tongue against mine, Logan broke the kiss.

"See you at five," he murmured.

"No, Logan."

"Ren—"

"No. I'm serious. This weekend's been…"

"Great," he supplied.

"I was going to say, pushing it. Boundaries have been blurred. I've given in on a lot, but not this. No dinners. No going out. No more spending the night."

I'd understated the part about the boundaries—they hadn't been blurred, they'd been obliterated. We'd eaten together, we'd watched movies together, we'd showered together, and slept together. On top of that, we'd talked—a lot. Nothing soul-deep or earth-shattering but the conversation between us had flowed from music, to travel, to favorite food, places we wanted to see, things we wanted to do.

I had to be smart. I couldn't let emotions muck up what we had.

Sex and only sex.

Mutual pleasure.

Then right before my eyes, Logan closed down and it wasn't until that very moment I'd realized how open he'd been all weekend. In that short amount of time, I'd forgotten how cold Logan could be, how dismissive, how aloof, and how badly it hurt when those indifferent hazel eyes looked straight through me.

Talk about a wake-up call. A much-needed reminder.

His hands slid away and he took a step back. The hollow feeling in my belly told me I was doing the right thing. It would be too easy to get attached.

Logan didn't say a word. He simply turned, walked out of the kitchen, snagged his keys off the coffee table, and walked out.

Ouch.

Yes, a much-needed wake-up call reminding me that Logan could be and still was an ass.

Ten minutes later I walked back to my bedroom, spied Logan's clothes from Friday night on my floor, and my heart clenched. Saturday morning before we showered he'd gone to his truck and brought back in a bag full of workout clothes and that bag was still sitting on the chair in the corner where he'd dropped it. I looked around the room— two unopened boxes of condoms, and a string of them on my ugly nightstand. More stupidity on my part. Lots of unprotected sex. Well, we were protected against pregnancy but I was not protected against losing my heart. And having sex with no barrier was a level of trust and closeness that I shouldn't've shared with Logan.

Shit.

I grabbed Logan's dirty clothes off the floor and shoved them into his bag but not before I caught a whiff of his cologne. Unsure if the offending odor was from his t-shirt or the sheets or the room in general, I decided it was best to zip the backpack, open a window, and strip my bed and wash the sheets.

So that was what I did. I busied myself with housework and thought about Logan. When I went into my bathroom to grab the dirty towels I thought about Logan. When I stood at my vanity to get ready for my day the toothbrush I'd given Logan mocked me.

By late afternoon I had to leave my house. Everywhere I turned I saw Logan. On the couch where we'd watched TV, him making fun of me when I admitted I had a deep affinity for The Munsters and had watched every episode multiple times. The only room he hadn't been in was my extra bedroom—that was nothing more than a junk room and I couldn't very well hide out in there.

So I fled my home and ended up at the grocery store, which was actually a necessary chore because Logan and I had pretty much cleaned out my fridge between meals and snacking.

I'd carb-loaded and found my orgasm limit all in one weekend.

I was tossing random shit into my cart because—you guessed it—I was thinking about Logan. I should've been paying attention to my surroundings. Situational awareness was what the men I worked with called it and they pretty much harped the topic to death. Yet I was lost in my head despite their many warnings, so I had no warning when a hand curled around my bicep and yanked me to a halt.

"Lauren."

Guy Stevens.

What the hell?

I wrenched my arm free and took a giant step away.

"Don't touch me."

Guy jerked and I had to hand it to him—he had the wounded puppy dog look mastered.

"Sweetheart."

I hated when he called me 'sweetheart'. And not like I pretended to hate it when Logan called me baby or Ren. I truly despised Guy calling me a pet name. It sounded slimy coming from him.

God, how dumb had I been to ignore all the tiny red flags? The small stuff that he did that I didn't like or found annoying yet I'd overlooked it all.

Had I really been that desperate?

Was I still being desperate, letting Logan trample all over my rules?

Yeah, I needed time for some self-reflection.

"Don't call me that. Actually, don't call me at all."

Having nothing more to say to my ex-scumbag I turned to leave but didn't get a chance to take a single step before Guy's nasty sneer hit my ears.

"Is that a fucking hickey?"

I lifted my hand and covered my throat as if I could feel a hickey.

"Fucking hell, it is. And bite marks on the back of your neck."

My hand slid around to cover whatever marks Guy was looking at. And since my hair was up in a high ponytail and I was wearing a racerback tank top I had no doubt he'd gotten an eyeful.

Damn Logan! I was going to kill him. Not so much because he'd marked me but he didn't tell me. Of course, anytime he was behind me he tended to suck on my neck and shoulder blade. He also liked to bite when he climaxed —something I found off-the-charts erotic but I didn't want to broadcast to the world my newfound kinkiness.

"If I'd known you liked to be treated like a whore I would've—"

I swung around and mocked, "You would've what? Paid *me*?"

"What's that supposed to mean?"

Of course, I couldn't tell him I knew he'd fucked a real-life bona fide whore and that was the reason I'd broken up with him and not the lame excuse I'd given.

"It means you're a dick and I want you to stop calling me."

"We were good together."

Was he serious or simply dense? I was choosing the latter. I was also choosing not to engage in any further conversation. As calmly as I could I walked to the front of the store, paid for the three things I had in my basket, and left.

It wasn't until I was lying in bed on my freshly laundered sheets that *still* smelled like Logan and sex—or maybe it was the room and it would forever smell of good times and future heartbreak—did I think about why Guy was at the grocery store two miles from my house when he lived thirty minutes away.

There had to have been twenty stores between my place and his.

I was deep in thought when my phone rang. It was after eleven and my mother always said no good news came in the middle of the night. Not that eleven was the middle of the night but it was close enough. I snatched my phone off my nightstand and ground my teeth when Logan's name flashed on my caller ID.

"It's late," I said as my greeting.

"Open your door."

"Why are you here?"

"Open the door, Ren."

God, I wanted to open the door. But a day spent thinking about nothing but Logan scared the hell out of me.

"Baby," he whispered. "Please open the door."

"I can't."

There was a beat of silence then he asked, "Why not?"

Are all men dense or just the ones I know?

"Because fuck buddies don't spend the night. They certainly don't spend two in a row. Besides I need to ice down my vagina and I haven't done that yet so I'm out of commission for the next few days and you should drink some protein mix or something to get your stamina back up. And..."

I squealed and dropped my phone when my bedroom door opened and Logan walked in.

"How'd you get in?"

"Picked the lock."

"I have an alarm," I reminded him.

"Yeah, baby, and who do you think services your system?"

It was mostly dark in my room, the only light coming from the open curtains and the hall light I leave on at night. I wasn't afraid of the dark or anything, but I was a woman who lived alone, one who was smart enough to have an alarm and not plunge my house in total darkness.

"You think my stamina's lacking?" he asked.

It was the slight tilt of his head that made him look boyish in a roguish sort of way that made me forget I was pissed at him for breaking into my house. "I think we need to slow this down and give ourselves some recuperation time."

"Right, because you need to ice your pussy."

So crass.

My eyes narrowed on him when I answered. "I didn't say pussy. I believe I said vagina."

"Right."

"Can you even say the word vagina?"

"Not without my balls retracting and my dick shriveling up."

Hm. Maybe we should try that. I was beginning to think a dickless Logan would be the only safe Logan.

You can think that all you want but you know you want Logan for more than his dick.

Stupid conscience.

"Why are you here?"

Stupid question. He was here because he wanted sex.

"I was in bed, tossing and turning, and couldn't sleep."

"So you thought, what the hell, I'll go to Lauren's, break into her place, and wake her up?"

"Were you sleeping?"

"That's beside the point."

"Then what's the point?" he asked and started walking across the room. "You weren't asleep."

"How do you know?"

Logan made it to the foot of the bed and I scooted so I could watch him. He tore his shirt off, shifted from side to side—toeing off his shoes I assumed—next, he pushed down his shorts and his cock sprung free.

He was not erect and I had to admit part of me was disappointed.

"I've had two mornings of your cute, sleepy voice. You were wide awake when you answered your phone."

Did he just say I had a cute morning voice?

In the blink of an eye, Logan was on the bed, pulling the covers back. Another two blinks and he had me tucked close with my head on his chest, and with nowhere else to put it, my arm over his stomach.

I belatedly asked, "What are you doing?"

"Your pussy needs to be iced down and apparently I need protein before I can perform again so we're going to sleep. But just to say, if you'd like me to demonstrate that my manhood should never be questioned I could get down to business and prove to you no protein is needed."

Going to sleep?

Logan was spending the night, again?

"Logan!"

His hand shifted through my hair, then his fingers massaged my scalp and I groaned.

"Sleep, beautiful."

I closed my eyes and said nothing.

What could I say? I was a spineless twit. And a sucker for a scalp massage. Something Logan knew because I'd told him.

Starting tomorrow I was going to wise up. No more sharing. Logan played dirty.

9

"You're smiling," Luke accused.

"What can I say, I enjoy punching shit."

I steadied the heavy bag and glanced around the gym, pleased this was a solo visit from Luke and he hadn't brought in reinforcements. Lauren and I had been at work for hours and other than side-eye glances no one had approached me to ask about Friday night. I was surprised it had taken this long before someone cornered me, though it was a Monday and the roster was full of training classes all day.

"Good weekend?"

I stepped away from the bag and pulled my knuckle guards off for no other reason than to make my nosy-ass friend wait.

"That's how you're gonna play it? Ask how my weekend was?"

"You didn't answer your phone or return your texts all weekend." Luke shrugged. "The way I see it you either spent the weekend nursing your broken heart because Lauren locked you out or you spent the weekend fucking her. I'm on the fence about which one I'm hoping for."

Something nasty curled in my gut. Of course, I had spent my weekend fucking Lauren, but hearing it come from Luke felt wrong. Lauren wasn't a fuck. I wasn't entirely sure what she was, but she definitely was more than a woman I'd picked up with the sole purpose of getting off with and leaving as soon as the mission was accomplished.

"I spent the weekend with Lauren. We were busy."

I didn't miss the skepticism in my friend's stare. He considered Lauren a friend and his protective streak was a mile wide. Hell, every man and woman in this building took loyalty and protection to the extreme. Even knowing Luke was only looking out for a woman who was his friend it pissed me off he thought he had any claim over her.

"Does that mean you pulled your head out of your ass?"

"It means that Lauren and I are adults and what we do outside of work is no one's business."

"You haven't pulled your head out of your ass," he mumbled. "Does she know?"

"Know what?"

"That you'll never commit to her. That there won't be a relationship. That when you're done with her your shield will go up and you'll walk away. That you think love's bullshit and she'll get nothing from you."

None of what Luke said should've pissed me off. He was right on all accounts. I didn't commit. I didn't engage in relationships and when I was done I walked away and never looked back. But the love thing he had wrong.

"For fuck's sake, for the last damn time, I know that people can love each other. I know what you and Shiloh have is good. I know you love her. But I also know that is something I will never feel. I don't have it in me. But that doesn't mean I'm not happy for all you sorry-ass saps that have found it."

"Does she know, Logan?" he pressed. "Lauren's not a woman out for a good time, happy to get what she can get and leave with a smile."

Now I wasn't pissed, I was inching toward furious.

"I know who Lauren is, brother. I know her better than you. And she knows exactly what we have and what we *don't* have."

It was me who was blurring the lines. It was me who pushed to stay at her place. It was me who broke all the rules Lauren had wanted in place. It was me who laid in bed last night and couldn't sleep without her.

"Did she tell you about her run-in with Guy? Jace's report didn't mention you were with her and I can't—"

"Come again?"

"Which part? Jace's reports are always thorough, did he miss you being there?"

Luke was correct; Jace Demby's reports were always on the mark. TC outsourced work to Jace when we lacked the manpower to follow a lead. And when Jace follows a lead he does it in a literal way. Jace was a PI of sorts, though he didn't run internet searches, he believed in up close and personal investigative work.

"Being where? Guy didn't come by Lauren's house."

"Kroger on Sunday afternoon. You weren't with her?"

Fuck.

"No, I went home Sunday morning to..." I shook that off; Luke didn't need to know why I went home. And he didn't need to know that Lauren had refused to allow me to take her to dinner. "I didn't go back to her place until later that night. And no, she didn't tell me she ran into Guy. What happened?"

"They had words in the snack aisle and Lauren left. Jace couldn't get close enough to hear the conversation. Which was three minutes and twenty-two seconds because you know he times that shit. Lauren walked away and Jace followed Guy out to his car. Oh, and Guy grabbed Lauren's arm—"

"He fucking touched her!"

"Whoa." Luke put his hands up and moved in front of me. "Calm down."

"Calm down? That asshat touched my woman and you want me to calm down? Fuck that."

I skirted around Luke and stalked to the gym exit and was down the hall before Luke could stop me. I rounded the corner into the reception area, happy to see Lauren not on the phone, meaning I wouldn't have to rip the cord out of the wall to disconnect a call.

"Logan!" Luke shouted from behind me.

Lauren jolted in her chair and looked up at me with wide eyes.

"What's wrong?"

"You saw Guy?" I ignored the way Lauren's shoulders snapped back and continued. "And you didn't tell me."

"How do you know that?"

Her eyes got narrow and I ignored that, too. She could dish out all the attitude she wanted and it would do nothing to alleviate my already red-lined anger.

"Answer me, Ren."

Lauren pushed out of the chair and belligerently crossed her arms over her chest.

"No. You answer me, Logan!"

"Guy's being investigated," I told her.

"So?"

"*Investigated*, Lauren. He's being followed which means

his movements are being reported. You had a conversation with him at the store. Why didn't you tell me?" Lauren's gaze shifted and I was feeling especially irate so I snapped, "Eyes on me."

"Your office, now."

Lauren moved from behind her desk, careful not to touch me as she passed, then sauntered through reception.

"Take a minute, Logan, and calm down," Luke advised.

I didn't take a minute and I didn't calm down before I followed Lauren. She was already in my office standing in the middle of the room with her hands on her hips when I entered and closed the door behind me.

"Don't ever do that again," she said deceptively soft. "Whatever we have going on outside of this office doesn't give you the right to interrogate me. Further, you never—and I mean *never*—have the right to speak to me like that."

"Speak to you how?"

"Like I'm some meaningless piece of—"

I should've listened to Luke and calmed down. Alternately, I shouldn't have approached Lauren at all.

"Meaningless?" I repeated. "You think I'd be this pissed if you didn't matter? You think I'd be this fucking furious to find out that after I left you yesterday Guy confronted you in a grocery store? That's what you think?"

"I don't know what to think. You come rushing up to my desk and start yelling and hurling accusations with your cold eyes and scowl."

"Honest to God, you don't know what to think?"

"Well, let's see." Lauren completed her sarcastic comeback with an eyeroll and my anger ticked up a notch. "You don't ask what happened and let me explain. Instead, you treat me like I'm guilty of something when I did nothing wrong. And just to say, even if I had done something wrong, you still don't get to yell at me, especially at work."

I felt the eruption bubbling, the venom started working its way to the surface, yet I still closed the distance between us.

Lauren stood her ground, not moving an inch when I stopped, leaving only a few inches of space between us, and hissed, "He touched you, Lauren."

"What?"

"Not only did he catch you alone and vulnerable he put his fucking hands on you."

"He didn't..." She paused and dropped her gaze.

When she didn't continue, my hands went up to cup her cheeks and tilted her head back until I had her eyes. "He didn't what, baby?"

"I was going to say he didn't put his hands on me, but he grabbed my arm. Though he didn't hurt me."

"I don't give a fuck if it hurt or not. He touched you."

"You keep saying that but he didn't actually—"

"Did you ask him to touch you?"

Lauren stiffened and she shook her head. "No, of course not."

"Right. No man ever puts his hands on a woman when he knows damn good and well the woman he's touching doesn't want that. And no fucking man ever puts his hands on a woman in anger."

"Well, he wasn't exactly angry until he saw the hickey you left. Then he called me a whore and...um...never mind."

"Oh, no, please continue."

"I don't think I wanna tell you what he said when you're looking at me like that."

What the fuck?

Sour hit my gut and I dropped my hands. After I took a step back I said, "I'd never hurt you."

"What are you talking about, hurt *me*? I'm worried about you hurting Guy. You're right, he shouldn't have touched me. But honestly, it wasn't a big deal. He grabbed my arm to get my attention. When I turned around and saw it was him I pulled away and he didn't hold on. The whole thing start-to-finish lasted about a minute. It wasn't until I was walking away did he see the hickey and bite marks. He said he didn't know I was a whore and started to say something about not knowing I liked it like that. I cut him off and left." Lauren stopped and shook her head. "You should've told me you left marks on the back of my neck."

My body reacted to the reminder of the marks I'd left but not enough to cool my temper. This right here was a red flag, the reason I had no business being close to a woman, ever.

"And I didn't tell you because it wasn't a big deal," Lauren said.

"How many times has he called you since you dumped him?"

Lauren winced then she gave her best attempt at a stern stare but she missed the mark by a mile. The woman was tough but she was a bad liar and worse at evasion.

"What makes you think he's called me?"

"Ren, a man doesn't get dumped by a woman like you and not call to gauge his chances at reconciliation. So, the question isn't whether or not he called, it's how many times has he done it."

"But..." She stopped and I was learning she paused mid-thought when she was trying to find a polite way to say something.

"Just say it. Whatever you're thinking, spit it out and don't worry about niceties."

"We hadn't even had sex."

It was time to put that topic to rest once and for all.

"It's a good thing you didn't fuck him, Ren, because since the day I walked into Triple Canopy and saw you sitting behind your desk you belonged to me, and the thought of that asshole touching you in any way sends me over the edge."

"Right. But *you* didn't belong to *me*."

The insinuation I'd fucked other women was there behind the veiled remark. Yeah, it was time to clear that up, too.

"Haven't fucked a woman since I moved to Georgia."

"Say what? That was like over a year ago."

Trust me, honey, my dick knows exactly how long it'd been.

"I'm not gonna lie and tell you I haven't hooked up, because I have. But as hard as I tried to fuck someone else, *anyone* else, I couldn't stop thinking about you. I'm so fucked-up inside, Ren. I wanted to protect you from the darkness. But I couldn't stop thinking about you. I couldn't stop dreaming about you. I couldn't stop myself from *needing* you. And that's dangerous for both of us."

"Why is that dangerous?"

"Because I'm fucked-up, Lauren. So fucked-up I'm never gonna change, I'm never gonna get married, have kids, live in some fake domestic bubble. I don't have that in me; it was beaten out of me."

"Beaten out of you?"

We were not going there.

"Did you hear what I said?"

"I did and I'm wondering why we're having this conversation."

It was Luke's fault for making me question our arrangement, and guilt had started to worm its way in. I wouldn't be another asshole who broke Lauren's heart.

"Because I want to make sure you understand, I'm never gonna love you, baby. The only thing I can promise you is I will never fuck you over."

No sooner had the words left my mouth than acid coated my throat and bile swirled in my gut. Wrong. So fucking wrong I wanted to tell her to forget I'd said them. But I had, and when she flinched my heart hurt like a motherfucker.

"I'm not hard of hearing, Logan. Nor am I stupid. And I'll take this opportunity to remind you, Friday night I went into this with my eyes wide open. We're obviously attracted to each other, we've ignored it, and it didn't go away. So we *fucked*." Lauren pointed at me and went on, "I told you to leave Saturday. You stayed. I didn't ask for that. I didn't ask you to come over last night. I know the only thing I'm going to get out of you is great sex. So, again, why are we having this conversation when you're the one who needs the reminder I'm nothing to you but a warm body with a vagina?"

So we fucked.

Christ, I wanted to bleach my memory of ever hearing Lauren say those three words.

Before I could think better of it, I pulled her into my arms and my mouth was on hers. As if I could expunge what she'd said with the stroke of my tongue. As if I could swallow those words and take them from her so she'd never think them again. The longer we kissed the deeper it became until she was moaning into my mouth and my dick was begging for relief.

Without thinking, I had her skirt around her waist, her

ass on the edge of my desk, and my erection free. I pulled her panties to the side, rubbed the head of my dick around her clit, then down through her excitement. When her hips bucked and she groaned I drove in. And like all the times before, Lauren went wild. She pawed my back, my shoulders, yanked my hair, and wrapped her legs around my hips.

Lauren was like dynamite—once the fuse was lit the explosion was imminent and catastrophic. She was so hot, so sleek, so goddamn wet it took her no time at all to get me to the edge. Her pussy felt so good, it was *too* good. I couldn't hold back with her. I couldn't stop the tidal wave of sensations. I couldn't stop the euphoria. But the part that scared the holy fuck out of me was I couldn't stop the emotions. I was all too aware I could never just *fuck* Lauren. It could not and would never be a detached act of mutual pleasure.

Her hips bucked, her pussy spasmed, and I went at her harder, getting her where I needed her—swallowing her mews and whimpers. In return, she muffled my grunts and growls. Finally, her back arched and her inner muscles clamped around my dick so I let go and came with her.

I released her lips and Lauren dropped her forehead to my chest with a muttered curse.

"Look at me, baby."

"That can't ever happen again."

Oh, it was going to happen again. I was just smart enough to pick my battles and not argue about it.

"Ren, baby, I need you to look at me."

Slowly her head came off my chest and she tipped her eyes up to meet mine. She had her shields up and the irony of the situation wasn't lost on me. Lauren looked to be completely unaffected and there I was wanting to lay it out. All of it. Everything. But first, something needed to be addressed.

"You're not a warm body with a vagina. And serious as fuck, I hear you ever say that shit again I'm gonna be pissed the fuck off."

The corner of her mouth twitched and her lips pinched together.

"I'm not being funny," I told her.

"You were wrong."

"About?"

"Unless your balls retracted and your dick shriveled, you can indeed say the word vagina."

Seeing as my dick was still rock hard, I pulled out and drove in hard, prompting a sweet-sounding groan.

"I don't know, Lauren, what do you say, did my dick shrivel?"

She shook her head and concluded, "Seems to be in working order."

The thing about Lauren was, as soon as we were done I was ready to go again. I couldn't get enough, which led me to wonder why I'd denied us for so long. And when she smiled, I had the sick feeling she'd be right; I was the one who needed the reminder that I couldn't keep her. But the harder she pushed me away the more I wanted to pull her closer. And when she talked about love being for fools, even though I'd said the same thing thousands of times, I wanted to show her how good love could be.

"We're at work," she whispered.

"Yeah."

"This is wrong."

In so many ways being with Lauren was wrong. Being with me would put her in danger.

"Sometimes wrong is the path to right."

"You're the most confusing man I've ever met."

And she was the most mystifying woman I'd ever met. But I didn't tell her that.

Remembering we were at work and I had a mother-fucking asshole to track down and set straight, I pulled out. As soon as I did my gaze automatically went between Lauren's legs. I was beginning to think there was something seriously fucking wrong with me when my pulse quickened and I reached out to swirl my finger in our combined release. I didn't do this in an effort to clean it from her but to push it back in.

When Lauren tilted her pelvis to chase my retreating fingers, all thoughts of work flew out the window.

I pressed and rolled my thumb around her clit and kept working my fingers as I leaned close and whispered, "You're gonna have to be fast, Ren. Fast and quiet. You think you can do that, baby?"

She bit her lip and nodded.

It was like she was made for me.

10

I'm never gonna love you, baby.

It had been three days since Logan had uttered those words and I could still taste the heartbreak. Which was stupid because I didn't want him to love me and I didn't want to love him. But it still hurt to hear him unequivocally confirm what I already knew. And in those three days, Logan had become more confusing. Every night after work he'd shown up at my house. Not for sex. Oh, no, not Logan. He ate dinner with me, we watched more TV, laughed, talked, teased. You know, all the things I was going to get smart about and not do. Yeah, well, I didn't wise up. I fully participated in the madness. This was because I found I enjoyed Logan's company.

When we were at home...whoa, *whoa*, whoa...when we were at *my* house he was a totally different man. He was quick to laugh and faster to smile. And each night he loosened up even more. We were coming up on a week and we'd slept in the same bed since the first time we'd been together. If I didn't know any better I'd say we were in a relationship. But then I'd remember, *I'm never gonna love you, baby,* and my heart would splinter before I glued it back together and added a steel plate to reinforce the damn organ.

This was going to be painful.

Yet, I didn't put a stop to it.

Logan's mom and twin sisters were flying in from Michigan tomorrow night and staying until Sunday. The timing was perfect. Two days to cool things down and get my head straight.

The front door sensor beeped and I looked up to see Addy at the keypad punching in her code. Liberty, Shiloh, and one of Addy's clients, Chelsea, were jogging their way from the parking lot.

Thursday workout.

I was still thinking up an excuse that would be a total lie to get out of working out when Addy walked in with her hand up as if she could read my mind.

"No excuses. You're coming with us," Addy barked and Shiloh gave me wide eyes.

"Wait, I'm confused. Are you Adalynn or Hadley?"

Addy didn't miss my sarcasm. It had taken me a few months to be able to differentiate the identical twins but after years of working at Triple Canopy and being close friends with all the Walkers, I knew without a shadow of a doubt it was Addy standing in front of me. Though the attitude she was throwing was more along the lines of Hadley's normal snark than Addy's.

"I'm pissed at you," Addy snapped.

"Oh, shit, little sis is on a tear," Quinn muttered and stopped at my desk. "Maybe I'll bow out of class tonight. I don't feel like getting my ass kicked."

"I'm pissed at you, too," Addy continued.

"Me? What did I do?"

"It's what you *didn't* do, *sister*."

Then in the worst timing in the history of bad timing Logan, Matt, and Luke walked into the reception area. I didn't miss Luke's wince as his gaze slid around the room. Though when his eyes landed on his fiancée Shiloh he smiled. Matt didn't look around, he'd zeroed in on Chelsea. *Interesting.* However, my observation was cut short, because bad timing turned into something so much worse when Logan opened his mouth.

"Ren, baby?"

"Huh?"

I started to look at Logan but froze when I heard Addy growl.

Sweet Addy growled like a bear—a cute polar bear—but still, she growled.

Ren, baby.

Shit, damn, and fuck my life.

"I'm gonna be late tonight. Luke, Matt, and I have to run to Richmond Hill."

Richmond Hill? That was where Guy lived.

After Logan had found out that not only had my ex cornered me in a grocery store but that he'd also frequently called—which I never answered—and texted, Logan was off-the-charts irate. Nothing I said calmed him down, not even when I explained that after the first ten or so texts that consisted of me telling Guy there was nothing he could do to change my mind and to please leave me alone, I'd stopped responding altogether. The more I tried to appease Logan the angrier he got, so I'd dropped the subject Tuesday night and decided Logan was going to do whatever he thought he needed to do to make Guy leave me alone. I didn't want Guy bothering me so I actually didn't care what Logan said to Guy. Though him taking Luke and Matt out to Richmond Hill sounded like a disaster waiting to happen.

"Why are you going out there?"

Logan gave me a look that said I knew why and his one-word alpha answer confirmed it.

"Babe."

"He's a five-foot-eleven computer geek, Logan. I hardly think there's a need for *three* former SEALs to show up on his doorstep. Just the sight of you alone will make him pee his pants."

Logan's smirk was a clear indicator he not only agreed with my assessment but he also took my comment as a compliment.

"He'll be pissin' into a bag he thinks to fuck with you again after today's visit."

"Logan—"

"And Matt and Luke aren't going to be seen. Luke's putting a tracking device on his car since it's parked in the driveway and not his garage. Matt's going around back to take down a nest a damn bird built right in front of one of the cameras and I'm pulling double-duty laying out what I will not be tolerating while causing a distraction."

"I hate to interrupt," Chelsea cut in, not sounding like she hated it at all. "But why didn't someone stop the bird while it was making the nest? I mean, what if there's eggs in there? The poor mama bird's gonna wonder where her babies are."

"I think having eyes on the dipshit's backyard is more important than a few bird eggs," Matt returned.

"Whatever you say, bird killer," Chelsea huffed.

I glanced over at Matt and waited for him to volley but all he did was scowl.

Yes, very interesting.

"We good?" Logan asked.

"Sure."

"Then we're leaving. I'll see you later tonight."

"I'm busy tonight," I blurted out.

Logan's lips quirked up into a knowing grin right before he winked.

"Yeah, you're busy tonight all right."

Addy made another sound, this one not quite a growl but more than a grunt, and all eyes went to her.

"I'm so totally pissed at everyone."

"Ren?" Logan said from beside me—right beside me, as in so close when I turned my head I was easy pickings and had no way to stop Logan from kissing me.

Kissing me in front of everyone.

Thankfully it was a short, closed-mouth peck but it was still a kiss and his lips were still on mine and people were watching.

"Have fun."

And with that, before I could kick his ass he and the guys strolled out the door. But not before Luke stopped in front of Shiloh and kissed her goodbye. Luke's smooch was not short and closed-mouthed. It was the type of kiss a man gives the woman he loved.

I wasn't jealous.

Nope. Not even a little bit.

The door had barely closed behind Matt when all eyes came to me.

"What?"

"What?" Addy screeched. "You're going out with Logan and all you have to say for yourself is 'what'?"

"I'm not going out with Logan."

"She's not going out with Logan," Addy mocked. "Is she crazy?"

"*She* is right here, you know!"

"I'm not talking to you. We're supposed to be friends.

Friends call their friends when they land the hot guy they've been crushing over. Friends call their friends when they hook up with the hot guy they've been lusting after for-freaking-ever. And friends call their friends when the hot guy practically moves in. But, no, not you. You don't call. I have to hear it from Shiloh."

"Logan hasn't moved in," I said to Addy but I was now staring at Shiloh.

"Don't look at me. I thought she knew. I mean, everyone else knows. How was I supposed to know that her man's not keeping her up-to-date like Luke's keeping me?"

The man Shiloh was referring to was Trey. He was another former SEAL who worked at Triple Canopy.

"Brice talked to Jackson who got it from Carter that Logan's spent every night at your house since Balls last Friday," Quinn put in. "That's basically living together."

Brice was Quinn's very-soon-to-be-husband. He was a firefighter who worked with Jackson Clark. Obviously, neither of those men worked at Triple Canopy but Carter Lenox did, and not only was he one of Logan's best friends he was also Jackson's cousin.

"I'm sorry, but do the men that work here have nothing better to do than gossip?" I asked snidely.

"You've worked here longer than I have," Quinn pointed out.

And she need not explain further. All of the men gossiped worse than old church ladies.

"Logan's not living with me. We're not in a relationship. We're not..." I stopped and reconsidered. "Okay, we're hooking up. But that's it. Nothing else."

"Um...I'm sorry, was she not here when that man called her 'Ren, baby'?" Chelsea asked. "Because I was and I

swooned a little. Which is code for my panties got a little
damp and the 'baby' wasn't even directed at me."

"You just wish Matt would call you 'baby'," Addy
snapped.

"Hell yes, I'd like for Matt to call me baby. Have you seen
him? You know the only reason I'm still rehabbing with you
is so I have an excuse to come here. Can you say, eye
candy?"

"You have the hots for Matt?" I chirped. "That's cool.
Matt's a great guy."

"Stop trying to change the subject. You're not off the
hook." Addy pointed at me.

Jeez.

Someone had their panties in a twist.

"Fine, I'm sorry I didn't tell you, but *I* haven't actually
told anyone."

"And why is that, exactly?" Quinn asked.

"Because we're..." I trailed off.

What were Logan and me? Bed buddies? Fuck friends?
Were we even friends? Yes, I could admit we were friends,
which was one of the reasons it was going to hurt so badly
when this ended. I genuinely liked Logan as a person. That
was when we were alone and he let down the stone wall he
kept around him.

"Lauren?" Addy called.

"We're just having fun," I answered. "It'll never be
serious and I'm okay with that. I don't want a relationship."

Quinn busted out laughing. Her body shook so violently
she bent at the waist and slapped her thighs. "It's like déjà
vu," she sputtered. "I'm having flashbacks. Only...Logan's me
and Lauren's Brice."

"What does that mean?"

"Stop freaking her out," Liberty spoke up.

"Too late, I'm already freaked. What does that mean: I'm Brice and you're Logan?"

Before Quinn, Brice Lancaster was the quintessential playboy. With his good looks, it was no surprise women had fallen at his feet, or into his bed as it were. But after Quinn had talked him into a neighborly friends-with-benefits arrangement, an arrangement that made Brice admit he had feelings for her and get over some deep-seated internal struggles that were holding him back. Now they were getting married in a few weeks.

Wait.

What?

"I am not Brice and holding out on Logan. And trust me, friend, Logan's not you. He legit doesn't want anything more than what he's getting from me."

"And what's he getting from you?" Liberty inquired.

"Lots of sex."

"You know I love you, girly," Liberty started. "From the bottom of my soul like a sister but you need to open your eyes. Logan does not, for any reason, ever, spend the night with a woman. And he doesn't spark up friendships with the women he sleeps with."

A funny sensation—one that felt a lot like betrayal—rumbled in my belly.

"He told me he hadn't slept with a woman since he'd been in Georgia." I heard Addy suck in a breath and Quinn made a strangled sound that sounded like a laugh. "So how would you know that?"

Liberty's eyes slowly drifted closed but not before pain flashed and her mouth turned down.

"Liberty?"

"What has he told you about his dad?" she asked when she opened her eyes.

"He said his dad was dead."

And that was it; Logan hadn't elaborated but his non-verbal reaction to my question had left me feeling horrible for asking so I didn't push. I loved my dad so I could totally understand the topic being a sore subject, and from the way Logan's body had turned to stone I knew he wasn't over his father's death.

"He is," Liberty confirmed. "I wasn't speaking from first-hand knowledge, I've never seen him with a woman. I just know what Drake has told me. And Logan does not get involved with women. Not ever, Lauren. I mean that he actively avoids getting into a relationship and he has his reasons. I don't agree with them, but Logan wholeheartedly believes down to his bones he should never be close to a woman."

I'm never gonna love you, baby.

"What does 'should never be close to a woman' mean?"

"That's not my story to tell," she whispered.

"But there's a story?"

"Yes. One that he needs to tell you. I thought you knew."

I didn't know. And I was thinking I *should* know.

My gaze went to Addy and she looked deep in thought. "Do you know what she's talking about?"

"No. Trey just said Logan has his reasons and I should leave it be."

No help there—Addy would never lie. I glanced at Quinn, but before I could ask her she was shaking her head.

"I don't know anything and if Logan has shared something with Brice he hasn't told me."

A thought struck me. After Logan had laid out all of the things he *didn't* do with women he was adamant that was *not* how he was with me. That implied I was different. I just didn't know what different meant. Why did *he* insist on spending the night? Why did *he* insist on coming over every night? As far as mixed signals went, the ones he was giving off were so twisted and knotted I couldn't figure out what he truly wanted.

"After what happened with Guy I'm not looking for anything serious. Logan has his reasons and those are not my business. I don't want a relationship—"

"Seems to me like you're already in one, sister. A *serious* one if he's spending the night every night and calling you 'baby,'" Chelsea tossed out.

"You need to talk to him," Liberty encouraged.

Nope. No way. I wasn't asking anything personal, nothing that would cement a friendship that had an expiration date. The more I learned about Logan the more he got past my defenses. If I wanted to come out of this without being totally shattered I would not be asking him why he'd kept an emotional distance from women.

Women who are not you.

As quickly as the thought popped into my head I pushed it away.

I didn't want to be different.

Liar.

I ignored Liberty and addressed Addy. "Are you still pissed at me?"

"Kinda."

"Then I'm bagging on Thursday workout night. On a normal night, I leave sore. No way am I going into the gym with you mad at me."

"Whatever," Addy mumbled. "We're doing a light workout tonight. I have to meet my mom later to go over wedding plans."

"I'm still impressed you got Trey to hold off a whole nine months when he swore up and down he wasn't waiting until after my wedding to marry you," Quinn told her sister.

"I didn't do anything. Emily Walker spoke and Trey listened." Addy shrugged. "At this point, Dad's offering us money to elope. Two weddings in two months and you know how he gets. I thought after Delaney got married and he was a grouch it was just because it was his first daughter getting married. But he was the same way when Hadley married Brady. And he's already in a bad mood and your wedding hasn't even happened yet."

Jasper Walker was not grouchy, he was emotional. I knew my dad loved me, but there was something different about the way Jasper loved his daughters. I'd never seen anything like it until I started working at Triple Canopy. And it wasn't just Jasper. Nolan Clark loved his sons, Jackson and Nick. Carter Lenox was the same with sons, Carter and Ethan. Then there was Levi McCoy and the man positively adored his daughter, Liberty. But it wasn't just love, it was the way the four men showed it. It poured out of them so pure it was beautiful to see. Over the years I'd heard the girls bitch about how protective the men in their lives were. While I knew my dad loved me and he was proud I was a good person, he was not an overly protective man. I would never admit it to any of my friends but secretly I was a little jealous.

What would it be like to have someone love you so much they would do anything to protect you?

A question I'd never know the answer to.

11

"It's a good thing you didn't end up in the clink." Lauren's breath fanned across my neck.

"The clink?" I chuckled.

Lauren moaned, then I returned the groan when her pussy clamped tight.

"The can, the joint, the big house."

"Yeah, baby, I know what the clink is."

"Well, I'm glad you didn't end up there or I would've never experienced a triple. And, honey, just so you know, now that I've had this awesome experience I'll be expecting more in the future."

"A triple?"

"Three back-to-back orgasms," Lauren explained and tightened her legs around my hips.

Right.

Lauren must've developed amnesia.

"Ren, hasn't been a night this week you haven't had three."

"That's different."

"How so?"

"Well..." She stopped and tried to hide her face.

"Oh, no, baby girl, you started it. See it through and explain to me how me getting you off with my mouth before I get you there with my dick is different."

"That's just it, one with your mouth. A triple has to be executed in one go."

Yeah, I wasn't seeing the difference but she had indeed had three orgasms that I'd barely been able to hold out giving to her and I was spent. Thus, I felt it best to agree.

"Sorry, baby, seems before tonight I've been slackin'."

Lauren's body under mine started shaking and when her giggle escaped I closed my eyes. Never before had I experienced such a sensation. I'd always been quick to disengage and go someplace in the back of my mind. I'd always known that made me an asshole. But now I was pleased as hell; Lauren was my first. The first woman I'd slept beside. The first I held until I fell asleep. The first I laid in bed and talked to. And she sure as fuck was the first I'd laughed with while my dick was still buried deep.

"I need to clean up."

She did, then we had a lot to talk about. But first, I wanted a kiss and since her beautiful face was mere inches from mine I didn't have far to go when I dropped my lips to hers and touched my tongue to her lips. Instead of opening and letting me take her mouth Lauren touched just the tip of her tongue to mine before she swept it over my bottom lip. She took her time, sweet and tentative, and the scar tissue around my heart thinned.

"You have great lips," she murmured and kissed the corner of my mouth.

The reverence in her tone should've put the fear of God in me. The soft touches should've had me running for the hills. Instead, I wanted to stay. I wanted to wrap her up and keep her in bed and never let her go. I wanted to cocoon us in her sheets so outside forces couldn't invade. Build a fortress around us and block out every bad memory.

I was in way deep with Lauren and I didn't give the first fuck. That above all else should've told me now was the time to make a clean break.

But there was zero chance I was going to do that.

I pulled out and smiled when I heard her mew when she lost me.

"Clean up and hurry back."

Lauren made an annoyed face and rolled her eyes to the ceiling. Keeping them there she muttered, "Always so damn bossy."

Reminding her my bossy was what had given her a 'triple' would've delayed her getting up, cleaning herself off, and coming back to me. I rolled to the side wondering when the fuck I became the sort of man who ordered a woman to hurry back. The fuck of it was my urgency had nothing to do with the conversation we needed to have and more about wanting her near.

Yeah, I was in way too fucking deep, sinking deeper, and not giving a shit.

My eyes followed her to the bathroom and I wondered when we got so comfortable in each other's presence she didn't bother closing the door. Neither did she try to cover herself up. Lauren was completely at ease in her nudity and it had taken less than a week. This was not a complaint. Merely an observation.

She came out of the bathroom, tagged my tee off the floor on her way back to bed, and had it on before she crawled back onto the mattress and flopped down on her belly, resting her head on my stomach, face turned in my direction, eyes pinning me in place.

"What's on your mind, Ren?"

"Will you tell me about what happened at Guy's?"

"Camera's functional again. A tracker's been put on his car. And I made my point that you are to be left alone."

"Just like that?"

If I hadn't already known what a pansy-ass Guy was after my brief conversation with him I would've questioned if the idiot had a pair of balls. He caved surprisingly fast.

"Yep. Just like that."

"Huh."

"Huh, what?"

Lauren was silent for a second and her gaze slid away.

"I don't like talking about him to you," she said.

Her ex wasn't my favorite topic either, but I wasn't fond of the expression on her face so the conversation needed to be had.

"He's not my favorite subject either, baby."

"I want to preface this by saying, I'm happy he got the message and he won't be contacting me again. But it's just strange that after calling me and texting me nonstop he'd just agree to not contact me. Again, I'm grateful but Guy likes to get his way and when he doesn't he lets you know he's not happy."

I felt it start, the sick in my gut, the stirring of the poison, childhood memories of my dad not getting his way and raging until I was beaten and bloodied—or worse, my mom was.

"Did he..." Fucking shit, I couldn't even say it.

"Oh, God, no. He never abused me or anything. He would just get pissy. It was totally passive-aggressive. Like he'd never come straight out and tell me why he was being an ass. He'd simply make snide jokes."

It was on the tip of my tongue to ask why the fuck she'd

put up with Guy's shit but I didn't want to know. And not because I didn't care about her answer but I knew it would in some way enrage me that my stupidity had driven her to him. If I'd manned up sooner, she never would've met the douchebag.

"I think Guy understands he's not getting you back and it's in his best interest to forget you exist. Besides, in a few days, he'll have more to worry about than trying to call you."

Dylan was finding all sorts of interesting threads, placing Guy in multiple cities where Lucky's drugs had been distributed.

"So you really think that Guy's involved with Lucky somehow?"

Seeing as Lauren was a trusted member of TC she wasn't kept in the dark about who and what the team was investigating. She'd made the travel arrangements for the team and when we got behind she'd type up our SITREPS. So Lauren knew about Lucky and the drugs.

"Yes, I think he's involved. The question is, how deep."

"Damn. I'm not gonna lie; that creeps me out."

There was a lot I'd do for Lauren, but helping her process her feelings about Guy was not one of them. I was getting ready to move the conversation along when her finger traced the scar on my stomach.

"How'd you get this one?"

I grew cold and I could feel, muscle by muscle, the stiffness as it crept up my body. Each labored breath felt like I was being suffocated. Lauren's hand stilled and anger clawed at my throat.

"I'm...I'm sorry, Logan. I shouldn't've asked."

No one had ever asked about my scar. The guys knew because I'd told them. They never asked. No one ever fucking asked. I wasn't sure which was worse, her asking or her tracing all the ugly with her beautiful, clean touch.

"Up, Ren."

I couldn't take it. Not another second of her looking at me with wide, scared eyes. Not her head on my lap. Not her skin touching mine.

She never should've asked.

Lauren scrambled as quickly as she could, coming up on her knees on the other side of the bed.

Fight or flight.

I'd seen that reaction in my mother so many times I'd lost count. Seeing Lauren look at me in fear made my stomach revolt.

"What's going on?"

Weak and small.

Fucking Christ.

I'd heard that, too. Every time my dad was getting ready to blow, my mom's voice would wobble.

"Logan?"

I needed to get up and get the fuck away from her. Away from all the venom clogging my mind. But with the oxygen stuck in my lungs, I couldn't move.

"Hey," Lauren called and lifted her hand.

"Do not fucking touch me."

"Explain to me what's going on," she demanded.

"I'm leaving."

I rolled out of bed and had my pants pulled up when Lauren rounded the bed and grabbed my hand. With a flick of my wrist, I yanked my hand free and stepped back.

"Do not fucking touch me," I raged.

Jesus fuck, I even sound like him.

"Okay, I won't touch you. Now tell me what's happening. I touched your—"

"Don't fucking say it," I growled.

Lauren's back shot straight. Her eyes did the squinty thing they did when she was seriously pissed and she stared at me. No, not at me, *through* my tissue, bone, organs, straight to my soul.

"Talk. To. Me."

I didn't talk, I also didn't move.

"How'd you get that scar?"

My teeth clenched so hard I wouldn't have been surprised if I'd chipped a tooth.

"Was it in the Navy?" she pushed. "An accident. A childhood—"

That was when I broke.

"My dad gave it to me."

"Your dad?" She sucked in a breath. "Were you in a—"

"No, babe, it was no accident. The motherfucker stabbed me. That was after I stopped him from kicking the shit out of my mother. But before he could turn to one of my sisters."

"What?"

"Oh, yeah, he just sunk that blade in, no hesitation. He wasn't ready to let up. Came home early and pissed, wasn't even in the door five minutes before he started in. I heard it, came downstairs, and he was dragging my mom into the kitchen by her hair shouting about why his dinner wasn't ready. Not the first time he beat the fuck out of her, but it sure as fuck was the last."

Lauren's gaze was steady but her chest was heaving.

"Did you kill him?"

"If you're worried you're fucking a killer, hate to tell you this, but I figured you knew with my prior occupation and all, that I've killed—"

"Shut up!"

"No, Lauren, you should know who've you got in your bed."

"I would've killed the bastard if he'd beaten my mother and stabbed me."

I couldn't stop it. Sweet little Lauren talking about killing a man—the absurdity of it had me rolling with laughter. And once it started it just kept coming.

"Are you done laughing at me?" she snapped.

"No."

"No? You're not—"

"No, I didn't kill the asshole. But that's only because I was lying on the kitchen floor in a pool of blood."

The hollow, raw, darkness scratched its way to the surface. My mom's shrill screams. The burning pain in my gut. The helplessness. The impotence of youth. The anger at a dead man. All of it tore through me, ripping me to shreds.

Still weak. Still helpless. Still in pain.

"It was beaten out of you," she oddly whispered. "That's why you don't believe in love. That's why you hold yourself apart. I get it now."

"Do you?" I spat. "Do you understand that he's part of me? That I have that in me, too?"

"Yeah, I can understand why you think you do. The man who was supposed to teach you how to love your wife, love your children, love your family, failed you. The betrayal is so deep, the depth of it is unfathomable. All he taught you was pain. All he showed you was hatred. And you gathered all those lessons and you hold on to them so tightly you can't see what he actually left you with."

What the fuck is she talking about? The motherfucker left me with nothing.

"Every time I look in the mirror I *see* what that fucker left me."

"I'm not talking about the scar, honey. He left you with way more than that."

Lauren wasn't wrong. My dick of a father had left me with way more than a scar. I had a headful of trauma.

"You'd never hit me or any other woman."

"Lauren—"

"And you'd never in a million years hit a child."

"Stop—"

"He left you with *that*, Logan. That's what you can't see. You're denying yourself a life because of the pain he caused."

"No, Ren, I'm living my life in the absolute refusal to become what he was. I will never take the chance of losing my temper and lashing out at the people I love."

"You were pretty angry with me earlier when you found out I didn't tell you about what happened with Guy at the grocery store. Did it cross your mind to lash out and smack me?"

Was she insane? I'd never smack her.

"Fuck no!"

"Right. And just now, having to relive something painful, something that caused you great harm, was your first thought to beat me to shut me up? Did you want to inflict pain on me to detract from yours? Did you want to take your anger about your dad out on me?"

"I would never hit you, Lauren. For any reason."

"Are you listening to yourself, Logan?"

I clamped my mouth shut and shook my head. She didn't understand. It was there, in me, and one day it might escape. One day I might not be able to contain it.

"I will never take that chance."

"I'm not saying you should. I'm just asking if you're hearing what you're saying. You said you wouldn't take the chance of lashing out and hurting the people you *love*. You said you'd never hit me for any reason. I could be wrong, but I don't think I am, when I conclude that your father wouldn't have thought twice about using his fists to get himself out of a situation he felt was uncomfortable. And I'd venture to say, he didn't love a single person, including himself."

"Wife beaters always say they'll never do it again."

"Logan, I'm not trying to talk you out of feeling how you feel. You have to live your life how you see fit. Do what makes you comfortable. Only you can decide if the way you've been living makes you happy. You didn't ask my opinion so I'll keep it to myself and not tell you how wrong I think you are."

That was a backhanded way of giving an opinion if I'd ever heard one.

I needed to leave.

"I should go home."

"Okay."

What the fuck?

"Okay?"

"What do you want me to say, Logan? Beg you to stay? Tell you, you can't leave? That's not what we have."

Jesus Christ, that fucking hurt.

"So you're fine with me coming over, fucking you, then leaving?"

What the hell was wrong with me asking such a stupid question? She couldn't win; either answer was going to piss me off.

"This is what we are. This is how it should've been all along. I've thought a lot about what you said and I still think you're right. Love and relationships aren't for me. I feel too much and I'm the one who's left hurt when the relationship ends. I'll take the sex, maybe even some companionship, but I don't believe in love. Not for me."

This is what we are?

"What are we exactly, Ren?"

I needed to hear her say it, to pour more salt into my wounds. Remind me I was useless.

"We're friends who enjoy each other's company."

"Bed, baby. And before you get in, lose the shirt."

"Thought you were leaving."

"I changed my mind. I feel like *enjoying* my friend's *company* a little more."

Lauren didn't hesitate when she pulled my tee over her head and tossed it aside. She didn't dally getting back into bed. And she didn't protest when I slid inside of her and took my time making love to her.

12

If there were ever a time when I wished I wasn't an only child it was now. I wished I had a sister to confide in. Or better yet, I wished I had the kind of relationship with my mom that Addy, Hadley, Delaney, and Quinn had with Emily or Liberty had with Blake. I knew my mom loved me but she wasn't the kind of mom who became your friend when you became an adult. But right then I needed a sister or Emily/Blake/Lily/Reagan-type mom. There were so many thoughts battling in my mind I couldn't organize them in an orderly fashion. I was so confused I actually had a headache.

Logan was a contradiction.

He said one thing then did another. He said something then in the same conversation he'd contradict himself. The inconsistency would've been more confusing if I didn't understand why he was the way he was.

Logan was a liar.

I didn't think he even knew he was lying. He believed what he said, not realizing his actions and sometimes his words were not jibing with the persona he presented. The

Love Is Bullshit façade was just that. He loved people, he knew it was real, he saw it all around him. He simply wouldn't let himself have it. And I'd be a hypocrite if I ridiculed him for that.

His father had literally beat something out of him—it was the 'what' that was in question. What exactly did the asshole beat out of Logan? It wasn't the capacity to love, it wasn't his strength or his honor. It wasn't his compassion or his morality. No, it was Logan's faith in himself. He had zero self-worth. He didn't believe in himself.

Logan actually thought that one day he would hit a woman and he'd accepted this as fact. I mean, why wouldn't he? Plenty of people say abused children turn into abusers. I wasn't one of those people. At least not in Logan's case. I was not afraid of him and that wasn't naïveté. Last night, Logan had been wrecked. He was right back to a time when he got the shit beat out of him. I saw it come over him, I witnessed the pain that leaked out, and I knew there was more that was buried but he'd worked hard not to let me see. A man who feels that kind of pain then spends his life actively thinking about the possibility that he could turn out the same way *does not* inflict pain on others. He doesn't see how self-aware he is. He doesn't understand that a man who is going to beat his wife and children doesn't think and worry about it every day. And I'd venture to say there had not been a day in Logan's life when he hadn't dwelled on the what-could-happens or the what-ifs.

Confused and exhausted. That was what I was. And for the first time in all the years I'd worked at TC I was looking at the clock, counting down the minutes until I could go home and go to bed.

"Are you busy Monday night?" Quinn asked, pulling me from my musings.

"I don't think so."

"Addy wants—"

"No way! I'm not working out two days a week. My ass muscles are so sore I can barely sit."

"Halt!" Brady said, joining Quinn at my desk. "There is not enough ear bleach in the world for you to finish whatever you were talking about."

"Aw, is my brother-in-law squeamish?" Quinn teased her brother-in-law.

"About why a woman who is not my wife has a sore ass? One hundred percent."

"It's sore because of Addy. She's a menace. I am deeply ashamed I made fun of Trey all those times he left PT bitching and moaning."

"Trey's a wimp," Brady returned.

"I heard that," Trey called out as he walked into reception.

"Can the two of you please leave so I can talk to Lauren?" Quinn griped.

"Is it about work or gossip?" Brady asked and I rolled my eyes.

"Please, you men gossip more than Lauren and me." Quinn said what I was thinking. "And it's business."

"Jeez, you Walkers are snippy. I was just walking past to leave," Trey delivered with a smile.

"You know you're marrying a Walker, right?" Brady chuckled.

"Yep. The sweet one."

"You used to call my sister the Devil," Quinn reminded Trey.

Trey's face lit the way only a man in love's face could and his smile tugged higher, pulling on one of the scars on Trey's cheek.

I'd seen pictures of Trey before the mission that had left his face marred with scars and his leg severely injured. It could be said, Trey could've been a model. He was incredibly good-looking. But to me, the marks on his face added to his masculine beauty.

"What can I say? Turns out I like it a little rough," Trey joked. "Catch you all Monday."

Brady made a disgruntled snort and I took pity on him. "What can I do for you?"

"Did Dylan send you the Lucky files?" he asked.

"Yep. I printed them out and highlighted the cities that matched against Guy's credit card statement. As I was going through the files there were a few dates Guy told me he was going out of town that weren't on his credit card statements but the dates corresponded with the DEA report." When Brady stared at me I rushed on. "I didn't mess the report up, did I? I can print another one."

"No, you didn't mess anything up. We haven't found a digital calendar and his phone's clean so we've only been going off of Guy's credit card statements. Thanks for including those dates."

"Can I ask you something about the case?"

"Sure."

"Why haven't any of you asked me about Guy?"

Brady took me in with his gray eyes that used to hold so much pain. Since he'd finally pulled his thumb out of his ass and admitted he was in love with Hadley Walker, they were normally full of life. But right then, they held compassion I didn't understand.

"No one wants to upset you."

"Upset me? Talking about Guy doesn't hurt me."

"Just tell her," Quinn piped up.

The look Brady gave Quinn would scare the pants off

anyone else. Quinn being a ballsy, outspoken, badass was not affected by her brother-in-law's scowl.

"My dad told the guys not to drill you for information. He doesn't want Guy's...extracurricular activities to be rubbed in."

Jasper Walker.

The man's heart was too big for his extra-large body. Some time ago when a man called Roman Kushnir waltzed into TC looking to avenge his father's death and use Liberty as the vehicle to deliver his retribution, he beat me unconscious. Liberty and the team had all been out on the range and I was alone in the building. At the time the front door had no security—now it does, by Jasper's decree. Clark, Levi, Lenox, and Jasper had paid the medical bills that insurance didn't cover and Jasper and Emily wouldn't hear of me recovering alone at home so they'd taken me in. I might've been staying with Jasper but my convalescing was a collective effort and each of the men and their wives had stopped in daily to help.

The thing was, I wasn't physically hurt that bad. It was more that I was so afraid after being attacked I couldn't sleep. Jasper had talked me through the nightmares.

"He loves you," Quinn rushed out when she misinterpreted my silence.

"I know he does. Sometimes I forget how protective he is."

Quinn snorted and shook her head. "That's because you didn't grow up with him."

This was probably true. As an adult, I could appreciate his love and care. As a teenager, I might not have liked it.

"So, now that we've got that out of the way please let me help," I told Brady. "I wasn't with him long and I never traveled with him but I'm sure I know something that can be of use."

Brady still looked skeptical so I started blathering on about what I knew about Guy Stevens.

"He told me he was from Florida. And I realize all of this could be a big fat lie since he's a lying asshole but he told me he dropped out of college because his family couldn't afford the cost. He decided to get his Microsoft certs and went into networking. After a few low-paying positions, he figured out the corporate world wasn't for him so he started freelancing. He moved to Georgia about five years ago after he did a job up here and liked it. He has an office in Savannah."

"Wait," Brady interrupted. "Guy has an office? Have you been there?"

"That's what he told me and no, I've never been there."

"Do you have an address?"

"No. I've been on the phone with him when he's supposedly left the office to meet a client at the Henderson Country Club. That conversation lasted about five minutes. I teased him about choosing an office space so close to the golf course."

"Five minutes from the club would put an office in Midtown," Quinn said, looking down at her phone. "Assuming he was telling the truth that he left his office. East of the club is all residential. North is the Savannah River and marine terminals. South is more residential until you cross Victory and there's no way with traffic it would take five minutes to the club from there and there's always traffic."

"He doesn't have an office space rented in his name."

"He must've been lying to me then." I shrugged.

"What about his family? Did he talk about them?" Brady asked.

"His parents live in Miami. His sister moved to Texas and he has a brother who lives in St. Augustine. Finn the Fisherman is what Guy called his brother."

"Fisherman?"

"Yeah, I guess Finn owns a sportfishing boat or company, however you say that. Anyway, Finn's into deep-sea fishing and charters his boat. I remember that because Guy made fun of his brother's name but also, Guy said he gets seasick and has never been out with his brother."

Brady was quiet and I wondered if Guy had gone as far as to lie about his family. It seemed there was very little he'd told me the truth about. And funny enough, it didn't hurt as bad as one would think. I was more embarrassed I'd been swindled. But grateful I'd held back and not slept with the asshole.

Can you say, VD?

Just because my feelings weren't hurt didn't mean I was above wishing he'd get a flesh-eating bacterial infection and his dick would rot off. But that had more to do with my pride and the ass cheating on me than me being sad.

"Does he not have siblings?" I inquired.

"He does. Finn and May. May lives in San Antonio with her husband and children. Finn lives in Jacksonville. But he's not a boat captain; he's disabled and lives off social security and a settlement from his previous employer from a work accident that injured his back."

Another lie.

Whatever. It had already been established Guy Stevens was a skilled liar.

"One more thing," Brady started. "Other than the Samsung did you ever see him with another phone?"

Samsung?

"Guy doesn't have a Samsung. He has a Kyocera. He

called it a tough phone or something like that. Said it was totally waterproof and he could run it over with his car and it wouldn't break."

"Are you sure?"

"Positive."

Brady mumbled something under his breath then thanked me for my help before he beat a hasty retreat down the hall.

"They could've asked and saved themselves weeks of investigating him," I muttered.

"Yeah, well, you know the TC crew are always trying to protect their women. Which brings me to the business I need to talk to you about," Quinn stated.

"Right. Monday night. I'm available as long as there is no exercising involved."

"Promise."

"Are you going to give me a hint about why we're meeting? Wedding stuff?"

"Strategizing for a new business venture. Liberty and Shiloh came up with the idea. Addy jumped on board and Hadley has even agreed to leave her position at the library to help."

"Really?"

Hadley loved being a librarian. Her whole life seemed to revolve around books and literacy outreach.

"Yep. Liberty wants to call it Women Inc. but Hadley's fighting her and wants it to be called Heroines. They'll hash that out but we'd like your input and participation."

"Um, I have a job and so do you."

"Liberty talked to the Uncles. They're fully onboard. Monday we'll go over the specifics."

The Uncles were Jasper, Levi, Clark, and Lenox—the original owners of Triple Canopy. I suppose they still own

TC or at least part of it but they've stepped down from the day-to-day operations.

I loved my job but I wouldn't miss an opportunity to work with a group of women who were strong, smart, and motivated.

"Okay."

"Awesome. After work, we're meeting here in the conference room. Prepared to be wowed." Quinn smiled. "Now, go home and enjoy your weekend."

Yes, my weekend.

Alone, since Logan was with his family.

Something I thought I needed, but now for some reason alone sounded *lonely* and boring.

13

"So, Logan, your mom tells me you were in the Navy," Ian Webster said from across the table.

I'd been internally debating which grated my nerves more—the motherfucker sitting next to my mother or the sound of his voice. At his attempt to start yet another conversation with me I decided it was his voice that pissed me off, but when his hand covered my mom's on the table my opinion quickly changed.

This was not a good idea.

Not my mother and sisters insisting I meet the man or us having dinner together. I thought I could hold it together for the two days they'd be in Georgia.

I'd been wrong.

"Logan, Ian's talking to you," my mom needlessly pointed out.

"Yes, Ian, I was in the Navy. My sisters tell me you were once married but have no children."

I was being a total douchebag. I knew his wife had passed away and I knew they had no children due to her cancer treatments early in their marriage.

"Logan," my mom gasped.

Jill and Jackie both huffed. Jackie kicked me under the table. Not to be outdone her twin, Jill, pinched my arm.

"It's okay, DeeDee," Ian soothed. "I was married, yes. We were unable to have children. She passed ten years ago."

I didn't offer my condolences or any other platitudes that would smooth over me being a dick. I was caught back on Ian calling my mother a nickname. Her name was Deandra, but everyone called her Dee. I'd never heard anyone call her DeeDee and I didn't like hearing some asshole calling her a pet name.

"What's wrong with you?" Jill leaned over and muttered.

"Me? What the hell is wrong with you? Some guy's circling Mom and you're okay with this?"

"Ian's not a shark circling his prey, Logan. And why does everything have to be so damn difficult with you?" my sister pushed.

"Maybe because I love Mom and I don't—"

"Stop it, both of you, we're in public." Jackie the sensible twin scowled. "You're embarrassing Mom."

There was no doubt my mother was embarrassed. Her face was a deep shade of red and her perfectly manicured eyebrows were pinched together. And sitting there staring at her I wondered if she still woke up every morning and kitted herself out because that was what her abusive dickhead husband had demanded of her, or if she did it for herself. Dee Haines was always presentable.

"My son believes that it's his job to protect the women in our family," my mom said conversationally. "There was a time when that was the case. A time when I relied on him to oversee his sisters and keep them from harm. That time has long since passed but Logan has never stopped standing between us and anyone who he deems a threat."

What the fuck?

"Mom—"

"As Jackie has pointed out we are in public and now is not the time to air our dirty laundry, but, Logan, it's time for all of us to talk about what happened."

My hand went to my stomach and anger swelled.

"I vividly remember what happened."

"We all do, son. It's just you who cannot move past it."

I shut my mouth and clenched my jaw.

On more than one occasion Luke had accused me of being a mama's boy. He wasn't wrong. I adored my mother and my sisters. But it was my mom I had a soft spot for. It was my mom who had saved my life. It was my mom who had endured countless beatings to protect me and my sisters. I'd never been able to deny her anything.

But I wasn't sure if I'd be able to get through this dinner watching a man hold her hand.

"I love you, Ma."

"I know you do, son." She gave me a tentative smile that succeeded in making me feel like a huge asshole. "Now, let's talk about my girl making partner."

Yep. I was a horrible son and an even worse brother.

Seeing as Jackie was a vet tech and Jill an account manager for an advertising firm I knew which sister my mom was talking about.

"You made partner?" I asked Jill. "And didn't tell me?"

"I just got the news last week and wanted to tell you in person," she chirped.

No, she wanted her good news to be used to cut the tension. My sister was no dummy and knew exactly how I'd react to meeting Ian.

Fucking shit. I was going to have to get to know this guy. If he was going to be in my mom's and sisters' lives I had no choice.

"Proud of you, Jilly. Tell me all about it."

Jill filled me in on her new position. Jackie told us hilarious stories about the mishaps at the vet clinic she worked at. My mom injected her own stories about work—she was a receptionist at an attorney's office which was where she met Ian. Throughout dinner Ian smiled and let the girls gab, only adding something when Jill, Jackie, or my mom asked him a question. He didn't engage with me again until we left and he shook my hand and thanked me for buying dinner. Something I did to piss in my corner, something he saw right through and didn't bother to argue about.

By the time we parted ways, Ian and my mom going to their hotel, my sisters going to my house to stay with me, I was unsure how I felt.

But Jackie, she knew how she felt and the second I started the engine she let me have it.

"I love you, Logan, but you're a monumental prick."

"Jackie, calm down," Jill called from the back seat in an unusual twist.

Jill was the twin who was quick to blow her top while Jackie was the one to interject common sense.

"I'm not going to calm down. Mom deserves to be happy. And if you hadn't been such a prick at dinner you would've seen for yourself how happy Mom is. But instead, she was uncomfortable and on pins and needles and that's on you, Logan. God! She was nervous enough bringing him to visit you. I'm so mad at you right now I could bleach all of your clothes."

Right, so as a result of my father's constant abuse in the house no one threatened violence. My mom never scolded us and threatened a spanking, nor did she administer them.

My sisters would argue and threaten the most bizarre retribution but never said they would hit, smack, or physically harm each other. When they were pissed at me they'd proclaim they were going to shave off my eyebrows in my sleep, throw away something I valued, use hair removal cream on my legs. That had not changed.

"You bleach my clothes, Jackie, we're gonna have problems."

"Problems like you being a jerk to Ian, bringing up his wife? Or problems like you bringing up an incredibly painful reminder he doesn't have children because his wife went through chemo and they didn't have the option to preserve her fertility. But you knew that because I told you. What I didn't tell you is that both Ian and his wife wanted to freeze her eggs but they couldn't afford it. Wanna know why? Because she couldn't work due to her illness and Ian had to cut back to the bare minimum at his job—just enough hours to keep his insurance so he could take care of her. He refused to allow anyone else to see to her care. So they barely scraped by the whole time she was sick. That's the man you were a supreme fucking asshole to. A man who loved his woman so damn much he practically starved so he could care for her."

Fuck.

That dagger my mom stabbed into my heart with her sad smile was being twisted.

"Just give him a chance," Jackie pleaded.

"I can't."

Jill sat forward and popped her head through the front seats. "What, why not?"

"I don't know. I want Mom to be happy. But I can't fucking watch a man touch her."

"He is not Dad, big brother," Jackie whispered.

"You're right, he's not. But he could turn into him."

"I'm disinviting you to my wedding," Jill mumbled.

I swerved and righted my car and growled, "What? You're getting married?"

"One day, yes. And I'm preemptively disinviting you unless you at least talk to Ian."

"Jesus Christ."

"Yes, brother, now's the time when you should start praying before the hell you force yourself to live in becomes eternal," Jackie added sarcastically.

I stayed silent the rest of the drive. I grunted and pointed when we got into my house. Neither of my sisters said another word about my obnoxious behavior.

I waited for them to settle in the guest room for the night, then not bothering to attempt to sleep in my own bed, I grabbed my keys and left.

14

It was official; I was a prune.

I'd been in the bath so long I'd had to warm the water three times and I was a quarter of the way through a new book. For as long as I'd been in the tub I should've been further along but my mind kept drifting to Logan.

He'd been a total grump when he'd left work, bitching and complaining about his mother dating. Had he not told me about his dad I would've been totally confused. Logan was closing in on forty, far too old to be put off by the idea of his mother being with a man.

Since I'd been home from work, I'd had to stop myself from calling Logan to check on him. Dozens of times I'd picked up the phone to call but then I chickened out. Calling him would mean admitting we were more than what I was trying to convince myself we were. Finally, I'd gotten in the bath and left my phone in the kitchen to alleviate the temptation.

But truth be told, I was worried about him.

I checked the time on my tablet and it was almost nine. *I*

should get out and text him. A text wasn't the same as a call. A text conveyed friendship. A call said other things. Faster than I cared to think about and what my urgency said, I got out of the bath and dried off.

I opened the bathroom door. My eyes fell on my bed and I screamed, narrowly escaping cardiac arrest.

"You scared the shit out of me, Logan!"

"Sorry, I didn't want to interrupt your bath."

He won't interrupt my bath but he'll break into my house and get in my bed?

His voice was flat and monotone and upon further inspection, he looked...crushed.

"What happened?"

"I can't do this, Lauren."

The dreaded Lauren. Not Ren. Not baby. Lauren. My heart rate spiked and I braced for the end of us. Sure, I knew it was coming, but I figured we had more time.

"Do what?" I asked and clutched the towel tighter around my breasts.

"I can't give my mom what she deserves. I can't give my sisters what they want. I can't fucking do it."

I spotted Logan's discarded t-shirt on the floor, picked it up, and slipped it over my head before I pulled the towel free, let it drop, and climbed into bed next to Logan. Once I was situated next to him—both of us on our backs, our eyes on the ceiling, not touching—did I debate how to start the conversation.

Sisters. That seemed the easiest course of action.

"What do your sisters want?"

"For me to get to know Ian."

"Ian?"

"My mom's boyfriend."

Logan spat out "boyfriend" like saying the word was akin to eating raw whale blubber. Like he was going to vomit if he had to say it again.

Oh, boy.

"You met him tonight at dinner, right?"

"Yep."

"You're gonna have to help me out here. Did you not like him?"

"I was a total dick to him," he admitted.

Maybe his age didn't matter. Maybe thirty-eight-year-old men didn't like seeing their mommies move on. Or maybe Logan's instincts were telling him this Ian fella was no good. I'd learned the hard way that Logan could read people.

"Did you get a bad vibe or something?"

There was a long bout of silence and in the quiet, I listened to Logan's heavy breathing. Each inhale sounded like he was gasping for oxygen. His exhales rattled around the room and the longer this went the more my heart hurt for him.

His struggle was real even if I didn't fully understand what had him tied up.

"Why would you ask me that?" Logan asked softly.

"If you got a bad vibe?" I took Logan's grunt as my answer and went on. "Because you're a good judge of character and you've been trained to read a situation. If you were a dick to him I suppose you had a reason."

Logan blew out a breath then confessed, "When my sister called and told me my mom was seeing him, I ran a background check on him."

Of course, Logan ran a check. Knowing he couldn't see me I rolled my eyes and pinched my lips.

"Did you find anything?"

"Not a goddamn thing. Everything he told my mom and sisters checked out. He's had one speeding violation in the last ten years. He has no personal debt beyond a mortgage he could pay off. Moderate business debt. Healthy checking and savings, both personal and business. Never been arrested, no complaints have been filed. He's not wealthy but he's far from hurting."

"What'd he tell your mom and sisters?"

"He's a widower. His wife had endometrial cancer when she was twenty-three. She beat it but years later she developed bladder cancer. It was aggressive and spread quickly. Ian's wife passed ten years ago. Since then, he's submerged himself into business. I couldn't find a hint he's had even a date since his wife passed."

None of that was bad. All of it said great things about Ian and his devotion to his wife. Which meant Logan's issues were not with Ian but with his father.

"Until he met your mom," I whispered.

I didn't miss Logan's growl. I also didn't miss the way he lay beside me perfectly still and stiff.

"I don't know how to help you."

"Why can't I let it go? Why the hell can't I move on? Why can't I be fucking normal like everyone else?"

Each question he rapped out sounded like Logan was being tortured. Each question more painful than the last to hear.

"Honey, you *are* normal."

"No, Ren, I'm toxic. I'm so broken inside I can't give the woman who saved my life what she needs. I was a dick to a man who loved his wife, is honorable, and very clearly likes my mother. But I can't be happy for her."

"You think he's gonna hurt her? Physically hurt her."

"She killed him."

Deader than dead. Totally devoid of any emotion. A tone that sent a shiver through me, so when I reached for Logan's hand, mine was shaking. But I still managed to curl my fingers around his.

"Who?" I asked, with a squeeze of my hand.

"My father. I think my mom knew he'd finally cracked and it was only a matter of time before he went beyond his normal beatings, so months before that, she bought a gun. She killed him the night he stabbed me."

Holy shit.

Holy, *holy*, fucking shit.

"Logan," I breathed.

"Tonight with Ian sitting close to my mom all I could think about was how she used to cover her bruises. And when Ian held her hand all I could see were all the times my dad would grab her and yank her around." Logan paused and cleared his throat. "He was going to kill me. He was pulling back to stab me again when my mom shot him. I closed my eyes knowing it was coming, he was going to end me, I couldn't watch. I heard the bang, then my mom's hysterical screaming. Not before and not after, even with what I saw in the Navy, have I ever seen a woman so undone. And it wasn't just that night, it was for months after. It took years for her not to be skittish. Years for her not to jump at the slightest noise. Years for her not to flinch if she heard an argument when we were in public. I just don't fucking understand why she'd do it again."

"She's not doing it again, Logan."

"Same road, different man."

Logan's stomach might have been stitched up but the wound was still gaping, and with all the years that had passed without attempting to heal it, infection had set in. His father's abuse had turned into a virus and Logan allowed it to poison his every thought about love and relationships. It was no wonder he was the way he was.

I couldn't say that if I'd lived through what he had I wouldn't completely close myself off. Hell, I'd let a few bad boyfriends and one cheating, lying prick cause me to retreat and turn my back on everything I once wanted.

My heart sank and I could no longer bear the desolation, the kind of hurt that came out as a sound but sliced straight to the bone.

I had no idea how I was going to do it but Logan needed to open his eyes.

"I think you should spend some time with Ian. While he's here, take the opportunity to talk to him."

Logan's hand convulsed in mine, then tightened so tight I squeaked in pain but he didn't loosen his hold. He didn't move. I was unsure if he was breathing.

"I can't."

"Logan, you can."

"No, Ren, you don't understand. I cannot fucking do it. I cannot—"

"Stop!" I jerked his hand as hard as I could. "You *can* do it, Logan. You didn't get where you are by quitting. You didn't get here by cowering away from obstacles. And I know you didn't do the things you've done and see the things you saw and help the people you helped because you allowed fear to rule your life."

"Lauren—"

"Listen to me! You're gonna do this because you love your mom. You're gonna spend time getting to know him for your peace of mind. You're gonna do it so your family can

heal. What your father did to all of you is beyond compre-
hension. It was horrible—the worst. But, Logan, good men
do *not* hit women. They do *not* hurt children. They do *not*
stab their sons. What he left in you when he hurt you,
honey, is still eating at you. It's still inside of you and the
only way to stop it from festering is to deal with it."

Logan didn't reply verbally. He tugged my hand until it
was on his chest then he rolled into me and shoved his face
in my neck. He didn't speak, he didn't move, he just curled
into me with his heart pounding against my shoulder, his
breath fanning over my neck. We laid there in silence—me
perfectly still, him vibrating with pent-up anger and pain.

And that was how I fell asleep—with Logan clinging
to me.

The next morning I woke up in bed alone and I wondered if
I'd imagined last night until I heard Logan's raised voice
coming from the living room. A few seconds later he walked
into the room and gave me a pinched look that was a
reminder that last night not only happened but sleep hadn't
miraculously soothed his soul.

"Sorry, baby, I tried to put them off but they're on a
mission and on their way over here."

"What?" I blinked. "Who's on a mission?"

"Jill and Jackie."

"Your sisters?"

"Yeah, Ren. I only live five minutes from here and they
were walking out the door when I was talking to Jilly."

I didn't have time to process how cute it was that big
brother Logan called his baby sister Jilly.

"You live five minutes from here? Who's driving, Mario Andretti?"

I'd never been to Logan's house but I knew he lived about ten minutes from Carter and Delaney which would put him thirty minutes from me.

"Bought a house two months ago."

Was he serious? He bought a house? How did I not know this? Why hadn't anyone told me?

"Thanks for inviting me to your housewarming party," I snapped.

I wasn't sure why it hurt that I didn't know he bought a house but it did. It also rankled that I hadn't known he was looking to buy a place.

"Men don't have housewarming parties."

"They don't, really? I seem to remember Jackson had a big blowout when he moved in with Tuesday. And Trey and Hadley had a party in that huge mansion he calls a house."

Logan smiled and my breath caught. First thing in the morning, hot and sweaty from a workout, late at night, tired, it didn't matter—Logan had a beautiful smile. When it was real and the lines around his eyes appeared, his smile could light up a room.

"I'll rephrase that; single men don't have housewarming parties."

"You didn't have a housewarming party?"

"Ren—"

"Did you buy a house?"

"Yes."

"Then you have to have a housewarming party. It's the law, Logan. You have to have a party to celebrate. It's good luck."

His smile beamed. Then there was a knock on my front door and his smile faded.

"Out of time, baby. My sisters are here."

"Here? As in, at my door first thing in the morning, here?"

"Did you miss the whole beginning part of this conversation when I told you my sisters were on a mission and on their way over?"

"No, I didn't miss it. I blocked it out in the hopes that I heard you wrong."

"Hate to dash your hopes, but they're here."

"Why are they here?"

There was another knock accompanied by my doorbell and Logan mumbled something unkind about cutting his sister's hair off before he stomped out of the room, closing the door behind him.

What the hell is going on?

I rolled out of bed, glanced at the clock on my nightstand, and I felt my eyes bulge.

Noon?

Shit! It was not first thing in the morning, it was the middle of the day. How in the hell had I slept so late? I heard Logan's rumbling voice followed by a female's and I remembered why. I might've drifted off to sleep quickly but I'd woken up several times throughout the night hot, sweaty, and pinned under Logan's big body. Each time I'd awakened he was in the same position—on his side facing me, heavy arm across my chest, leg cocked with his knee resting on my thighs, and his head was resting on my shoulder. It was a weird reversal of how we normally slept with me cuddled into him. It was like, throughout the night he was holding on to me for dear life.

Now Logan's sisters were in my house for an unknown reason. Something I couldn't process until I got dressed and got some caffeine in me. I wandered into my bathroom, did my business, rushed to find something presentable to wear, and was getting ready to go out into the living room when the door flew open and I stumbled back, narrowly escaping a concussion.

"My mom and Ian are here," he announced with a face full of thunder.

It was safe to say my head was getting ready to explode, and by the look of Logan, his would follow.

I had a lot of questions as to why Logan's family was in my living room. But the only thing I got out of my mouth was, "Why?"

"Jill and Jackie woke up this morning, found me not there. Jill called me and when I told her where I was she started to scheme. An hour later she calls back to inform me we're all going to lunch. During this hour Jill had to plot she called my mother. Now they're all here and we're going to lunch."

That sounded great. Maybe I could hide out in my room until they left and save myself the embarrassment of a modified walk of shame. I mean, it was my house, so it wasn't like I was leaving somewhere in last night's clothes. But they all knew he'd spent the night. Not that we'd had sex last night, but they didn't know that. And Logan was wearing yesterday's jeans and a shirt that was clean only because he'd left it over and I'd washed it.

"Well, you guys have fun."

Logan blinked and tilted his head.

"Ren, you're coming with us."

"Um. What? No way."

"You wanted me to get to know the fucker, so you're coming."

I would swear that I felt my eye twitch and my cheek jump and my neck spasm all at the same time.

"Don't call Ian a fucker, Logan, that's not nice."

"See, that's why I need you there. You can point out all the ways I'm not being *nice*."

Logan might've been making a joke about needing me there but there was some truth in his statement. The tightness around his mouth and the way his hands were curled into fists told the real story. He didn't want to go to lunch and he seriously didn't want to be around Ian.

"Will me pointing them out make you stop?"

"Likely not."

At least he was being honest.

"Then we're stopping at the pet store so I can buy you a shock collar, one made for a Bernese Mountain Dog. No, a cattle prod. Better yet, an elephant tranquilizer and I get to shoot you with it every time you say something mean."

"A taser might be easier for you to conceal," he offered.

"Do you have one?"

"Not on me."

"That's too bad," I muttered, only half-kidding.

"Get ready, baby. I'll keep them occupied until you're done."

I was such a sucker.

"Is that safe?"

"You're right, it's not. I should shower with you."

Suddenly I didn't care if it was unsafe and my living room caught on fire and the house burned down. There was not a chance in hell Logan was showering with me while his family was waiting.

"Get out before I change my mind."

Logan stepped closer, one hand went around my back, the other went to the side of my neck, and he dropped his forehead to mine.

"I can't do this without you, Ren," he whispered.

Then he let me go and was out the door before I caught my breath.

Yes, I was a sucker.

I was also a fool because no matter how hard I tried I knew I was falling in love.

15

"I think we should go to Tybee," Jill announced as she opened and closed Lauren's cabinets hunting for a coffee cup.

"Can you please get out of Lauren's kitchen?"

"I would if you didn't suck as a host and offered me a cup of coffee," she shot back.

"Tybee sounds sublime," Jackie added. "We should totally do that."

"Mom, what do you think?" Jill asked as she helped herself to a cup of coffee.

"I think your brother's right; it's rude to go through Lauren's kitchen."

Jill, being the sister with no boundaries, opened the fridge and helped herself to half and half before answering.

"I doubt Lauren would mind. She's practically family."

It was at that moment Lauren appeared at the mouth of the hallway looking freaked the fuck out. She was, as ever, beautiful in a knee-length sundress, her hair down, makeup-free, with flip-flops on her feet. Beautiful but freaked.

"Ren, baby, come here so I can introduce you."

I ignored my mother's sharp intake of air and my sisters' very loud, very overexaggerated sigh and focused on Lauren. She was glancing around her house full of my family with wide eyes.

With no one saying anything and Lauren not moving, fucking Ian spoke up.

"Lauren, right?"

Lauren did a slow blink then her gaze went to him and my jaw clenched when she smiled.

"Yes. Sorry. I was..."

"Overwhelmed?" Ian supplied. "My apologies for taking over your home without notice."

"No, it's fine." Lauren waved her hand and I felt a molar crack.

Who the fuck did this asshole think he was—the head of the family, the patriarch, the goddamn mouthpiece for *my* family?

"Yes, Lauren, our apologies," my mother piped up. "I was under the impression you knew we were coming." My mom's gaze sliced to Jill and lingered before she walked to Lauren with her hand extended. "I'm Dee by the way."

"Dee, it's a pleasure to meet you." Lauren returned the handshake and the room plunged into awkward silence.

Yeah, I couldn't do this. Not even with Lauren by my side. Between wanting to strangle my sisters and my ever-growing need to punch Ian in the face it was safe to say I was struggling with not ordering everyone to leave.

"Oh my God," Jill groaned. "This is the best coffee I've ever tasted."

"It should be considering it's forty bucks for half a pound." Lauren smiled. "I stopped getting weekly manicures just so I could afford my expensive coffee addiction."

"You spend forty dollars on coffee?"

"Yes, Logan, you've tasted it and you can't deny it's worth every penny."

I wouldn't go that far. It was good but I'd still reach for the fifteen-dollar brand at the store.

"I'm Jackie. The rude one who helped herself to your kitchen is Jill."

"So I'm just gonna put this out there now. Please don't be offended if I see you again and you have to tell me who is who. Logan said you were twins but not identical."

"We're used to it," the twins said in unison.

"So, Tybee?" Jill pushed.

"Jill, there's no way we're gonna find a hotel." My mom injected wisdom.

"I'm sure we can get a VRBO or one of those Airbnbs, DeeDee."

Fucking DeeDee again.

No fucking way was I sharing a house with my mom, sisters, Lauren, and Ian. I'd poke out my eyeballs before that shit happened.

"The kids wouldn't want to stay with us, Ian."

The kids.

Jesus fuck. I was going to vomit.

"Jill," I snapped but got no further because Lauren loudly cleared her throat.

"There's a six-bedroom VRBO on the beach right next to that ice cream shop Mom loves," Jackie said and looked up from her phone. "And it has a pool and hot tub."

"Jack—"

"Logan." Lauren smiled sweetly.

"Ren," I warned.

"Zap. *Zap*," she returned her own warning with an edge to her voice but the smile still firmly in place.

I was going to zap her ass as soon as my family left.

"Lauren, would you like to spend the weekend in Tybee with us?" my mom asked.

"Um. Thank you but I couldn't impose on family time."

"Oh, no, baby, you're imposing," I told her.

If looks could kill I'd be severely maimed by the daggers Lauren was aiming my way. I could almost feel the heat from her anger radiating from her.

"Great, that's settled. I'll book the house before someone else does." Jackie's thumbs flew over the phone's screen.

I didn't miss the cat-like smile that tipped up the corners of her mouth.

My sister outplayed me.

Fucking shit.

"Cool, we'll have lunch at the beach," Jill bossed.

"Jackie, use my card, sweetie," Ian offered and reached for his wallet.

Sweetie?

I felt that fire in my gut ignite, the burn that would turn into an out-of-control blaze sparked to life and I took a step closer to Ian. The man had to leave.

"Lauren, you have a beautiful home," my mom commented.

"It's totally boring but I appreciate you saying so. I rent so I've never really decorated. I have a great landlord and every year he has the carpets professionally cleaned and last year he had the inside repainted but it still feels...I don't know, boring's the only word for it. One day I'll buy something."

"Logan just lives around the corner," Jill helpfully put in. "That's convenient."

"Yes, my son, the homeowner. Mind you, I've never seen

his house and he didn't even invite us down for the house-warming party," my mom told Lauren.

Lauren's gaze came to me, one eyebrow quirked up, expression set straight to *I told you so*.

"I didn't have one," I reminded her.

"That's just crazy. Who doesn't have a housewarming party?" Mom chided and Lauren's brows went up higher.

"Since Jill and I Ubered here we'll drive with Mom and Ian. That will give you and Lauren time to pack and we'll meet you there." Jackie cut into the ridiculous house-warming conversation. "I texted you the address."

Sure enough, my phone vibrated in my back pocket.

This was happening. I was going to spend the night in the same house as Ian Webster. Totally fucked. See-you-laters and nice-to-meet-yous were exchanged and two minutes later Lauren and I were alone.

She looked seriously displeased. If I wasn't such a selfish asshole I would've let her off the hook and told her she didn't have to come. But the disturbing truth was as much as I loved my mom and sisters and wanted to spend time with them, I couldn't bear the notion of Lauren not being there. I needed her and that need went beyond anything that was healthy. I was a grown-ass man, I'd lived through a plethora of dangerous situations, but I couldn't face one night and two days with my mom and her boyfriend without Lauren by my side.

"Logan?" Lauren called. "Are you all right?"

"Fuck no."

At that, Lauren rushed to me and didn't stop until her chest was fitted to mine. Her arms went around me and she held tight.

"What do you need from me?"

Christ.

I had to force air into my lungs before I could answer, "I just need you."

Lauren tipped her head back but she kept her arms locked tight.

"No, Logan, I mean how do I help you?"

A new kind of pain burned, a different kind of agony, the kind that felt so damn good you'd do everything in your power to feel it over and over. To keep it, to feed on it, to drink it in and savor it.

Kindness I wasn't worthy of but not stupid enough to let slip away.

"I will never in my lifetime do anything to be the kind of man you deserve. I know you deserve so much better. I know it, but, baby, I cannot let you go. It's gonna have to be you."

"What's gonna have to be me?"

"I won't ever walk away from you, so it's gonna be you. When you're done putting up with my shit, and you've figured out what a cocksucker Guy Stevens is, and you realize everything he did was because he's a fuck-up loser and it had nothing to do with you, you'll remember. And when you do you're gonna leave me."

There it was, the truth hung between us. I would never leave Lauren. I would never find the strength to be the better man and step aside so she could find love and happiness. I would linger like a black cloud, selfish in my need. Desperate to hold on to her.

"Is that what you think?" Disdain dripped off every word. "That I don't know that what Guy did was about him? I didn't snort coke off a hooker's boobs. I didn't cheat. I'm not a criminal and liar. He is. And that's not why I've decided I'd rather be alone. Well, that's part of it. But mostly, I've decided I'm never going to be someone's sucker ever again. I like myself too much to let myself get walked on again. I'd rather be by myself and be happy than have my heart broken."

"Ren—"

"Drop it, Logan. I need to pack so we can leave."

"You don't have to come."

"Yeah, I do, unless I want to bail you out of jail later. Or alternately bail one of your sisters out of jail after they attempt to drown you in that hot tub Jackie was so excited about."

And here I thought Lauren missed the dirty looks Jill and Jackie were casting my way.

"You're observant," I noted.

"No, they weren't hiding their irritation and your mom looked like she was on pins and needles. The only one who looked perfectly at ease was Ian. He's not stupid, Logan. He knows why you don't like him, and one look at him and the way he acted says he understands."

Screw Ian Webster and his understanding.

Lauren breathed an impatient sigh and loosened her arms. But before she pulled away she rolled up on her toes and kissed my jaw.

"Just watch and listen tonight," she whispered. "Give him a chance to prove he's who he says he is or prove he's really a bastard. But you won't know if you don't get to know him."

With that Lauren walked away.

I watched as she disappeared into her bedroom, thinking the fuck of it was I believed Ian was who he said he was. I believed he loved his wife. I believed he was a man of character. Yet I still couldn't untwist the memories that plagued my mind.

"I like her." My mom beamed.

This felt like a trap. Either she was hoping I'd return the sentiment and tell her I liked Ian or he was at least growing on me or she was fishing for information about me and Lauren. So I kept my eyes on the front door of the store my sisters and Lauren had gone into and shoveled another spoonful of ice cream into my mouth.

"I like that she's a little shy. I think she balances you out. Though she warmed up to Jilly and Jackie quickly."

"Are you saying I'm a jabber jaw?"

"No. But you don't need to talk; it's your presence that's commanding. Lauren softens you."

Not that I'd tell my mother, but the last thing Lauren did was make me soft. I'd been fighting wood for the last three hours we'd been on the beach. It didn't matter Lauren's one-piece bathing suit covered more than any of the other women under fifty. The pale yellow made her skin glow and the deep V in the front couldn't hide her cleavage.

That reminded me. "You need to tell Jill and Jackie to buy new bathing suits."

"I think they're way past the age where they'll listen to me. All of you are."

It was my mother's exhalation that told me she was gearing up for a Mom Talk. One I'd been studiously avoiding all day. But now that Lauren and my sisters were shopping and Ian was down the street making reservations at the restaurant my mom wanted to go to, we were all alone.

Fuck.

I needed Lauren.

"I'm scared for you," my mom whispered.

"What?" I shifted on the bench and the look on my mom's face cut deep.

"I'm scared that you're so caught in the past, in bad, that you cannot see the blessings in front of you."

My mouth filled with saliva which was unfortunate because that meant I couldn't stop my mother from continuing.

"You know, for ten seconds after I killed your father I felt relief. I felt joy. I felt the chain break. We were free. But, Logan, son, that eleventh second comes, and the fifteenth, and the thirtieth, and relief turns into doubt. It turns into guilt."

"Guilt? That asshole beat you. He beat me. Why the hell would you feel guilty? You saved us."

"You misunderstand. There's never been and there never will be a moment when I've felt guilt or remorse for killing him. Truth be told I should've done it before that day. The guilt comes from what I did to *you*. In that eleventh second when the relief waned I saw you on the floor bleeding, staring up at me with wide eyes, and your father was next to you dead. *I* did that. I killed him in front of you. And for that, I will forever feel guilt."

No.

No more.

I couldn't stomach any more.

"Mom—"

"You have this picture of family in your mind and you won't let it go. The way you grew up, what you saw, son, that image is warped. It's not right. And I need you to erase it so you can break the cycle. You're squandering your life, Logan. You're denying yourself happiness."

I forced my body to remain still, forced myself not to jump off the bench and run, forced myself to breathe.

Break the cycle.

That was what I was doing by not falling in love. Not finding a wife. Not having children. I was breaking the fucking cycle. No wife meant I couldn't beat her. No kids meant I couldn't hurt them.

"I can't take the chance," I told her.

"What chance?"

"That I'm like him."

My mother gasped and her hands slowly lifted like they always did when she reached out to touch one of us. Her movements were gentle, slow—soft so as not to scare us. It had been a long time since I'd flinched when someone reached for me. A long time since I'd felt helpless. A long time since I was a little boy powerless to stop my father from hurting my mom, but she still moved gently. But when her hands cupped my cheeks they were anything but soft.

And just as fiercely as she was holding my face she rapped out each angry word. "Listen. To. Me. You are nothing like him. Not one goddamn thing!"

I was unsure which was more shocking—my mother saying a curse word or the way she'd jerked my neck around as she spoke.

Someone behind me cleared his throat and I knew it was Ian. My mother's gaze went over my shoulder and I waited. When I was a child this was when she'd close down. When my father caught her hugging me, cuddling me, speaking quietly to me, my father would rage and tell her to stop making me into a pussy. My mother's eyes would flash, then she'd back away. She'd learned what happened if she didn't. It wouldn't be her who would get a beating, it would be me. He'd yell that I needed to toughen up and he'd slap me around a few times to drive his lesson home.

But as I watched and waited, no change came over my

mother. Sadness shown in her eyes. She didn't mask her pain from Ian. I couldn't process what that meant.

"I'm sorry to interrupt," Ian began. "The only table the restaurant has available is in ten minutes. I'll go back and cancel the reservation. We'll find somewhere else for a later time."

No anger.

No irritation at possibly canceling a reservation he'd walked two blocks to secure.

Something like that would've sent my father into a rage.

"No. I'll go get the girls," I told him but didn't take my eyes off my mom.

"It's fine, Ian. We were just finishing up." My mom's gaze came back to me and smiled. "One day, my beautiful son, you'll believe me. And if you'd open your eyes to what is right in front of you it'd happen sooner than you think."

Fuck me, she wasn't wrong. I knew I was in love with Lauren. But I also knew it was wrong.

I wasn't safe to love anyone.

16

Jackie had found the perfect house.

Close to the beach, restaurants, shops, the rooms were beautiful, the house was spacious, the pool was awesome, but the hot tub was the best. And that was where I was currently sitting with a full belly and a glass of wine Dee had poured for me. I was also alone. Jill and Jackie had cornered Logan and carted him off into the room the twins were sharing. I was supposed to be running interference but I was exhausted after dinner and I figured Logan could handle his baby sisters, and if he got his boxers in a twist I'd untwist them later.

It wasn't that dinner was horrible; it wasn't. Apparently, during their last trip to visit Logan, that trip Lucy and her wife had joined them, they'd discovered the restaurant we'd gone to. Dee had declared it her favorite. Upon finding this out, Ian being the kind of man who wanted Dee to have anything she wanted, demanded we go there for dinner. It had been the only time since we'd arrived in Tybee that Ian had voiced an opinion. The food was excellent, the ambiance was beautiful, and since I'd relaxed, I enjoyed the company.

Logan was the only one uncomfortable. He wasn't rude or brash or behaving like a dick, he was simply quiet. Almost reflective. Which made Dee watchful. Which made Ian watch Dee. Which made Jill talkative. Jackie and I were the only two at the table who were attempting normalcy.

The good news was I no longer wanted to kill Logan for dragging me on an overnight trip with his family. Dee was sweet and funny. Ian was a nice guy. And Jill and Jackie were hilarious. They reminded me so much of Hadley and Addy. I wished they lived closer because I'd so be friends with them.

Watching them also reminded me I didn't have what they had. My parents were not bad people, they called me occasionally, I called them, we exchanged emails but we were not close. We didn't let loose and laugh with each other. Up until I started working at Triple Canopy I hadn't realized how disconnected we were.

One of the three sets of French doors that faced the flagstone patio opened and Ian came out with a beer in hand and a friendly smile.

"Would you mind company?"

"Of course not."

He didn't get into the hot tub, instead, he pulled a chair closer and sat next to it. Night had fallen but the backyard was lit like a tropical oasis. The blue lights in the pool illuminated the water perfectly, the artfully placed solar lights in the flower beds were dim but still highlighted the landscape, and both ceiling fans under the patio overhang were on, casting a warm glow.

It was so beautiful it made me wish for a house of my own. One I could decorate and landscape without having to ask my landlord for permission. Not to mention, it'd be a waste of money if I landscaped my rental.

Why hadn't I done that yet?

"Have you been here before?" Ian asked.

"To Tybee?" Ian nodded and I answered, "I've lived in Georgia for years and this is my second time out here."

"It's funny how we get so busy with our daily lives we forget to explore the world around us."

Wasn't that the truth?

"When we moved to Michigan, Nicole and I had all these ideas for day trips and vacations. Harbor Beach Lighthouse, boating on Lake Huron, visiting Niagara Falls. In the ten years we lived there we made it to the falls once. Take this advice from an old man with a mountain of regret—don't forget to have fun while you can."

That sounded like good advice.

"Why'd you move to Michigan?"

Ian smiled, and for the first time since I'd met him, it was a real, happy smile. Not that he'd been disingenuous or fake throughout the day, he'd just been a little guarded, and with Logan's mood being on high alert, no one could blame the poor man for being watchful.

This was also the first time I'd heard Ian say his wife's name or bring up anything personal.

"When I met Nicole I was living in Chicago. Niki had gone to design school there, fell in love with the city, and stayed. After she got cancer I think we both realized how important it was to have family around. My parents had me late in life and they'd passed, so we moved closer to her family. They lived in Flint but Niki and I didn't want to be in the city anymore but we wanted to be within an hour of her family so we looked at a map. She saw the town Bad Axe, and said with a name that cool good things were bound to happen there. And she was right; good things happened there. Now it's your turn. Are you from Georgia?"

"Nope. I grew up in Arizona, outside of Sedona. My parents still live there and they will until the end of time. My mom's a jewelry maker and sells her pieces to the local shops. My dad owns a tour company and stays busy scouting new locations."

"Why'd you move?"

Why did I move? I left Arizona so long ago I'd almost forgotten why.

"I guess I wanted an adventure. I love my parents, they're good people. Sedona was a beautiful place to grow up but I wanted to see something else, I guess. A friend lived in Savannah and I came out to visit, loved it here, and decided to stay. I was thinking about moving back to Arizona when I was offered a job at Triple Canopy. I was a waitress then and working at TC meant better pay and steady hours. I thought what the hell, I'll give it a try. I like my job, but I love the people I work with. I found a second family working there."

"And Logan works there," Ian noted.

I took a sip of my wine to buy myself time. Ian and I were having a pleasant conversation and bringing Logan into it felt like a betrayal of sorts.

"I didn't mean to make you uncomfortable, Lauren."

"You didn't," I semi-lied. "Yes, Logan works there. He joined the team when he left the Navy."

"DeeDee worries about him. I think she was hoping after he left the Navy he'd decide to become an accountant," Ian huffed out a laugh. "One look at Logan and it's clear as day he is not a man who'd be happy crunching numbers."

"No, he is not. It's hard enough to get him to fill out an expense report on time. Listen, Ian—"

"You don't need to say it, Lauren," Ian interrupted.

"Again, DeeDee's worried. I am not. I know the history. I know what happened. I would be concerned if Logan didn't have his reservations about me being in his mother's life. He's the head of the family and has been since he was a teenager. I know it will be a long time before he warms up to me or the idea that DeeDee and I are together. I don't judge Logan for not wanting me around. He loves his mom and sisters. It will take time, and a good amount of it for him to understand I do, too. But I will not hide who I am or how I feel about DeeDee, Jill, Jackie, and Lucy. I adore all of them. That's something that Logan and I have in common. Something we can build from when he's ready."

That was good. That was smart, giving Logan time to adjust.

I was looking at Ian thinking it was a shame he didn't have children. I bet he would've been a good dad.

"Why the serious faces?" Dee asked as she joined us on the patio. "Oh, darn it to heck, I forgot my wine."

Dee turned to go back into the house when Ian called out, "Come sit down, sweetheart. I'll get it."

Dee turned back and smiled so huge it split her face.

And it hit me, something that Logan had said to me way back at Drake and Liberty's wedding.

A man doesn't let his woman get her own drink and he sure as fuck doesn't let her get his. He makes sure her ass is sitting and enjoying herself then he goes and gets her *a drink.*

We'd been arguing about Guy and why I was at the bar getting a drink instead of sitting with my friends while Guy got them. The truth was, Guy had offered, but I saw Logan at the bar. My errand was two-fold—keep Guy as far away from Logan as possible and find an excuse for me to be close to him. Since the day Logan came to work for TC I'd found a multitude of excuses to be near him.

"Do you like to furniture shop?" Dee asked bizarrely.

I wasn't sure where she was going with her question so I answered with one of my own, "Um. I guess?"

"The girls report that Logan has a couch, a TV, a bed in his room, and a lumpy old bed in his guest room. No other furniture. I was hoping you could talk him into furnishing his home so the next time I visit I can stay with my son and not in a hotel."

Oh, boy. When that happened I hoped she came solo, or Logan's attitude would redline at the thought of Ian staying at his house.

"I didn't raise that boy to eat sitting on the couch. That was a rule in our home—food stays in the dining room only. No eating in the living room or bedrooms. Besides, it's rude to have your girlfriend over and not have a table to offer her to sit at."

Oh, shit.

"Dee..." I started, needing to explain that Logan wasn't my boyfriend. But I stopped because I couldn't very well tell her that her son and I had a friendly sex arrangement.

I was back to wanting to strangle Logan.

"We spend most of our time at my house. Actually, I've never even been to Logan's house."

Yeah, and that kind of stung admitting that.

"You've never been to his house?"

"We've only been seeing each other a week. We're very..." I was stammering like an idiot. I was so going to choke Logan. "We're new."

Dee blinked, then blinked again, then smiled hugely.

"I never would've guessed, the way you two behave. You're very attuned to my son."

"We've known each other a while. But he and I being together just started."

"It might've just started, but it doesn't change the fact that you put him at ease. He looks to you to calm himself. A touchstone if you will. I like that he's found that in you. He's never had that. Someone who he can look to when he's anxious. And someone who will pinch him when he's getting ready to open his mouth and be rude."

Damn. I had indeed pinched Logan. Twice when I felt him getting ready to say something obnoxious. But I thought I'd been stealthy about it. Apparently, I had not been.

My face flamed hot and suddenly the water in the hot tub felt like it was boiling my skin.

"You caught that, huh?"

"A mother, she worries about her children. Being a parent doesn't stop when your child turns eighteen. It's a job that lasts the rest of your life. After what happened to my family, I was most worried about Logan. He endured the most to protect his sisters. He saw more. He felt more. I worried his childhood would jade him, and I was right to worry. It has. I never thought my son wouldn't allow himself to find love. Yet, he has, and now he's struggling with what to do with it. He is not what his father showed him. Logan would never hurt you."

I was caught on the part where she thought her son was in love with me. Which he wasn't and I needed to disabuse that notion before Dee got her hopes up. But first, there was something more important to address.

"I say this with respect, Dee, but I know Logan. And from everything I've heard about his father, he is nothing like him. As a matter of fact, he is the opposite in every way. Logan is a protector. Not only would he never raise a hand to me or any woman, but he'd also put himself between me and anyone who tried to harm me. He knows I'm not afraid of him and he knows this. He also doesn't believe me because he doesn't trust himself. He thinks that deep down a monster lurks. And there is nothing you or I or anyone can say to him to convince him otherwise. It is something he has to figure out on his own."

"Yes, you know my son well."

"I do. I know him to be a brave man, one with honor and integrity. I also know he's as stubborn as the day is long."

"Pool time!" Jill shouted and ran across the patio.

Her cannonball into the pool had Dee shaking her head. But the smile on her face told the real story. She adored her children.

"I swear that girl never left her teen years. She's just as wild now as she was back then. Drove Logan insane. Jill has no fear. Jackie at least exhibits some common sense. Thank God for Lucy; she's my level-headed one."

"I'm sorry I didn't get to meet her."

"Next time," Dee declared.

I didn't inform her there probably wouldn't be a next time. I was too busy swallowing the lump in my throat. Damn Logan, why'd he have to introduce me to his family? Why'd they all have to be so nice and welcoming? Why did I wish with my whole heart that there'd be a next time, and a time after that, and a time after *that*?

17

Fuck. I was going to do it.

The women were all in the pool. Ian was sitting in a lounger next to me, the only thing that separated the chairs was a small wooden table. And I was going to initiate conversation.

Fuck.

"My sisters told me you own a security firm."

Of course, I didn't tell him, my background check confirmed this information.

I didn't need years of training to see the way Ian's shoulders tensed, and the tic in his jaw didn't go unnoticed, either. Nor was he attempting to conceal his surprise that I was speaking to him.

To his credit, he answered, "Yes. I fell into the business by accident. I started off writing software for some of the larger alarm companies. Years ago a friend of mine ran into some financial issues and needed someone to bail him out. I offered him the capital but I wanted a percentage of the company as collateral. The arrangement worked well until he wanted to retire. I had a good amount of money tied up in the company and it was finally profitable so I bought the business from him. The problem was I didn't know anything about alarm systems, the equipment, or how to install them. I knew how to write software and how to monitor the systems in place. My friend stayed with the company for a year after I bought him out while I went out on every call with our installers. He didn't actually retire until I learned what I needed to know to oversee that part of the corporation. And even then, I hired someone to manage the installs."

"What software?"

"Access."

"No shit? We use Access or parts of it to monitor our systems. The more comprehensive systems use Future."

"I wrote that, too."

"It was before my time, but there was an issue at Triple Canopy. Someone was able to walk in, get to Lauren, then proceeded to gain access to the back hallway. After that, my bosses added safety protocols at all points of entry. We use Future to run those systems as well as to monitor the perimeter detection."

"Get to Lauren? What does that mean?"

And fuck me, Ian sounded genuinely concerned.

"The man came in wearing an S-vest to prevent Lauren from alerting the others. He beat her unconscious. She was alone in the office with the doors unlocked," I told him.

I hadn't been there but I'd heard from Brady that when he found Lauren his first thought was that she was dead. He hadn't stopped to check her pulse because there was a man with a bomb strapped to his body in the back hallway. From the story Brady and the others had told, Lauren's face had been a mess. The mere thought of some asshole touching her sent me into a fury that was best kept locked down.

Roman was dead; Liberty had seen to that. Then Drake and Brady had disposed of his corpse before the bomb could explode in the building.

"What scanners are you using on the front door?" Ian inquired.

"Keypad entry for employees. All visitors have to be manually keyed in."

Ian's mouth got tight but he said nothing.

"I take it you're not a fan of keyed entry."

"Too easy to bypass. Even with my software, if someone wanted in, they could get in. I'd use biometric and facial rec at points of entry. Not only for employees but for visitor access as well. There's a new feature in the Access software that you can run in tandem with Future. It will run facial rec through any database you connect it to. If there's a hit, you have to manually override the system to key the person in. Not only that but it will send an alert to everyone connected to the system that someone unsavory is attempting to gain access to the building."

I couldn't believe I was getting ready to ask what I was going to ask but Ian made a good point.

"If you have time, maybe you could talk to Dylan before you leave. He's in charge of building security."

Ian's gaze went to the pool and mine followed, taking in the women.

It couldn't be denied my mother was a beautiful woman. Seeing her sitting on the step, wine glass in her hand, smile on her face, water lapping around her lower body I could imagine what Ian was thinking. In the years since my father had died Deandra Haines had taken care of herself. The bruises were long gone, the shadows had lifted, she was indeed free and had been for a good long while. It was only me who still wore the chains. And the fuck of it was I was using those chains to tie her down. It was me who was holding her back from being happy. My father had held her hostage for thirteen years and now twenty-five years after his death I'd shackled her with my insecurities.

Christ, when did it end for her? When was it her time to have everything she should've had? If she'd never met my father, if she'd never been manipulated, brainwashed, abused, who would she have become?

I looked from my mom to my sisters. Smiling, happy, carefree. They had no recollection of our father. They lived through it but they didn't. Lucy remembered but she didn't allow those memories to hold her back. It was just me. I was the only one in the family who flat-out refused to let it go.

Lauren laughed at something Jill said and I had a sudden urge to pluck my woman out of the water for no other reason than to be close to her. I wanted to soak in her laughter. I wanted to absorb every smile. I wanted to make her love me and promise she'd never leave me.

"Not my place to say," Ian muttered but I didn't take my eyes off Lauren. "I reckon I'm also stepping out of bounds here but I'd be remiss if I didn't warn you that life is short. While it's happening, the day to day, you don't notice the time slipping away. You're too busy living. But one day it ends. Just like that, it's over and you're left wondering where the time went. You're left wondering if you did enough. You think back and try to remember if you gave enough of yourself and your time and your love."

"Did you give enough?" I found myself asking.

"No, there is always more to give. But what I do know is my wife died knowing I loved her deeply. She left this earth knowing that if we had more days, I would've given more. Before I met Dee I was a lot like you. I was going through the motions of life because that was what was expected of me. I had a business to run, employees I was responsible for, but I was dead inside."

Was that what I was doing, going through the motions of life?

"I'll make time before we leave to go to Triple Canopy," Ian finished.

Silence fell and neither of us tried to fill it. Both of us watched the women in the pool. In typical Jill and Jackie fashion, they'd ripped me a new one for not being "friendly" at dinner, then once the drama was over they were back to their fun-loving, happy selves. They clearly had taken a liking to Lauren and were eager to get back to their new friend, which meant I was saved from a lengthy lecture and instead they'd made it quick but no less effective when they called me out.

Needing to do the right thing, get it out in the open, get it over with, I blew out a breath that did not do one thing to quell the burn in my chest.

"I've been a dick to you, Ian, and that was uncool. I knew about your situation before we met and threw it in your face. That wasn't uncool—that was me being an asshole. You not drilling into me when you had every right shows you're a better man than me. I know you kept your shit because you didn't want to upset my mom and sisters and I appreciate that even if I deserved you handing me my ass for that dig. I am truly sorry I brought it up and the way I did it."

"Lots of different ways a man can be in pain. Lots of ways for a man to lash out. Lots of ways for him to hurt himself. I suspect your pain runs deeper than most. You got a family to protect and I understand that. I also appreciate you being the sort of man who can apologize. I hold no personal grudge but I will caution you to tread carefully when speaking about Nicole. Like you, I have a family to protect; that includes your mom and sisters, but also a good woman's memory. I wanted kids, Logan. I wanted them badly. I struggled with that, knowing I had to choose between my wife and the dream of having children. I believe I made the right choice but that doesn't mean I still don't struggle, especially now watching your mom and all that she has with you, Lucy, Jill, and Jackie. I wanted that. I wanted a house full of family. I wanted holidays and vacations. I wanted grandchildren. Instead, I got years with the woman I loved. That isn't something I regret, because I had Nicole.

"I know I'm luckier than most. According to the doctors, I had years I never should've had with Nicole. I'm grateful for that time. And then I found something different but no less beautiful with Dee. There's not one thing I can say to you to convince you I am not your father. I can't even call him a man, because men do not cause the people who love him pain. The only thing I can do is be myself and let you come to the realization on your own. But there's something you should know. While you're taking your time, I will be moving forward. You're a man who had the responsibility of taking care of a family at a young age. You raised those women into who they are, Logan. I know the story, I know your mom broke apart and day-to-day life fell on your shoulders. I also know you helped your mom put the pieces of her life back together. You might not want it, you might reject it, you probably don't trust me to take it, but you now have help. And my hope is one day, you'll come to accept that help. In the meantime, you need to know there will be no violence in my home, no yelling, no profanity, no pain. And the last thing I'll give you is this; I've asked your mom to move in with me. I also asked her to marry me but she said no. That answer will not change until you and your sisters are comfortable with me being in all of your lives."

Fucking shit.

Not until you and your sisters are comfortable with me being in all of your lives.

Translation: until *I* was comfortable.

I was not comfortable. I was extremely uncomfortable with the way an apology had turned into a heart-to-fucking-heart that I was not ready to have. I needed Lauren. I needed her to pinch me. Hell, we should've stopped somewhere along the way to Tybee to pick up the shock collar. How the hell was I supposed to trust a man I didn't know with my mother?

Fucking hell.

My mom set her empty wine glass down on the pool deck and prepared to stand, but before she could Ian was out of his seat.

"I got it," Ian said and nabbed the glass.

"Thanks. The bottle's on the table."

I stared at my mom, happiness radiating off of her in every direction. So much of it, I couldn't bear to see it. My gaze slipped to Lauren and our eyes locked. She, too, was smiling, but it was her eyes that spoke.

She remembered what I'd said about Guy letting her get her own drink. It wasn't near the same, or was it?

Lauren gave me a blinding smile before she turned back to Jill and continued her conversation.

Fucking, *fucking*, hell.

"I had a great day," Lauren muttered sleepily and snuggled closer. "Thank you for inviting me."

I dipped my chin and inhaled. Coconut, some flowery scent, and the faint smell of chlorine lingered even though we'd showered and I spent a good amount of time using my hands to soap her body and wash her hair.

We were now in the bedroom farthest from the one my mom and Ian were staying in. It might've been immature but the son in me couldn't stomach sleeping in the room next to my mom and her boyfriend, not when my brain wouldn't shut the fuck up.

"Didn't exactly invite you," I reminded Lauren.

"I know you didn't, Logan. You demanded my presence and didn't leave me an out unless I wanted to look like a shrew in front of your family. Luckily for you, I have manners and didn't want to cause a scene. Also lucky for you, I'm being pragmatic and pretending you extended an invitation instead of what you really did. *Also*, you're lucky I really like your sisters, and your mom's awesome."

I was damn lucky, and as we lay there with her head on my chest, our legs tangled, and my hand resting on her bare ass cheek, I thought she should know just how lucky I knew I was.

"Thank you for coming, Ren. I wouldn't have made it through today without you."

"You would've—"

"No, I would've bailed. Five minutes into lunch I would've gotten back into my car and left. And if not then, when you and my sisters were shopping and my mom laid me out I would've made myself look like a jackass and taken off. The only thing that's kept me somewhat steady is knowing you were near, and not wanting to let you down or embarrass you."

"He's a good guy."

Her whispered words fanned across my chest and my

hand cupping her ass convulsed. Not even I could deny her assessment.

"He asked her to marry him and she said no."

"What?" Lauren pushed off my chest and came up on her elbow so she was staring down at me. "She said no?"

"Yep. I guess she told him that until *we*, which really means *me*, are comfortable with their relationship she won't marry him. But she's moving in with him."

"Logan," she muttered. "Honey, your mom loves him."

Fucking hell.

"I know she does."

"He loves her, too."

"I know that."

"What are you going to do?"

I was going to man up and stop acting like a dick was what I was going to do. The problem was when the mere thought of my mom marrying Ian crept into my head I felt sick.

"I got no choice but to give my mom what she needs to be happy."

I said the words but that didn't mean my throat didn't feel scratchy. It felt less so when Lauren smiled. The prickly feeling was just receding when she lowered her mouth to mine and kissed me. I fought against taking control then taking us other places. The only thing that stopped me was knowing my sisters were in the room next to us. So that meant Lauren's kiss was soft. Sweet glides and sweeter brushes of her tongue against my lower lip.

"Proud of you, Logan."

My eyes started to sting, and since I'd never felt a sensation quite like it, I didn't know what it meant. But I did know it felt really fucking good. And when Lauren settled and curled her soft body into mine, I knew that felt better.

18

"Logan!" I panted and braced a hand on my headboard.

Apparently, three days without sex and Logan was feeling energetic.

"Not yet, baby."

Both of his hands were holding my hips and he was using his grip to pull me back as he thrust forward. I was so worked up I couldn't hold on, this was because he'd woken me up with one of his hands between my legs and the other up my shirt cupping my breast. Once I was fully awake, my shirt was discarded and he employed his mouth. Starting at my neck he licked and nibbled his way down, stopping only to tease my nipples into hard peaks, then he continued to his destination. Three days might've made Logan energetic but it also left him hungry. He showed no mercy when he ate me, he edged me close only to back off and then start all over. He tasted until he had his fill then turned me over and took more.

"So close, honey," I whimpered.

"Love your ass, Ren."

I knew he did. If we were in bed, Logan was touching my booty.

"Honey."

"Love the way you feel, baby."

God.

I could take no more. I dropped my forehead to the bed, tipped my ass higher, and fisted the bunched-up sheets under me. Logan drove in harder and moved one hand around and down, his finger hit the exact right spot and my pussy spasmed. Then Logan bent forward until his chest was resting on my back and his lips were at my ear. I could hear his heavy breaths, I could feel his big body vibrating, I could smell his spicy scent. It was sensory overload. I was hot and cold, felt like I was floating but held down, until pleasure ripped through me so hard it was painful.

"I can feel you, baby," Logan whispered. "Sleek and wet. Love your pussy, love how wet you get for me. Every time. Never gonna let you go, Ren."

He was still pounding deep, my mind hazy from my climax, but even still I heard him.

"Never, baby," he finished and groaned.

Three more strokes and he planted himself to the root and trembled.

"Won't ever let you leave me, Lauren."

Showered, dressed, travel mugs of coffee poured, I was ready to go to work.

Or more accurately, I needed to escape Logan.

Something had shifted and I wasn't the only one who had noticed.

Yesterday, at Sunday brunch Jill had openly gaped at her

brother. Jackie had been skeptical at first then rolled with Logan's mood. Dee had been overjoyed. And Ian had been... Ian. The man was nothing if not even-keeled. Steady as a rock and calm. I wouldn't go as far as saying Logan had been friendly, but he'd been friendlier and he'd engaged in conversation with Ian.

The change was obvious, his family welcomed it, but it confused the crap out of me.

Not only had Logan's attitude softened toward Ian but something had certainly changed between us. He'd been openly affectionate with me, way more than he'd been in the last week even when we were in private. He held my hand, he kissed my temple, he'd put his arm around me, or his hand on my leg. Bottom line was, if I was close he was touching me.

This I could tell pleased his family. It seemed to make Ian happy as well.

Now I was more confused than ever. Whatever was going on between me and Logan was based on a big, fat, honking lie. Not that I meant to deceive Logan, but looking back I'd been in love with him for a long time. I loved him before I'd dated Guy, I loved him while I'd been dating Guy, and I continued to love him after I told Logan that I agreed with his life motto that love was for fools or idiots and whomever else was dumb enough to fall into the trap.

I'm a fool and an idiot.

I was in love with a man who'd straight-out told me he'd never love me.

But then he said he was never going to let me go. And he said he was never going to let me leave him, but that was said in the heat of the moment. Right before his orgasm had taken over at a time when endorphins were coursing through his body and he was feeling good.

See? Confusing as fuck.

My mind was racing a mile a minute vacillating from elation to doubt. And it had been doing that for the last twenty-four hours. After brunch, we'd left Tybee. Everyone was exhausted and retreated to their respective accommodations—Ian and Dee back to a hotel, Jill and Jackie at Logan's, and Logan at my house. No one batted an eye when he told his sisters he'd be staying with me. I argued that Logan should go home and spend time with his sisters. Jill said it would be a waste because she and Jackie were going to crash as soon as they got to his place. Then I'd tried to get him to go with his mom, which was met with Dee's rebuff explaining that Ian had treated her to a spa day and she'd be getting a massage and facial.

I fell asleep on the drive home. Two days of eating good food until I was stuffed, walking around in the sun, swimming until after two in the morning, had caught up with me. Once we were home, Logan propped me in front of the TV, made grilled cheese sandwiches for dinner—which for the record were the bomb. He'd sprinkled parmesan cheese into the butter and patted it down into the bread before he'd grilled them and he used three slices of cheese—cheddar, pepper jack, and provolone. I was concerned with the smorgasbord of cheeses but the end result was divine. Later Logan carried me to my bed because I'd once again fallen asleep. And he cuddled me close.

That was three nights of no sex but cuddling.

Mixed signals and confusion.

"We're gonna be late!" I yelled from the kitchen. "What are you doing in there?"

"Sorry, I had to shave," Logan explained as he walked into the living room fresh-faced.

That was too bad. He hadn't shaved while we'd been in

Tybee and the scruff looked hot. Not to mention, it felt awesome between my legs.

Logan's burst of laughter made me jump.

"What's funny?"

"Babe, your face."

"My face is funny?"

"Yep."

I felt my eyes get squinty.

"Wanna explain why my face looks funny?"

"I'm not sure if you're pissed or disgusted but the nose scrunch is cute. So is the way your forehead wrinkles when you're thinking. But it was the frown that got me. I think I can take from your reaction you liked the beard."

As Logan spoke he'd made his way into the kitchen so when he stopped speaking he was standing right in front of me.

"I'm not disgusted. But I'm gonna be pissed if we're late to work."

"Ren?"

"Yeah?"

"Babe, you want me to grow the beard back?"

I shrugged even though I kinda did. "It's your face."

"Yeah, but you're the one who has to look at it."

He had a point. But admitting I liked the beard and wanted him to grow it back felt like something a girlfriend might have a say in and I definitely wasn't his girlfriend.

However, as previously mentioned, Logan was stubborn and if I wanted to get to work on time, I was the one who had to give.

"Fine. Yes, I liked the beard."

A soft, whisker-free cheek rubbed against mine and I closed my eyes. Logan smelled like my shaving cream. That felt...weird...intimate...the same way him using my toothpaste did. It made no sense; it was shaving cream for crying out loud, but it was mine, it was the girly kind, and Logan using it meant he'd shaved in my bathroom after spending the night.

"Was that so hard to answer?" he asked softly.

"Yes," I admitted.

"Is it the way it looks or the way it feels that you like best?"

Just once, I wished I could pull one over on Logan. Just one damn time I wished he wasn't so freakishly observant that he could read my facial expression and my mind.

"Both."

"I think you like the way it feels better. You damn near suffocated me when I got my mouth on your pussy."

"Is that a complaint?" I snapped.

"Fuck, no. You wild and wet, grinding your pussy on my face, begging me to tongue-fuck you is my new favorite way to wake up."

I suppressed a groan and covered up how affected I was by barking orders, "We need to leave. Now. Or we're gonna be late."

"Best part of my morning is watching you take my cock. Hearing you whimper, feeling you wrapped around me, seeing you come apart and beg for more. Second best part is watching you get dressed. Knowing what's under your clothes, knowing that I watched you put it on, and later it will be me who takes it off. Third best part is listening to you bitch we're gonna be late when you know damn good and well we have plenty of time."

Logan had a gift for being sexy and annoying at the same time. He was the only man I knew who could turn me on and irritate me at the same time.

"Well, I'm glad you enjoy hearing me bitch. Because today, we're really gonna be *late*."

I tried to step back but was waylaid when Logan's arm went around me and he pulled me close.

"Never had that, Ren. Never had anything to look forward to. Never went to bed excited to wake up the next morning. Never left work eager to get home. Never woke up happy. Thank you, baby, for giving me something good to wake up to."

Holy crap.

I melted into him and my confusion grew. I had to come clean. I had to tell him he couldn't say stuff to me like that. I was in too deep. I was already drowning and when he said sweet things, meaningful things, loving things, it made it hard for me to breathe.

"Anything but country," Logan griped as he drove.

"Passenger controls the station," I told him.

"My car, my music," he returned.

"You wouldn't be subjected to my music if you would've let me drive myself."

"No use you driving when you're going with me later to the airport."

Right. The airport. I was going with Logan to see his family off. I was unsure why I was doing this, seeing as they were all coming to Triple Canopy before they left. Ian because Logan had asked him to speak to Dylan about some security software. To say I was shocked when Logan told me he'd invited Ian to TC would be the understatement of the year. Dee, Jill, and Jackie were tagging along so they could see where Logan worked. That shocked me, too, that they'd never been to TC even though they'd visited Logan in Georgia before.

"Don't you want alone time with your family?"

"Nope. I've had thirty-eight years of alone time with my mom and twenty-six years of alone time with the Disastrous Duo."

"Don't call them disastrous, Logan. That's not nice."

"You like them."

It wasn't a question but I still answered.

"I adore them. I wish they lived closer. They'd fit right in with the rest of the girls. Hadley and Addy would love them. And Liberty and Shiloh would think that Jill was hilarious. Not that Jackie's not funny, but Jill's the mouthpiece for both of them. And Delany and Jackie would totally hit it off. I wish we had more time, I would've loved to introduce them to everyone."

Logan's nonresponse made me look from the radio to him. His jaw was clenched and his eyes were darting from the rearview mirror to the side mirror, pausing only a moment to watch the traffic in front of him then back to the mirrors.

What on earth?

"What's wrong?"

"We're being followed."

His terse reply took a moment to sink in but when it did panic hit.

"What?"

Logan didn't answer, the music abruptly cut off, and the sound of a phone ringing filled the silence.

"Yeah?" Drake answered.

"Where are you?"

"Leroy coming up on 84."

"I have a black Merc tailing me," Logan told Drake. No

inflection, no worry, like it was no big freaking deal. "We're on 84, traveling west. I'm gonna hit Lewis Frasier and try to ditch him on the back roads."

"Copy that. I'll use Holmestown; if you keep west I can intercept."

"I'll do that. I've got Lauren with me, go easy."

"Fuck," Drake clipped. "I'll call it in, you stay alert."

"Always."

The line disconnected and Logan accelerated. His Mustang shot forward and I held my breath. I saw the road he wanted to turn onto up ahead but he wasn't slowing down. I continued to hold my breath. The median barrier ended and I knew from experience turning onto Lewis Frasier you had to cross two lanes of oncoming traffic. I also knew the Jersey barrier restarted about ten feet from the turn.

Logan needed to slow down.

He didn't.

In the scariest maneuver I've ever experienced, Logan made a hard left narrowly missing getting hit. And I mean narrowly. I'd be shocked if the other car hadn't kissed Logan's bumper as he flew by.

I shrieked. Yes, my shrill voice echoed in the car. It wasn't my finest moment, but it wasn't every day I was in a car that was being followed, with a badass behind the wheel thinking he was on a racetrack rather than a busy Georgia highway.

Logan ignored my outburst and answered his ringing phone.

"Yeah?"

"You got a plate for me to run?" Dylan asked matter-of-factly.

What the hell was wrong with these men? Was no one concerned?

"Negative, no front plate on the Merc. I lost it when I turned but now I got a white Charger or Challenger and he's on my ass."

"Change of plans, Matt's close. He's moving your way using Bill Carter Road. He'll be waiting for you at the intersection. He needs space to cut off the car so put some distance between you and the Charger."

"Not sure if that's gonna be possible, Dylan."

"Find a way."

That call disconnected and it was safe to say at this point my stomach was feeling woozy.

"Ren, open the glove box and grab my Sig."

I didn't argue. I reached for the glovebox and fumbled with the latch. On the third attempt, I got it open and pulled out his gun.

"Calm, baby, everything's gonna be fine."

Was it? *Was it really*? I glanced at the speedometer and I couldn't see how driving fifty miles an hour over the thirty-five miles an hour speed limit equaled "fine".

I didn't verbalize this.

"Take the Sig out of the holster. Safety's on but keep the barrel pointed at your door."

"I think your version of fine and mine are two very different things."

"I'd never let anything happen to you, Ren. The gun's a precaution."

Logan's eyes narrowed on the rearview mirror and the air in the car changed. It sizzled and charged with something so unpleasant my stomach bottomed out.

"Get down!"

Logan didn't give me an opportunity to follow his

command. His arm shot out, his hand grabbed me around the back of my neck, and he shoved my face to my knees.

One second.

One heartbeat.

One breath later the first gunshot rang out. Glass shattered, something hit my back, and there was a loud thud.

Without missing a beat, Logan reached between my chest and legs and deftly pulled his gun from my hand.

"Do not move, Lauren. Not a fucking muscle, we clear?"

Fuck yes, we're crystal clear.

"Clear," I mumbled.

The second and third bullets hit the car.

I closed my eyes and listened to the engine whine as Logan pushed his Mustang to go faster.

"Call Matt Kessler," Logan barked.

"Calling Matt Kessler," Logan's car returned in a British accent.

British, really?

"I'm in place." Matt's voice came over the speakers.

"Shots fired," Logan calmly conveyed. "I've taken three."

"Can Lauren—"

"No!"

"How much space you got?"

"Two car lengths, at most."

"That's not enough room. She needs to return fire."

"Not gonna happen."

"Brother—"

"Not gonna fucking happen, Matt. I've got ten miles until I'm at the intersection. Where's Drake?"

"He went down to 119 to cut around. If you won't let Lauren handle it now, I'll take him from behind."

Another bullet slammed into the Mustang and the car pitched right as I felt the car's back end slide. Logan swerved back on the road, all the while cussing a blue streak.

Fuck this.

Fuck cowering with my head between my knees.

Fuck being shot at while Logan argued with Matt.

I knew how to shoot. I'd been taught by the best.

"Give me back the gun," I demanded.

"Stay down!"

"Give me the damn gun, Logan, before we die."

"We're not gonna die."

"We damn well are if one of the tires get shot out while we're going a hundred miles an hour. Give me the gun and you concentrate on driving."

"Godmotherfucking!"

Logan handed me the gun.

I unbelted and started to crawl into the back seat when I stopped to stare at the missing headrest.

The headrest my head had been resting on one second before the bullet hit it.

Reality hit hard. I'd almost died. I would've died if Logan hadn't shoved me down.

"Lauren, ass in the seat, belt back on!"

His demand snapped me out of my stupor and I crawled through the front seats and balanced on my knees on the back seat. The back windshield was blown out courtesy of the assholes behind us. Good news was I had a clear shot. The bad news was glass was digging into my knees and shins.

Safety glass doesn't cut, right?

"Two miles," Logan called out.

Two miles didn't mean shit to me; I was unclear what was supposed to happen when we got to the intersection where Matt was waiting for us. All I knew was I didn't want either of us to die.

I flicked off the safety and raised the gun, trying my best to balance. My first shot hit the road in front of the white car.

"Easy, Ren. Breathe, baby, and aim."

Shit. Right. Aim.

On an exhale I remembered everything Jasper, Trey, Carter, Luke, and Logan had taught me about sight picture. I remembered what Luke had told me about trigger control. *Press, don't pull.*

I lined up, did my best to calm down, and slowly pressed the trigger. I hit the hood, quickly adjusted, and took another shot. The windshield of the white car spider-webbed and the driver slowed and swerved. I counted out five seconds and as soon as the driver righted the car, I fired again, and again, and again, and didn't stop until I was out of bullets and the car behind us was no longer moving.

"I see you!" Matt's muffled voice boomed.

"I'm gonna blow by you and head to TC. The car's five hundred yards back," Logan answered.

"Copy that. Good work, Lauren."

I could barely make out Matt's words over the ringing in my ears.

"Come back up here and belt up, baby."

"My ears hurt really bad," I told him.

"I know they do, Ren. Come up here," he repeated.

I scooted to the edge of the seat and winced as the pain registered. Not only from my ears but safety glass did cut, or the tiny shards dug in enough to break the skin. It felt like I was being poked with five million needles.

I somehow managed to get back into my seat but I

couldn't get my seat belt back on. After the third try, Logan reached across me and latched the belt.

"Your legs," he growled.

"Please don't talk. Every word feels like a screwdriver is piercing my skull."

Logan had slowed and it was funny how after going a hundred-plus miles an hour fifty felt like a crawl. There were a thousand questions I wanted to ask. A thousand things I wanted to say but my head was throbbing and my stomach was so queasy I was afraid I'd be sick.

So we drove in silence the rest of the way to Triple Canopy.

19

As soon as I pulled through the gate I saw Nick, Jason, Quinn, and Carter waiting outside. It was Quinn who worried me. She was going to rush Lauren.

I slowed and disconnected my phone from the Bluetooth before I called Carter.

"I see you," he answered after one ring.

"No Quinn."

I spoke as softly as I could but with my ears still ringing I might've been shouting.

"Shock or drop?"

"A little of both."

"Shit. Okay, I'll talk to Quinn. Your mom, sisters, and Ian are here."

Fucking shit. I forgot about their visit.

"Can you please ask Quinn to explain the situation to them?"

"Yeah. We'll clear them out of your office and put them into the conference room."

I glanced over at Lauren—face pale, eyes screwed closed, a grimace on her face.

"Gotta go."

I dropped my phone into the cupholder and pulled into a parking space.

Lauren didn't move. *Fuck yeah, shock's setting in.*

I turned off the Mustang, threw open the door, and rounded the trunk not bothering to close the door. I pulled Lauren's open, reached around her, unbuckled her belt, and scooped her out of the seat. She didn't open her eyes or protest.

Fuck.

By the time I made it to the men, Carter had the front door opened. Nick and Jason gave me identical chin lifts and scowls.

"My gun's somewhere in the car."

"I got it," Jason said and jogged off.

"I'll get the medkit and meet you in your office," Nick said and he, too, jogged away.

"Drake and Matt are on-scene," Carter started. "Trey and Luke are on their way there now. Ethan's been notified and my dad and Jasper are coming here. Levi and Clark are going to the scene."

Lauren shoved her face into my neck and groaned.

"Ears," I told Carter. "Let me get her settled then we'll brief."

I made my way through reception, down the hall, and I was able to slip into my office without my mom or sisters seeing me.

"Ren, honey, I'm gonna set you down."

She nodded and I carefully lowered her into the chair and immediately knelt in front of her.

"Open your eyes."

She shook her head then moaned.

I opened the bottom drawer, pulled out my Bose headphones, then shifted so I could wake up my laptop. I quickly found my white noise app and checked to make sure the headphones were connected and the volume was low.

"I'm gonna put my headphones on you. White noise is playing. I know it doesn't make sense but it will help with the ringing in your ears."

"No—"

"Ren, please listen to me, it helps. I promise. The volume is low, it won't hurt."

She nodded her agreement but still didn't open her eyes.

"After I put these on you, I'm gonna go wash up. Carter's gonna stay in here with you."

Lauren nodded again.

As gently as I could I placed the headphones on and adjusted them over her ears. When she didn't flinch or make any sound I got to my feet.

"Logan—"

"I need a minute."

After that, I stalked out of my office. I felt it coming—the ugly, the hate, the toxins that I had to work to keep buried. It was all bubbling up faster than I could choke it down, faster than I could suppress. I barely made it into the hallway before the first wave hit—anger so sharp I vibrated with it. Every step I took was taken with malicious determination. As soon as the gym door clicked shut behind me, I unleashed. My fist pounded into the heavy bag, then the other, again and again until I was breathless. Unchecked rage drove me to push on. Over and over I pummeled the bag.

"Enough!" Lenox shouted from behind me.

It wasn't nearly enough.

It would never be enough.

The fire in my gut was nowhere near extinguished. The

anger still pulsed through my veins. The fear still clogged my throat.

"Logan, stop!" Jasper called. "Enough, son."

Son.

I wasn't his son.

I was no man's son.

"She's asking for *you*, Logan," Lenox told me.

I took one last swing, stopped the bag, then turned to face my bosses.

Lenox's gaze dropped to my hands and his scowl deepened. "Feel better?"

"Nope."

"Dig deep and find it," Lenox ordered.

"How in the hell am I supposed to *find it* when I never *had it* in the first place?"

"Had what?" Jasper asked.

"That's just it, I don't have anything. The only thing my old man taught me was this." I lifted my bloody knuckles. "Violence. Anger. Hatred. This is all I know. How the fuck am I supposed to dig deep and find something I never fucking had in the first place?"

"You think men like you are taught?" Jasper carried on. "Men like you are *born*. That asshole did his best to beat it out of you. But he failed. You *are* the man you were born to be. There is no lesson to be taught. You have it in you or you don't. And you cannot stand there and tell me it's not inside of you."

"Jasper—"

"He's right, Logan," Lenox cut in. "That beast that lives inside of you, that fire in your soul, you misunderstand it. You think your daddy gave you that? You think some weak, wife-beating, child abuser fool had it in him to make you who you are? He didn't give you shit. He didn't make you who you are. He didn't have the power or the strength to make you into the man you are."

I felt the blood dripping from my fingertips, but I felt no pain. Air rushed over my dry lips, but I felt no oxygen entering my lungs.

Fuck.

"I can't—"

"You can't," Lenox sneered. "Only a pussy says I can't."

"Christ," Jasper bit out and my gaze went to him. Ice-cold green eyes stared back at me. "Did you just ring the bell?"

The old BUD/s reference had my shoulders squaring but before I could utter my ready response that I wasn't a goddamn quitter Lenox rejoined.

"Whatever's going on in your head, it's not your sacrifice. Whatever it is you think you can't do, that's not your burden. Time to wake up, Logan."

"Not my sacrifice? What the hell are you talking about?"

"Right now, you're thinking about all the reasons you shouldn't go back to Lauren. All the excuses you've compiled. They're junk, all of them. Throw them out and man the fuck up."

"Junk?" My laugh sounded rusty and humorless when I lifted my bloodied hands. "This is what you call junk? An excuse? I get pissed and overwhelmed I resort to violence. How in the fuck is that not a damn good excuse to stay away from Lauren? How is this right here not the reminder that I can't be trusted?"

I fucking knew better than to get involved. I knew better than to fall in love. I knew this would happen. Something would set me off and *he'd* come out. The motherfucker I couldn't expunge.

"I'm gonna tell you the truth." Jasper took a step closer

and I fought against retreat. Twice I'd seen Jasper angry. Twice I'd witnessed him lose his composure. Thankfully, neither time was his ire aimed at me.

Now it was.

Now he was advancing on me not as a boss, not as a friend, not as a man I respected, but as the formidable warrior he was. "And I hope to God you listen closely. You did not take your fists to Lauren. You didn't take your anger or your fear out on her. You walked away to do what you needed to do to let it out. It shocks the fuck out of me that I need to remind you you're not the only man in this building who needs a physical outlet. Do you really think you're the first of us to come back here and beat the fuck out of the bag? Why the hell do you think it's here?"

Logically, I knew I would never hit Lauren. I fundamentally knew that. But there was still this little voice in the back of my mind that nagged. It was relentless with all the what-ifs.

The door slammed open and Lauren stomped in. Red-hot pissed with dried blood dotting her knees and shins.

The anger came back tenfold. Not only could she have died but she was injured.

"Are you done?" she hissed.

That was a loaded question.

Was I done having a bitch fit? Probably not.

Was I done second-guessing myself? Again, probably not.

Was I done pretending that I didn't love her? Ab-so-*fucking*-lutely.

I was so done with all the bullshit.

"Baby, why are you up?" I asked. "You still got glass—" I clamped my mouth shut when Lauren growled.

"Smart choice," Jasper mumbled.

"You left me." Lauren's accusation was high-pitched and frantic. "I let you because I knew you needed it. But you're taking too long, Logan. You left me and I need you."

"Ren—"

"I let you! I wasn't so far gone, I didn't know you needed it. But my head was almost blown off and I *need* you."

Her words hit like spears. The recrimination lingered in the air. The censure in her voice hurt like a sonofabitch. But it was her understanding that I needed a minute to gather myself that cut through.

"Come here, Ren."

I made the demand but I met her halfway, and when she was close, my arms swept around her and she did what she always did when she was in my arms—burrowed close.

"Are you done?" she demanded to know.

"Yeah, baby, I'm done." I felt her head give a slight nod then she pressed deeper. "I was coming back to you. I just needed..."

Fuck, I didn't know what I needed.

"To get it out," she finished for me.

Something like that.

"Let's get your legs cleaned up."

"And your hands." Lauren's head lifted off my chest. I tipped my chin and I caught her watery eyes. "Next time will you please wear gloves so you don't bloody your knuckles?"

"Yeah, Ren, next time I'll wear gloves. How are your ears, still ringing?"

"A little but the white noise helped."

"Good."

I scooped her up and started for the gym door.

"I heard your mom and sisters are here with Ian Webster," Lenox called out.

Shit, damn, and hell.

194 RILEY EDWARDS

"I forgot they were here," I admitted.

"Carter told me Ian's in Dylan's office helping him go through traffic cams and Quinn's in the conference room with your mom and sisters. I'll call Lily, see if she can come down and keep the women company."

That translated into Lenox taking my back and my mom's by calling in his wife to keep my mom calm.

"I appreciate that."

"Don't mention it."

I stepped into the hallway and saw Carter and Nick leaning against the wall.

"Sorry, brother, I couldn't stop her," Carter muttered irately.

"I should've kicked you harder," Lauren returned.

"You kicked Carter?"

"I asked nicely first but he wouldn't move."

"You didn't ask nicely, you threatened to cut off my... manhood if I didn't move. I didn't have a chance to move because I was in shock. Never seen you mad and I definitely have never heard you say..." Carter trailed off, frowning.

"Oh, please, there are no children around; you can say the word dick, Carter, we're all adults."

Carter's eyes widened and he shook his head. "Please make her stop saying that."

"Baby, Carter's shy about his dick; he doesn't like it talked about."

Lauren's body started to shake with amusement and her lips thinned in an effort to keep from laughing out loud. She lost the battle and started to sputter, then she shoved her face into my neck and the sputters turned into an outright laugh.

I slowed my steps and savored the weight of her in my

arms. The sound of her giggles. The feel of her breath on my throat.

Alive, breathing, and laughing.

And in my arms.

Yeah, I was absolutely done pretending. It was time to get shit straight.

20

"Good Lord." Dee's wide eyes came to mine. "That boy can yell."

That boy was Logan and she wasn't wrong. Logan sounded pissed. But Ethan Lenox sounded more pissed.

I should back up.

After Logan carried me back to his office he left me again. This time it was just to wash up. When he came back he pulled the chunks of glass out then doused my legs with hydrogen peroxide. And by that I mean he poured half a bottle on my right leg from the knee down and the other half on my left. And, he'd refused to blow on my knees, spouting off some logical crap about introducing germs into my cuts. It hurt so freaking bad, germs were the last thing on my mind. Nick had come in and helped Logan mop up the mess on the floor.

Once we weren't bloodied up Logan carried me into the conference room. Our arrival was met with Dee busting out into tears, necessitating Logan to quickly set me in a chair so he could comfort his mother. Since I was no longer in their brother's arms that gave Jill and Jackie full access to me.

Quinn waited as patiently as she could, but since Quinn was a Walker and the one thing Jasper hadn't taught his girls was to idly stand by, she gave Jill and Jackie approximately three seconds each to hug me before she horned her way in.

Dee asked what happened and Logan deflected. Jill asked and Logan changed the topic. Jackie asked and he flat out said what happened wasn't going to be discussed.

Then Detective Ethan Lenox showed up and for some reason, his presence caused Logan to go on alert—high alert —full-on protection mode alert. He excused himself and took Ethan in the hallway to talk. Whatever they were discussing had obviously deteriorated because now they were yelling.

And now Dee, Jackie, Jill, and Quinn knew most of what transpired thanks to the conference room not being sound-proof and both of the men shouting.

"Jesus, Logan, I'm a cop. You can't say that shit in front of me." Ethan's voice carried through the door. "I need to inter-view Lauren and get her statement, that's all."

"Is everything okay?" Jill asked.

I didn't answer because the door swung in and Logan came right to me—as in right into my space—and bent down so he was all I could see.

"This is your choice. You tell me you're not ready, then we go home and you talk to Ethan after you've had a rest."

"What?"

I wasn't tracking what the big deal was. I knew Ethan well. Yes, he was a cop but I hadn't...oh, *shit*.

"Did I..." I couldn't finish my question. With everything that happened since we'd gotten to TC, and before that with my ears ringing and my head throbbing, I hadn't thought about what I'd done. The possibility I'd killed someone.

"No, baby, you didn't."

Thank God!

"Did I hurt someone?"

Logan's jaw clenched.

I'd hurt someone.

"Is Ethan going to arrest me?" I whispered.

"No," he growled. "But they found blood in the car. Not a lot, but you clipped the passenger."

I shot someone; how was I not being arrested?

Holy shit! I shot someone.

I felt my eyes start to water. Logan saw the tears brimming and suddenly he hauled me out of the chair and plastered me to his chest. It could be said that being close to Logan was my favorite place to be. However, for the first time since Logan and I started I didn't feel safe in his arms. I felt fear and a lot of it.

"We're done here," he rumbled.

His voice was loud enough that the whole room could hear but his tone was so low it was guttural. Unmistakably displeased but not full of anger. There was something else laced in his tone; threats and undertones of *something*, I just didn't know what.

Then he started bossing. This was not his normal bossiness; it was over the top and left no room for argument.

"Mom, go with Quinn and pack up Lauren's shit. Jill and Jackie, I need groceries at the house. Don't forget the coffee Ren likes and she needs vanilla creamer, the kind in the white bottle with the flower on it."

Um. Wait.

I was busy freaking out about Quinn and Dee packing my shit but not so busy I didn't hear Logan remember my coffee or that he'd noticed not only the creamer I liked but the brand as well. It was sweet and thoughtful he'd ask—

well, he didn't ask he demanded, but whatever—his sisters to pick some up for me.

"What's going on?"

"You're moving into my house."

"What?"

"We were followed from your house. Which means someone was outside watching and waiting."

In my current state, I couldn't think about the creepiness of someone watching my house. Which, if I thought about it too hard, would scare the shit out of me. Any other morning I would've been driving to work alone. What would've happened if Logan hadn't been there? If he hadn't been the one driving?

My head came up and I whispered, "Guy drives a black Mercedes."

"He does. He also left his house at six, drove straight to yours, and parked. Then he followed us out to the highway but didn't turn off. And his car right now is at the airport and he's on a flight to Nashville."

That was creepy and weird and it pissed me off that Guy was not getting the message that I didn't want anything to do with him. But it was scarier that Logan had talked to Guy and he ignored Logan's warnings. And it scared me because I knew nothing good was going to come from Logan's inevitable second chat with Guy. I figured that chat wouldn't be had with words but with fists.

"Please let Ethan handle this," I begged.

I held Logan's stare and watched as determination seeped in. I was wrong; the chat wouldn't be bad, it would be a disaster.

"I thought I made myself clear. I didn't. I promised you Guy would no longer be an issue for you. I didn't keep that promise. But mark this, Ren—he's gonna pay. He's gonna feel every second of your fear. He's gonna feel every piece of glass you had embedded in your skin, every cut, every bit of blood that leaked from your flesh. He's gonna feel it ten-fold."

"Man, you have to let me handle this," Ethan pleaded.

Logan turned but he didn't take me with him. He let go and pushed me behind him so he was shielding me from Ethan.

"I'm taking Lauren back to my place. She's gonna rest and you can come in the morning and get her statement."

"I need it fresh in her mind."

"Do you? No disrespect, Ethan, but would you let anyone near Honor after she was involved in a high-speed chase? A chase that led to a bullet going through the back of the seat her head was resting on two fucking seconds before that bullet hit? Would you let anybody near her to question her when that shit was still *fresh*? Not only that but say Honor was *forced* to take your firearm, crawl into the back seat while you were driving fast, no seat belt, no restraint, knowing all it would take was the motherfucker behind you getting in one lucky shot and your tire was gone and your woman would be dead. But you have no goddamn choice because again, one lucky fucking shot and my tire's gone, and at the speed we were traveling we'd both have been dead. So, you drive and you do it knowing you got no fucking choice but to let your woman put herself in danger to protect both of you. With all of that, you think I'm gonna let you or anyone near my woman, you think wrong. Tomorrow you come to my house, and we'll give you every-thing you need."

Holy shit.

With all of that, you think I'm gonna let you or anyone near my woman, you think wrong.

His woman?

"I didn't know it was like that," Ethan grumbled.

"It's exactly that," Logan returned irately.

"You're right, I wouldn't let anyone near my wife. But, Logan, I can't delay too long. You got until tomorrow morning."

"Mom, you and Quinn get on packing up Lauren, yeah?"

I glanced to my right and found Quinn biting back a smile. I didn't see anything amusing about the situation and neither did Dee. Her face was pale and her eyes were bright with tears. Jill had an arm around her mom and Jackie was next to her sister holding her hand.

"It wasn't that bad," I blurted out in an effort to ease some of Dee's fears. "Logan had everything under control. He's good at what he does, the best actually. It wasn't safe but it wasn't as dangerous as it sounds."

Okay, that was a lie; it was really freaking dangerous. We could've died, but I hated seeing Dee and Logan's sisters so scared. I didn't want them to think that Logan didn't know what he was doing.

"Shit," Logan muttered under his breath, then called, "Mom, come here."

Dee didn't delay; she was across the room and had her arms around her son in a flash. I tried to move away to give them space but Logan's hand went to my wrist and kept me behind him.

Still shielding me even though there was no threat.

In that moment a few things became clear. It was not anger that fueled Logan. It was fear. He wanted me close, wanted me behind him, wanted complete control because I'd lied earlier—Logan didn't have control over the situation. I was in the car, in danger, and it was beyond his control. It was dangerous and there was nothing Logan could do about that. He could do his best to navigate us through but that didn't mean I was in less danger.

This is what it feels like to be protected.

With everything slamming into me at once I bent my neck and let my forehead hit Logan's back. He had his mother at his front, me at his back, and he was holding us both up at once. A testament to his strength. Proof he was more than he thought he was.

"Where's Ian?" Logan asked.

"Right here." I heard.

"Get Mom, yeah?"

That was *big.*

So huge I didn't need to see Ian's reaction to Logan's request—which wasn't a request as much as it was a sign of trust and respect—to feel Ian's response. It was immediate and it was beautiful. Dee was shifted to Ian, Logan shifted me around to his front, and his lips went to the top of my head.

"DeeDee, sweetheart, he's safe." Ian paused and I saw Dee's body buck. "He's safe, baby. Lauren's safe. He's got good men all around him. You have to trust in that."

Oh, boy, Ian had been holding back the public display of affection. Likely this was done for Logan's benefit. Hearing Ian now, seeing the way he held Dee, this was not the first time he'd comforted her. The scene playing out was familiar and comfortable for both of them.

I braced for Logan's reaction and didn't let go of the breath I was holding until I heard him sigh.

"You're a good man, Logan. You might not think it, but you are."

His arms went super tight, then he announced, "I'm taking Lauren home."

"I'll give you an escort." I jolted when Echo Kent's voice boomed.

I hadn't noticed he'd come into the conference room, which was a damn shock considering no one missed Echo Kent. The man was six-foot-five and built like a powerhouse. He would terrify me if I didn't know he was a big old softy under all that muscle. Not that I'd ever tell anyone I thought Echo was a softy but when Echo was around his sister Shiloh he couldn't hide it. He was as big as a gorilla but when his baby sister was in the room he turned into a cute Teddy bear.

"I'd appreciate that," Logan returned.

"Lauren's purse and your cell are on her desk," Ethan started. "A wrecker will pick up your Mustang for processing. It'll take about a week. Jasper brought a Suburban around for you to use until we sort your car."

"Junk it."

"What? You love that car," I protested.

"Ren, baby, not only do I never want to drive that car again but I'd never put my woman back into a vehicle—"

"That's crazy! You *love* your car."

And he did love that Mustang. I'd never seen it not sparkling clean inside and out.

"Yeah, I do. But straight up, I love you more. And your ass is never, not fucking *ever* sitting in a car where your head almost got blown the fuck off. And I'm never getting back into that fucking car knowing there was a fucking bullet lodged in my dash instead of in your brain."

So there were more than his usual 'fucks' sprinkled into that statement, thus it was safe to say he was more than a tad incensed. But that wasn't what had my lungs burning. His cursing wasn't what made my insides overheat while at the same making me shiver.

"You love me?"

"From the very first time you rolled your eyes at me."

Say what?

"I roll my eyes a lot," I informed him.

"Yeah, you do. And you did it about five minutes after I met you when you heard me and Matt giving Drake shit about being domesticated."

"I think I also called you an ass because you were making fun of him."

"Men don't 'make fun of' their brothers, they give 'em shit and bust their balls. And they do it as a way to communicate they're jealous as fuck their brother has found something worth having. Drake knew what he had, he knew Liberty was his future, he knew he wasn't going to be a dumbass and let her slip away. But *I* was the dumbass who was standing there knowing that ten feet from me stood everything I ever wanted yet *I* was going to let her slip away. So I gave my brother shit, and to my surprise that beautiful, shy woman rolled her eyes, called me an ass, and gave attitude. She had a strength under all that pretty. She was not afraid to call me out. She had Drake's back and Liberty's even though I was just messin' with Drake. And still, I knew I was going to be a dumbass."

I loved all of that so much. So, so much I couldn't speak. Then I could but only to say his name.

"Logan," I breathed out.

"Happily eat my words, I was wrong. So fuckin' wrong. And it pains me to admit it took me almost losing you to wake my ass up. But feeling that fear, knowing you could be gone in a way that meant I would never have you back—oh, yeah, it woke my shit up. Knowing that I could lose a future with you. Me or you or both of us gone and you never getting from me what you should've had from me over the last year. Not only the words, but everything. I love you, Lauren. From the bottom of my soul. No more bullshit. We agreed on honesty, so there it is, all of it."

That wasn't honesty, that was Logan in front of everyone laying himself bare. That was him giving me everything I ever wanted and him not caring we weren't in private.

I heard someone sniffle. I heard someone clear their throat. I heard someone's footsteps.

But my gaze remained glued to Logan's. I stared into his wary eyes until I could no longer see them because my lips were on his and my eyes were closed. Logan didn't take over, he didn't rush me—he gave and gave and let me take. And even though we had an audience I took my fill.

It wasn't until we were in the Suburban on our way to Logan's that the drama of the morning knocked the wind out of me. One moment I was sitting there staring at the window and the next second I was hyperventilating. I didn't know if it was a delayed reaction to the car chase, the knowledge Guy was basically stalking me, that I'd shot a gun out of the back of a car moving at a high rate of speed, knowing I'd injured someone, or the news that Logan loved me.

Weirdly I thought it was the news that Logan loved me. Don't get me wrong; I cared that I'd shot someone—I mean, who shoots someone? Even if that person was shooting at us, I didn't actually want to hurt them. I just didn't want to die. Now everything was tangling in my mind. The bewilderment that he'd announced his feelings in front of a room full of people. Logan seemed to blurt things out when tension was high. Maybe that was why I felt like I was going to pass out from the anxiety, worry, and relief that seem to be on constant repeat.

"Ren, you need to slow your breathing," Logan clipped.

"I...can't."

"Fuck."

"Echo, Jasper, and Lenox are right behind us," he assured me.

I knew they were; I saw all three men get into their vehicles. Further, I knew it was highly unlikely that we'd be involved in two high-speed chases in one day. But rational thought didn't stop the panic from bubbling up.

"You love me?"

"What?"

I kept my eyes on my lap and asked again, "You love me?"

"Yeah."

Weird, he didn't hesitate. That made it harder to breathe.

"I think I'm mad at you," I told him.

"Because I love you?"

"Yes," I hissed. "I tried so damn hard to get you to pay attention to me, to the point I embarrassed myself. Then I had to let you go, and that hurt. Then in an effort to get over you, I started dating a criminal and a loser. Then we get together and start having sex at which time you tell me you'll never love me, and that breaks my heart. Knowing, *unequivocally*, I'll never have you in any real way. Then you screw with my head more and tell me you're never letting me go. And that gives me hope but at the same time scares the hell out of me because I was trying so hard not to fall in love with you more. I was trying to be who I needed to be so when you left me you didn't rip me to shreds. Now—*now*—you say you love me. After all of that. After my heart broke, a stupid asshole cheated on me, you convinced me I was better off being alone than loving someone, now, *now* you love me."

Since I was speaking it would seem I could breathe, but my breath was coming out in quick, rapid puffs, and I was surprised I wasn't spitting out fire along with my words.

"I fucked up."

"You fucked up?"

I felt something hit my thigh and looked down to see Logan's hand, palm up resting there.

"Give me your hand."

The moment I set my hand over his, palm to palm, his fingers curled and squeezed.

"Way before I met you I fucked up by not dealing with family shit. I buried it, not wanting to examine how a father could stab his son. How a man could hurt his wife. I couldn't understand any of it so I shoved it down and did the only thing I could do. I built walls. I told myself lies and I repeated them so often they became my truth. Love couldn't be real. I needed to believe that to explain how Dave could hurt us."

Whoa.

Logan had never told me his dad's name. His sisters didn't either. It was like uttering the dead man's name would conjure up demons. Like Bloody Mary, say Dave Haines three times and somehow the man would appear.

"I needed a reason," Logan continued. "Every morning before he left for work he'd tell my mom he loved her. Sometimes I'd see them sitting on the couch and his arm would be around her and it was like everything was normal. We were normal. But if something set him off he didn't blink before he blackened her eye. He wasn't a drunk, he had a decent job, we lived in a nice house in a nice neighborhood, from the outside we looked like a regular family. In public,

Dave was a loving husband, a father, a decent man. And since I needed a reason and there wasn't one to be found I told myself that love was bullshit, it wasn't real, it made you stupid, it made you vulnerable to pain. But mostly I told myself that I had Dave inside of me and if I ever loved a woman, I'd use my fists to show her.

"So I fucked up. It started when I was a kid, it grew after Lucy was born and Dave hit me for the first time, and it got worse after the twins. I was older—he could hit me harder but I was also bigger, I was learning to stick up for myself. But it got worse when I turned thirteen. I was tall, I had a little bit of strength, and I had a whole lot of anger. He'd threaten Lucy and I'd step in and piss him off so he'd come after me. He'd go at my mom and I'd push him so he'd stop nailing her and turn to me. Dave *loved* us all—at picnics, at barbeques, during family get-togethers—after he beat the fuck out of us. He loved us then. How in the fuck is that love?"

Oh. My. God.

"Honey, that's not love," I said barely above a whisper.

"You're right, it's not. But how the fuck was I supposed to know that? That was all I knew. My mom would leave, he'd drag us back. My mom would leave again, he'd drag us back. She had not a single credit card in her name, didn't work, he controlled the money, and her family wouldn't help her. They didn't believe in divorce. I don't know if she ever told them how bad it was or that he was hitting us, all I know is they refused to help. So she'd go back to her husband that *loved* her so he could beat her more."

I was staring at our hands. My small one was engulfed by his much larger one. Battered and scarred knuckles, fresh cuts from hitting the heavy bag. A fist that could do so much damage. Fingertips that had touched me gently.

I couldn't fathom how he'd survived. How Dee had survived knowing Dave was harming Logan. How scared she must've been, trapped, imprisoned, tied to a horrible man. Twenty-five years ago there wasn't as much help out there for abused women as there was today. She must've felt so alone. I hated that for her, for all of them, for a thirteen-year-old boy who was born a protector yet could not protect his mom.

"I'm sorry I fucked up and hurt you, Ren."

My heart clenched and guilt crept in.

"I shouldn't have said that, honey. That wasn't fair. I'm the one who should be sorry. I don't even know why I said it."

"Because it's the truth. Everything you said is the truth. I was so afraid of hurting you I didn't see I was hurting you. I'd lived my life knowing I'd never get married or have kids or be in any sort of relationship. It was a given. Even after my friends found women and I saw what it meant, how when a good man loves and it doesn't cause pain how beautiful it is. I still knew I had Dave inside of me and I would never take the chance.

"But then I met you and for the first time, I cared. For the first time, I hated my life. For the first time, I questioned everything I thought I knew and came to the realization there is nothing that would ever make me raise my hand to you. For the first time, I loved someone and I had no idea what to do with those feelings. I fucked up and lied. I told myself new lies until I believed you were better off without me and everything I was doing was to protect you."

The SUV started to slow and I looked up. If this was Logan's neighborhood Jill and Jackie had wasted money on an Uber the other day; they could've walked to my place. The houses were newer and bigger in this section of the development. They were also on bigger lots and set back from the street.

I saw Shiloh standing on the sidewalk and looked at the house behind her. Two-story, three-car garage, dark-blue siding with stone accents, a large, welcoming front porch complete with stone pillars, and a well-kept yard. The house was nice, very nice, and way too big for Logan to live in all by himself. It was a family home in a family-friendly neighborhood. There would be no raging parties here. Not that Logan was a partier but he was a confirmed bachelor.

"We're here," he announced.

I bit back a snarky *no shit, Sherlock* and instead asked, "Why'd you buy such a big house?"

"Because it was close to you."

My mouth dropped open. I didn't know what I was expecting but it wasn't that and I certainly wasn't expecting him to admit that straight out even if it was the truth.

Logan's phone rang. He grabbed it from the console and answered, and a moment later he gave a curt response and disconnected.

"Echo, Shiloh, and Lenox are clearing the house. Jasper will wait outside with us," Logan told me.

"Clearing the house?"

"Just a precaution."

I didn't want to think about why precautions were needed but still, I pushed. "Is all of this necessary?"

"Absolutely."

"Logan, I need more than that."

"The car that was following us was stolen. Until we have a lock on the men who were inside the car every precaution is being taken. Guy was at your house. Until we know why he was there, why he followed us, and if he's connected to the men who shot at us, every precaution is being taken.

Shit like this can go from bad to worse in the blink of an eye and I'm not taking any chances. The good news is the men in the car fled on foot and they did it quickly, which means they didn't have time to wipe down the car. Even if they were wearing gloves there's a chance they left something behind. The bad news is, none of the cameras so far caught an image clear enough to run through facial recognition. And unless we send someone to Nashville we have to wait until Guy gets back to question him. Matt and Brady could go to Tennessee and track him down, but I'd rather have them here in Georgia and have extra coverage on you and my house."

Okay, so perhaps I was incorrect and I wasn't freaking out because Logan loved me. Maybe it was the chase, the shooting, Guy being a crazy weirdo, that had caused my panic attack because now I was finding it hard to breathe again.

"Ren, baby, you are safe."

I wanted to believe that, but watching Shiloh, Echo, and Lenox approach Logan's house all with guns drawn, while Jasper now stood outside of the Suburban still idling at the curb, I found it hard to. I also found it hard to believe I was safe when Logan was on high alert. His eyes were scanning the street and when they weren't they were checking the mirrors. That should've been comforting but it wasn't. It was a reminder that we were not safe but in danger.

"Logan?"

"Yeah?" He didn't stop scanning.

"I'm scared."

That got me all of his attention. And when I say that, I mean he reached over, unbuckled my belt, plucked me out of the seat, and dragged me into his lap. It also got me intense, hazel eyes that were full of concern.

"I promise you I will do everything I can to keep you safe. I promise you my brothers will do the same. It fucking kills me to hear you say you're scared but it fucking kills more that I don't know what I'm protecting you from. Until we understand what's going on, I'm not taking chances. I'm sorry if that scares you, baby, but I'd rather you be safe and scared instead of not scared and unsafe."

For some strange reason that made me feel better. Not so much his promise—though I knew Logan would never make a promise he couldn't keep—but the part where he'd rather I was scared and safe. I'd prefer that, too.

"Okay."

"I know you already got a lot on you but I need you thinking about something else."

I wasn't sure how much more I could think about after today's drama but I still said, "What do you want me to think about?"

"House is empty," he strangely told me.

"So I've heard your sister say."

"Right. So I don't have much to offer you but I want you to think about moving in, permanently."

Whoosh.

All of my breath left my body with one word, "What?"

"I wasted a year, I don't feel like wasting more. I told you I bought this house because it was close to you. But at the time, I didn't *really* get it, I didn't need a house this big. I didn't buy it because it was close to you; I bought it *for* you. For us. I want you to think about moving in."

Silence ensued and he let me have it until he was done. Then he called, "Lauren?"

"I don't know what to say."

And I didn't. Part of me wanted to dance a little happy dance while singing a really bad rendition of "Hallelujah".

Part of me wanted to be sensible and tell him it was way too soon to be thinking about moving in with him. A bigger part of me wanted to tell him yes. And a tiny part of me wanted to tell him he had shit timing. First, telling me he loved me smack dab in the middle of a trauma, then asking me to move in while his house was being cleared by two police officers and a former Army man, all of whom were armed. Oh, and I couldn't forget Jasper who was right there outside playing armed bodyguard.

Totally shit timing.

"Just tell me you'll think about it."

"I want it on record that if you ask me to marry you in the middle of a drama the answer is no." I felt Logan go stiff. Unfortunately, I wasn't paying enough attention because I sallied forth. "You have the worst timing of any person I know. Maybe I would've liked the first time you told me you loved me to be in private so I could return the sentiment without your family and my co-workers present. And maybe I would've liked you to ask me to move in with you when I wasn't sitting in your lap in a borrowed SUV because your car was shot to shit."

While I was blathering on I hadn't noticed Logan's body had turned to granite.

"Return the sentiment?"

Oh, crap.

"I...uh..."

"That's what you said, baby. You love me?"

Is he dense?

"Of course I do," I snapped.

Logan's lips twitched before they tipped up and he gave me a dazzling smile.

"Yeah, baby, you do." His hand lifted to my neck and his fingers curled around and at the same time, he dropped his forehead. "You have for a long time, same as me. I fucked up and fucked around and lost too much time. We can't get that back and that's on me. So, my timing might be shit, but that's part of me not wasting it. I'm not waiting. I feel it or want it, I'm saying it."

I felt the pad of his thumb skimming the side of my neck. My vision filled with nothing but Logan. With my heart fuller than it had ever been, thoughts of the last week invaded—Logan coming home to me, going to sleep beside him, waking up the same. I knew then as it was happening I didn't want it to end. Now, knowing that he loved me and I was free to love him I never wanted it to end.

Logan was right; we'd lost time and just this morning in the form of bullets I had the reminder that time was precious and more of it wasn't guaranteed.

"Okay."

"Okay, you'll think about it?"

"Okay, I'll move in."

And since Logan's forehead was resting on mine, I got to watch up close as emotion flashed in his eyes right before they slowly drifted close. I got to feel his fingertips press deep and his body relax under mine.

21

I watched Lauren walk back into the house, Shiloh and my sisters coming through the sliding glass door behind her, and I did this coming to terms with how badly I'd fucked up. Self-reflection sucked ass. Having to admit you were wrong your whole life sucked, too. But knowing you hurt the woman you loved was worse. And seeing that woman almost get a bullet through her brain made a man quickly reconsider his stupidity.

Lauren said I had bad timing. She was right but she was also wrong. Right in the sense I should've dealt with my shit months ago and told her how I felt. But she was also wrong —there was no time like the present and I wasn't going to let anything get in the way of getting what I wanted even if that meant telling her I loved her in a room full of people.

There had been a steady stream of friends coming in and out of my house in the hour we'd been there. First, Drake and Matt stopped by on their way back to the office. Both men had barged in and bee-lined to Lauren, wanting to see for themselves she was unharmed. They left with the promise they'd be back. Next was Trey and Luke. Much like

Matt and Drake, they were in and out after checking on Lauren.

My sisters had made quick work of getting groceries. By the looks of it they just threw whatever they came across into the cart; never had my kitchen seen so much food.

My mom had called to tell me that she and Quinn would be a while. Emily Walker, Quinn's mother, had shown up with Lily Lenox and they were going to the home goods store to pick up "odds and ends". Whatever the hell that meant, I had no clue, but I figured my mom would take care of getting what Lauren would need to be comfortable.

And lastly, Reagan Clark and Blake McCoy had shown with their husbands, Nolan and Levi, with a dining room table. I didn't ask where it came from. I didn't question it when Reagan turned to Lauren and asked her if the table was where she wanted. Further, I didn't bother examining why I liked Reagan asking and Lauren directing the men to move the table a few feet so it was center. I knew why. This was what I'd been waiting for. This was why I bought this house and left it unfurnished.

I'd been waiting for Lauren to make my house into our home.

Jesus, I was a dumbfuck.

Lauren walked past Jasper, Lenox, Nolan, and Levi's huddle and came straight to me.

"You have a great backyard," she told me when she stopped next to me.

"*We* have a great backyard," I corrected and watched Lauren's face gentle. "The realtor told me the people who sold me the house had plans to put in a pool and the permits were already approved."

"A pool?"

"Yeah, Ren, a pool. You want one?"

"Pools are expensive."

"Didn't ask you about the cost. Asked if you want one."

"You have to buy a new car."

"Insurance will cover the car and if it doesn't I'll buy a new one. You haven't answered, you want a pool?"

"Of course she wants a pool, you dumb lug," Jill interrupted. "And patio furniture, and maybe a hot tub."

A hot tub would be first.

Before I could tell my sister to butt out she continued. "Matt will be here any minute to give me a ride to the airport. That way, Ian's not interrupted. I wish I could stay, too, but with the promotion, I have to get back."

My mother had declared she was extending her trip, Ian had readily agreed, and Jackie was all for staying. I wasn't particularly fond of the looks Jackie had been casting Echo Kent's way and had suggested she go home with Jill but she'd refused.

As if on cue the front door opened and Matt walked in.

"Ready?" he called out. "Traffic's a bitch this time of day."

"Yeah, my bags are by the door," Jill told Matt then turned to me. "Walk me out?"

A sudden wave of remorse hit me. The same guilt that gnawed at the end of each visit. I loved my mom and sisters, I visited them when I could and they did the same, coming to wherever I'd lived, but I would never move back to Bad Axe and for some unknown reason, they still lived there with all the bad memories that came with our childhood. I knew they understood why I couldn't spend any more time in Michigan than I did but I still felt guilt over not being closer, being more involved in their daily lives, not being there to watch over them.

"Be right back." I bent to kiss Lauren's forehead but she

tipped her head back and offered me her lips. Christ, that felt good even if it was a soft touch. Hell, it felt good *because* it was a soft brush.

"I'll be right out, I want to say goodbye to everyone."

Jill grabbed Lauren by the hand and pulled her in the direction of the kitchen where, by the looks of it, the women were rearranging cabinets. I followed Matt out the front door and down the drive to the curb.

"How is she?" Matt asked as soon as he stopped by his mammoth jacked-up truck.

He was asking about Lauren.

"Freaked the fuck out."

"Dylan was still checking local traffic cams and he set Ian on airport footage in Nashville to confirm Guy got on the flight. Something's not adding up."

"No shit," I spat. "What are the chances that today was the day that Guy decided to make his approach, the same day two unidentified shooters decide to take me out? I don't give a fuck if Guy's in Nashville; it's not a coincidence. Whether Guy meant to take me out or grab Lauren or hell, take her out, he's fucking behind this."

"I agree. My gut says this is about us getting too close to whatever Guy's got going on. You taking his girl is a bruise to his ego, sure. But a fuckstick like him doesn't have it in him to go after you alone. He'd need firepower which makes me wonder where he'd find the connections to get it, and since he did, how he found it so quickly. Not to mention, where he came up with the cake to pay for it. His bank accounts are healthy, he's certainly not hurting for money, but he's not loaded and a hit costs a whack, which he does not have."

"I take it you looked, so were there any withdrawals from any of his accounts?" I asked.

"Nope. Nothing out of the ordinary. Which also raises

some red flags—his deposits and withdrawals are clean, too clean. Same amounts every month. Taxes are filed on time and sparkling clean, not a single questionable deduction, all income down to the penny reported. I don't know a single business owner who doesn't have ups and downs on their balance sheet."

"It's all bullshit."

I wasn't asking for confirmation or conversation. I'd done my own digging and I'd come to the same conclusion. Guy Stevens was in the drug trade; the only question was how deep.

"Yep. We can back off—"

"Fuck no," I interrupted him. "He's scrambling, we push harder."

"Lauren."

"The only way to make Lauren safe is to take Guy down. In the meantime, I'll cover Lauren."

Matt's response was interrupted by my sister's fast approach.

"Sorry I took so long," she said as she wrapped her arms around my waist. "It was good to see you, big brother."

"You, too, Jilly."

Her head tipped back and I braced when I saw the somber look.

"I like her, Logan. No, I *love* her."

"Good."

"Thank you," she whispered.

"Why are you thanking me, honey?"

"For being cool with Ian. It took you a minute but you came around. Mom's happy. Well, right now she's trying to figure out how to kidnap her adult son and his girlfriend and lock you both in her house so she knows you're safe. But in general, she's finally happy. And her seeing you with

Lauren, I think she'll finally be able to let go of the guilt she holds."

Fuck, I hated hearing that my mom was still holding onto guilt. Nothing that had happened was her fault. None of us blamed her for the nightmare that was our father.

"I should've let all the shit go a long time ago," I admitted.

"A long time ago, you didn't have a reason. Now you do."

Hell yeah, I did.

"Call me before you board?"

"Yes, big brother. I know the drill. Before I board, when I land, when I get to my car, when I get home."

"There are crazy people out there, Jilly."

"You don't say?"

After she gave me a tight squeeze she let go and turned to Matt's truck.

"Overcompensating much," Jill teased Matt.

"If you weren't my brother's sister I'd have a comeback for that."

"I bet you would," she shot back. "And I still wouldn't believe you."

"Again, Jilly, if you weren't Logan's sister I'd offer to prove—"

"Swear on all things holy, you finish that, *brother*, you'll have my foot up your ass."

"Damn, you're easy to rile up." Jill laughed. "You do know I'm not a—"

"Jillian," I warned.

"Love you, Logan," she singsonged and jumped up into the cab.

"Call me!" I shouted as she slammed the door. "You, too."

"Will do and I'll be back."

I watched as Matt's truck pulled away, passing Quinn's SUV pulling down my street and Lily's car behind Quinn's.

I waited at the curb to help carry in the haul. There was no telling what "odds and ends" my mother had picked up.

I did this smiling, despite one of my sisters leaving.

A few minutes later, I found that it was a good thing I'd waited but I also needed to call out reinforcements. Emily's trunk had been packed full and the back of Quinn's SUV was jammed full of stuff, too.

"Jeez, Ma, did you leave anything at the store?" Jackie laughed.

Lauren was staring at all the shopping bags with wide eyes, looking more than a little freaked.

"Yes, Jaclyn, I did," my mom snapped. "It's not every day a mother gets to spoil her son and her soon-to-be daughter. And since your brother refused a housewarming party and I refuse to subject Laurie to ratty towels and no soap dispensers, I took it upon myself to save Laurie the hassle of having to shop."

Laurie?

Since I was still staring at Lauren I didn't miss her reaction to my mom calling her, her soon-to-be daughter. It wasn't a flinch but there was definitely surprise when Lauren's eyes twitched.

"It's a good thing you saved *Laurie* from that, Mom. No soap dispensers sounds like torture," I teased.

Lauren's lips slowly curved up and when they finally formed a full-fledged smile my stomach bottomed out at the beauty. How I'd stupidly held out for so long was a major fuck-up. I could've had this—her in our house, smiling at me, knowing later she'd be sleeping next to me and the next morning I'd wake up and she'd still be there.

I was a fucking fool.

"Anything you don't like, we can take back," my mom told Lauren.

"I'm not picky, DeeDee. I'm sure whatever you bought will be perfect," Lauren responded to my mom but hadn't taken her eyes off of me.

"You should have what you want," my mom argued.

"I already do."

Fuck, Jesus Christ.

"Ren, baby, come here." My demand was gruff. It was also necessary because my muscles had seized. One step in her direction, which was near the base of the stairs leading to the bedrooms, would be one step too close to where I wanted to take her. Too great a temptation.

"Bossy." I heard Jackie mumble.

"You're telling me."

Lauren's words might've been misconstrued as a complaint if she weren't smiling and moving toward me.

When she was close, I tagged her around her middle and yanked her to me. Once I had her where I wanted I dropped my mouth to her ear and whispered, "You like me bossy, baby."

I felt her body quiver and I didn't miss the soft sigh of agreement.

"I love you, Logan," she whispered.

Fire and ice mixed in my veins. Heat skated over my skin as Lauren melted closer.

"Now who has shit timing?" I growled.

"I figured a little payback was in order."

"Oh, yeah, there'll be payback. Prepare, Ren; you haven't begun to see bossy."

～

"Don't stop, Ren."

The sexiest groan filled the bedroom and I fought to hold on.

"That's it, baby, fuck yourself harder."

My hands skimmed over her ass, over the dimples indenting the small of her back, up farther until I had a handful of her silky hair. With a twist, I had it wrapped around my hand, pulling her head up so I could see her face.

"Tell me," I demanded.

"I won't stop."

Her hips bucked as she drove herself down on my cock.

"No, tell me you love me."

"I love you," she moaned.

Fuck, yes.

"Again."

"I love you, honey."

Jesus.

"Again."

"I love you, Logan."

"I love you, too, Lauren."

My eyes drifted closed and I savored the words still lingering in the room. I reveled in the way my chest burned and my heart pounded.

I opened my eyes, took in the sight before me—the woman I loved naked astride me, riding my cock so hard she was panting. Then I decided it wasn't a sight to be seen, it was a sight to *behold*. So goddamn beautiful with her face flushed, her hair a wild mess, sweat dripping down between her bouncing tits.

"I'm coming," she mewed.

I didn't need to be told, I could feel it.

"Take it, baby."

She stopped bouncing and started grinding. Each rock of her hips brought me closer, each flutter of her pussy closer, every twitch closer. Until I couldn't hold back and came with her.

"*Logan.*"

A breathy groan. So damn sexy.

"Fuck, baby."

I could say no more. I was swept under, waves of pleasure washed over me. I released her hair only to hold on to her hips, keeping her rooted deep.

Rooted deep.

Me in her.

Her on me.

Exactly the way it was meant to be.

22

Being driven to work with an entourage wasn't something that I ever thought I'd experience. But there I was in the passenger seat being chauffeured by Logan with Echo and Lenox following us. And if that wasn't enough Jasper and Brady were standing out front of the building waiting for us.

Logan pulled into a spot, Echo parked on one side, Lenox parked on the other and as soon as Logan turned off the car he turned to me.

"Wait for me to come around."

Then without waiting for me to answer he was out of the Suburban and rounding the hood, his eyes scanning the lot. My door opened and I was hauled out—as in Logan reached in and scooped me out of the seat and set me on my feet. Once there, his arm slid around my shoulders, and if I hadn't already been freaked right the fuck out, Echo, Lenox, Brady, and Jasper meeting us at the car and flanking Logan and me as we walked across the parking lot would've done it.

By the time we walked into TC what little calm I had was gone. Not that I'd had all that much since I'd woken up and found Logan on-edge which only fueled my anxiety. The men dispersed and Logan halted me in front of my desk.

"Not taking any chances, Ren," Logan reminded me for the five hundredth time.

"I know."

The reminders started as soon as Logan had pulled me out of bed and guided me to the shower. He continued through getting dressed, coffee, when we walked out of the house and I saw Echo and Lenox waiting for us, and every five minutes on the way to work. I will admit I had difficulty being in a vehicle, and it didn't help that Logan lived around the corner from my house—or I should say my *old* house— so the route to work was the same. I knew if Logan could've taken an alternate route, even if it added an hour to our drive, he would've. But unfortunately, there was only one road for him to take.

"Ethan will be here in a few minutes."

This was a reminder as well. Ethan had called before we left the house to give Logan a heads up he was coming in this morning with his partner Jace.

"I know," I repeated.

"And Jackie—"

"Logan, I know Jackie's coming by to have lunch with me. I know Ethan's on his way. And I know you're not taking risks. I know you're worried about me but I'm fine."

That last part was a little white lie that I felt no guilt telling. Logan looked more worried than I felt.

"Plus, you'll be with me when I talk to Ethan and Jace. Everything's fine."

"You said you were scared."

"What?"

I tilted my head back and to the side so I could catch his

gaze. Logan helped accomplish this by dipping his chin and holding mine.

"Yesterday, you said you were scared."

I was wrong. Logan didn't look more worried than I felt. He looked conflicted.

"Yesterday I was terrified when we were being shot at. I was horrified when I had to return fire. I was scared about *everything*. I will admit driving in wasn't pleasant, it was a little scary being back on the same road. But I had you next to me. It's a little alarming having a police escort to work, but I understand when it's necessary and I'm not stupid enough to turn down people looking after us. And I'll remind you that last night you were worried I wouldn't be able to sleep and I did that just fine because I went to bed knowing you were there."

That was the God's honest truth. I slept like a baby in Logan's—now mine, too—big comfortable bed with super-soft sheets that Dee had bought, washed, and put on the bed. Incidentally, today after work we were all going back to my house to pack up and move more stuff to Logan's—personal items since Quinn had practically carted all of my clothes to Logan's yesterday. Then Dee, Ian, and Jackie would be staying there instead of at a hotel. Dee had declared she was staying until she felt Logan and I were no longer in danger. Ian being madly in love with Dee had backed her play and simply called his office to tell them he wasn't coming back as planned. Jackie seemed to be content to stay. That might have had something to do with a certain six-foot-five blue-eyed beast of a man, but I wasn't bringing that up to Logan.

"Lauren—"

"Will you stay with me?"

"Fuck yeah!"

"Then I'm fine."

"Ren, baby—"

"Stop, Logan. You're freaking out over nothing."

His eyes flashed and he leaned in closer.

"You being terrified is something. You being horrified is something. You being scared and there not being a goddamn thing I can do about it until I find Guy is something."

There it was—Logan couldn't hide his fear.

And he was pissed he couldn't control *my* fear. The same way he couldn't control his mom getting beaten, or his sisters getting hurt, or his own safety when he was a kid. Whether his protective instincts came naturally or they were beaten into him the way he once thought that his capacity to love was beaten out of him didn't matter. *He* was the one who was terrified but he wouldn't appreciate me pointing that out. So I took a different approach.

"What do you need from me?" I asked.

"Need from you?"

"Yes, what do you need from me to make you understand that even though I'm scared all I need is you?"

The worry slid from his features and a new look took its place. Something gentle—no, more than gentle—tender. It made my heart stop beating and my breath catch.

"Baby," he whispered.

I lost sight of his eyes when his face went to my neck and his arms wrapped tighter. I had no choice but to return the embrace—not that I'd ever choose differently. I was exactly where I wanted to be.

"We're going to get through this," I told him. "Ethan's a friend; you know he'd never hurt me. Jasper, Levi, Lenox, and Clark are kicking in with bodyguard duty. Echo is, too. All the guys are working double-time to find the driver and the passenger. Ian's helping Dylan. We have good men all around us pitching in, protecting us. And, Logan, I have you. I know I'm safe. I know you're safe. I'll be okay. But I need to know what you need so you're not—"

"You're right," he interrupted me. "About everything."

"As much as I like hearing I'm right, you still haven't answered."

Logan's head came up but he didn't loosen his hold when he said, "I need you to let me worry. I need you to let me be me and part of that is you understanding that I've got no control over the situation which pisses me the fuck off. I need you to let me do what I feel I need to do to keep you safe, even if that means I got men camped on the front lawn. And I need you to roll with that—me being me even if that means I go overboard."

He stopped and pressed his forehead to mine. It wasn't painful, but it was forceful. Logan had a point to make and he wanted my attention—all of it. "I cannot bear the thought of something happening to you. I wouldn't survive it. If I lost you I wouldn't go back to being the asshole I was before I met you. I would be completely dead inside. For the first time, I feel like I'm living, *really* living, not just going through the motions. You woke me up and gave me something I never thought I'd have. Never thought I wanted. Now I have it. I have you, and, baby, I will fight and die before you're taken from me."

I loved, no I *treasured* every word Logan said. But I hated them, too. I hated that he'd lived a life that was not full and happy but instead had been "going through the motions". I hated that he'd never wanted or thought he'd find better. I hated that he didn't think he deserved to have a life that included love and family. I despised the notion that he never thought of himself as good enough. And that was what it came down to, what Dave had left him with. I knew it wasn't from Dee or his sisters—they adored him, they thought the world of him, and they didn't hide how much they loved him.

"You can have anything you need, baby," I whispered. "And everything you want."

I felt Logan's body go tight, then it turned to granite. He was so stiff I was afraid to breathe, so I held my breath, unsure what I could've said that would cause that reaction.

"You'll give me anything I need?"

"Yes," I answered.

"You'll give me everything I want?"

Again my answer came quickly with zero hesitation. "Absolutely."

"Christ." The word sounded like it was torn from his chest. "*Christ*. I jacked you around, fucked-up, hurt you, kept you waiting, and you'll give me anything I need."

"Well, yeah. I love you."

"Christ," he rumbled.

"*Christ, what*?" I asked.

Logan didn't make me wait to explain what "what" meant. And when he did I learned that words could slice to the bone, deliver velvety blows, burn, and feed the soul all at the same time.

"All my life, baby, since I could remember, love hurt. It came with fists, lies, guilt, blame, and bad memories. My mom's love comes with guilt—she blames herself for not being able to get us away sooner. My sisters' love comes with the memories—them remembering what I took so they wouldn't. All of us lived under a black cloud of Dave's lies. For the first time in my life love comes with understanding and forgiveness. It doesn't eat at my soul; it *feeds* it. Your love is free and clear, it's clean, it feels good. Never had that."

"Logan." My breath hitched and I could get no more out.

"Love you, Laurie," he whispered, and I felt my throat clog.

I heard a manufactured cough—you know, the fake kind, and their sole intent was to announce someone's presence.

"Our timing sucks," I choked out, still fighting back the tears that were forming. "Maybe, in the future, we should schedule our heart-to-hearts; you know, so we can have them in private."

Logan lifted his forehead off mine, placed a soft kiss there, then tucked me to his side.

"Sorry to interrupt," Ethan muttered. Jace stood silently beside him.

"No worries." Logan graciously let Ethan off the hook. "Jace, good to see you."

"Shit reason, but good to see you. Lauren, you, too."

"Hi, Jace. Morning, Ethan."

"Conference room is ready for you," Lenox called out.

Without further conversation, we all filed into the conference room. I wasn't surprised to see the whole team gathered around the big table. I was, however, surprised to see Ian sitting next to Dylan.

"We're gonna let Ethan get his questions out of the way," Nick started. "Then we'll go over what we have."

Logan was pulling out a chair for me when he asked, "Did you find something?"

"Let's let Ethan go first," Nick reiterated.

Logan stilled at my side and I knew he was gearing up to get pissed. My hand went to his chest and I shook my head.

"Zap. Zap," I whispered and Logan's eyes narrowed.

"That only works when I'm getting ready to be a dick," he told me.

"Isn't that what you were getting ready to be?"

"No such thing as me being a dick when it comes to your safety."

"Fine," I sighed and sat down.

"Got an ID on the occupants," Ethan told Logan in what I was sure was a time-saving measure. "And you know, I'm not going to discuss that further until I get Lauren's statement."

I thought that was great news, but judging by the scowl on Logan's face he wasn't pleased.

"He gave it to us, brother," Luke interjected. "We didn't sit on it, now we've got more."

"But you didn't give it to me?"

Luke's gaze cut to me then back to Logan. "You had more pressing things to handle last night. Trust us to have your back the way you've had ours."

Logan exhaled and jerked his chin in Luke's direction but his body was still coiled and ready to strike when he sat next to me.

He reached for my hand, threaded our fingers together, and rested them on his thigh. He also scooted his chair closer to mine.

Sticking close.

Staying with me.

It took an hour for me to answer all of Ethan's questions. Jace hadn't interjected once. Or I should say he hadn't verbally interjected seeing as there were a few times when I'd caught sight of the angry set of his jaw and felt the immensely unpleasant vibes rolling off of him and I had to stop speaking because I'd lost my train of thought.

I knew we were done when Ethan declared, "Got everything I need for now."

To which Logan replied, "What'd you find?"

Since I had a job to do, I pushed my chair back in preparation to leave the conference room to set about doing actual work. I was waylaid by Logan's iron grip on my hand as he pulled me back.

"Where are you goin'?"

"To my desk, I have work to do."

"Ren, baby—"

"I'll go with her." Ian stood. "I need to show her the updates I installed."

Logan's gaze went to Ian, then to me, then back to Ian. Clearly, my man was struggling with letting me leave the room. Ian didn't miss this—no one *could* miss Logan's harassed expression or the tightness in his shoulders.

"I updated the whole system. The new scanners won't be in until the end of the week, but Drake added three new cameras and they're dialed in. All of the doors are secure, same as they've always been. No one's getting in the building unless they're buzzed in. The employee entry codes have been changed and there's a new code Lauren needs to unlock the front door. I'll go over everything with her then work out there until you're done."

I reckon it was the promise that Ian would stay in the lobby with me that made Logan relax.

"Don't leave the building," Logan demanded.

I fought rolling my eyes.

"I won't."

"Not even to go to one of the other buildings."

That time I fought against rolling my eyes *and* telling him I comprehended English and knew what 'don't leave the building' meant the first time.

Instead, I gave Logan what he needed, "Got it."

"If you need to go to the back offices, take Ian."

My jaw clenched but it clenched with me forcing a smile.

"Okay."

"I'll be out as soon as I'm done."

"Okay," I repeated.

Logan's eyes studiously roamed my face and I sat still and waited for him to take what he needed. Finally, he leaned over and gave me a lip touch. He was pulling away but still close when he muttered, "You did good."

"Thanks."

By the time I was on my feet, Ian was next to my chair. His hand went to the small of my back and he propelled me forward. Ian didn't drop his hand until we were at my desk. Then I sat through a ten-minute rundown of the updates Ian had done to the system and he showed me how to view the new cameras. There'd been a blind spot by the front gate and two in the back of the building that were now visible.

Triple Canopy didn't screw around with security, but there were now more cameras, motion sensors, pressure sensors, and motion lights than in most government buildings. You couldn't make a move anywhere around TC without someone knowing.

Ian had just finished when it happened—Liberty, Addy, and Shiloh showed up at the front door the same time Quinn's heels clicked around the corner.

"Ian, that's my sister, my cousin Liberty, and Luke's fiancée, Shiloh. They're all on the approved list."

From his computer, he unlocked the front door.

Addy yanked the heavy glass door open and stomped her way across the reception area.

"Is your phone broken?" she snapped.

"What?"

"Your phone? Did you lose it in the car chase? Did it get

smashed, tossed out the window? Stolen? Misplaced? *Broken?*"

"Um?"

Actually, I hadn't thought of my phone once. It was in my purse probably dead.

"Two of my sisters were kidnapped," she whispered. *Oh, no!* "One of them shot and left to die on the side of the road. When there's a drama you answer the goddamn phone."

Guilt assailed me.

Delaney and Hadley had indeed both been kidnapped. Quinn had been shot and left to die; actually, she did technically die but was brought back to life. One could safely say that it wasn't drama that surrounded these women—it was pure lunacy.

"I'm sorry. As you can see, I'm fine. Logan had everything under control."

Addy was still shooting laser beams with her beautiful eyes and she looked fit to be tied.

"I'm *really* sorry, Addy," I tried again. "I didn't think to call anyone. Yesterday was crazy. The chase, Logan telling me he loved me, asking me to move in, everyone in and out of his house. By the time I had a moment to think I was so tired I went to bed."

"He what?" Addy breathed.

"It was awesome," Quinn interjected. "First Logan gave Ethan shit about wanting to question Lauren. He was all, 'would you let someone near Honor?' Then Ethan was like, 'it's like that, huh?' Then Logan told the guys to junk his car because he didn't want it back."

"What?" Liberty interrupted. "Logan loves his Mustang."

"Welp, Cousin, he was clear he loved Lauren more than he loves his car. That's what he told Lauren when she said the same thing about him loving the car. He said he *loved*

her more. Loved her—straight out said it and he got all
growly and told her no way the woman he loved was sitting
her ass in his shot-up ride."

"You didn't tell me that last night," Addy accused her
sister.

"Nope. I wanted to wait to tell you in person. Besides, I
knew you were pissed and I figured you learning the news
that Logan loves Lauren would soften you up."

It was good to know that Quinn had my back but I really
was tired of talking about the car chase.

"Can we please change the subject?" I asked. "Why are
you all here?"

"He loves you," Addy whispered.

Wow. That felt good, hearing someone else say that
Logan loved me. My eyes were stinging and I didn't trust my
voice so I nodded.

"Told you so," she finished.

"Addy's the smartest of the Walker sisters," Liberty said.
"I'm really happy for you and for Logan."

"I'm happy. *Really* happy. But I'll be happier when all of
this is over and I can slow down and process. I mean, Logan
asked me to move in with him the same day he told me he
loved me. And with everything that was going on I didn't
even get to call my girls and bitch he asked me to move in
while sitting outside in the car while Shiloh, Lenox, and
Echo did a sweep of his house. It wouldn't be real bitching
of course because, *hello*, he asked me to move in, but he has
the shittiest timing. I told him if he asked me to marry him
in the middle of a trauma like he told me he loved me and
asked me to move in with him the answer was no."

"You told him that?" Liberty laughed.

"Yes! Did you miss the part where he told me he loved
me for the first time in a room full of people? This after he

told me he'd *never* love me? A little privacy would've been nice, you know, so I could've told him I loved him, too. Maybe give him a kiss without an audience."

I finished my rant and jolted when Shiloh clapped her hands.

"Game plan!" She all but shouted. "When this is over and you're settled, move-in celebration at your new house."

"Moved in, settled, and after my wedding," Quinn put in.

"And maybe after Delaney has the baby," Liberty added. "She told me yesterday she's been having some contractions."

"My mom's freaking out," Quinn admitted. "She's threatened to write me out of the will if Delaney gives birth at Aunt Reagan's house. At first, I thought it'd be worth losing her anniversary jewelry she's promised me to watch Carter freak out the way Ethan did when Honor had Hudson on the kitchen floor. But now, what started as a joke is starting to worry me. I don't actually want my sister to birth my niece or nephew on the floor. I just wanted to torture Carter with the thought of him being on the business end of childbirth the way Ethan was. I mean, who would've thought that Ethan's son would be born on his birthday, the day Laney surprised Carter with a wedding? It's an awesome story, we all laugh about it all the time."

They might laugh about it now, but I knew for a fact Ethan wasn't laughing about it when it happened. And if Delaney gave birth on his Aunt Reagan's kitchen floor he wouldn't freak, he'd go berserk.

"Maybe it would be a good idea to have an ambulance on stand-by in the driveway. So Jackson and Brice aren't putting their EMT training to use," I suggested.

"Excellent idea." Quinn snapped her fingers. "Maybe

she'll have the baby early. She has a week before I get married."

"Addy, how are your wedding plans?" I asked.

"Everything's done. All we have to do is show up. The last thing we needed to finalize was the reception but my mom said she had that sorted and I didn't need to worry."

There was the calm, cool, and collected Adalynn I knew.

"Oh, we're going to postpone our business meeting about Women, Inc," Liberty told me.

"I wouldn't get your hopes up about that name, cousin. Hadley's willing to fight until the bitter end on the name," Quinn said.

With all the chatter I'd forgotten Ian was sitting nearby. My gaze went from my friends gathered around my desk to the big, overstuffed chairs arranged near the wall and found him staring at us with a wide smile. He didn't look put out or annoyed he had to listen to us cackle and gossip. He looked thoughtful, and if his smile was anything to go by, I'd say amused.

"What else are you going to name a business that's run by all women, that's sole purpose is to lift up women?" Liberty asked.

"Lift up women?"

"Outreach," Quinn started. "Self-defense, employment readiness, navigating enrolling in college or trade school, help with finding scholarships, information on the military and what jobs the different branches offer, ASVAB, GED, you name it we're gonna do it. Women inspiring women. Aunt Lily ran a charity a long time ago when she lived in California. She's going to help us get started and the Aunts will help with fundraising but the day-to-day will be us. The women of TC. Us giving back."

Without having to think about it I said, "I love it. I'm in. Whatever you need me to do, I'll make the time."

"Are you sure?" Liberty inquired.

"Positive."

I felt eyes on me and looked back over at Ian. He was looking down at his tablet but he was doing it smiling a smile that was a little bit conspiratorial and a whole lot secretive.

23

I scanned the whiteboard Nick flipped over as soon as Lauren left the room, following the lines and information someone had spent a great deal of time drawing—dates, times, places, overdoses—all leading back to one person.

I felt the anger welling but before I could commit to the feeling Ethan spoke up. "We caught a break. A resident has been having issues with vandalism, kids knocking his mailbox over. He set up deer cameras at the end of his driveway and one on the other side of the street. The images are black and white, quality's bad, but they were good enough for our guys to run. Isaac Robinson and Everett Moore."

I heard Ethan but I couldn't stop staring at the name on the board.

How in the fuck...

Echo's aggravated voice interrupted my thoughts. "I know them. On the street Robinson's known as Candy. You want pills, Robinson's your go-to. Moore's mostly the muscle. He's been picked up for questioning but we've never had enough to make anything stick." Echo worked with the drug task force, so knowing the suspects was both good and bad. "Something else about Moore; he's never been caught in a sweep. We get intel he's there, we get a team ready, but by the time we're ready to kick down the door, he's gone."

"Who's Moore connected to?" I inquired, not taking my eyes off the board.

"That's the thing, we don't know. One week he's providing his services to a local gang, next week we'll get word he's providing transportation for a rival, and the week after that he's out of town playing bodyguard. The unit can't get a lock on him. How he operates is unheard of."

Echo was correct; dealers didn't like to share territory and they typically set up their own crews and trusted no one outside of their network. But I homed in on the out-of-town part of Echo's explanation.

"Where out of town and who's he protecting?"

"Not sure where exactly, but word is he works for a man called Lucky."

"Lucky?"

My gaze cut to Echo's but continued to move through the room when Jasper cut in.

"You know," Jasper started. "Just fuckin' once it'd be nice if everyone was on the same page. Shit might get done a fuckuva a lot faster if information was shared."

Jasper was correct. It was annoying as fuck that the flow of information from the feds to local law enforcement was seriously lacking. Hell, there was even an issue locally— with all the different departments, intel moved at a snail's pace.

"What information?" Echo's question clearly conveyed his irritation.

"An old colleague of Jason's from the DEA came to us about three months ago asking for help. A new date rape drug's popping up in different cities. But just as fast as it hits the street it goes away. But then weeks later it's back but with a different formula. The DEA believes Atlanta's the test bed. New versions of the drug hit the market there first before they're distributed," I explained. "They also have a new distributor, Lucky. Chemistry's different than anything the DEA or locals have on record. Most of today's heroin comes from Afghanistan, but this comes from the old Golden Triangle, specifically Burma, and it's cut with creatine. One specific brand is always used."

"Burma?" Lauren squeaked from the doorway, Ian standing closely behind her. "Guy loves Burma. He has this huge picture on his wall of this circular rock that sits on the edge of a cliff. The rock is painted gold, and on top of the rock is this pagoda. He told me he took that picture when he visited Burma a few years ago."

"Are you sure? There's no record of Guy visiting Burma," Lenox asked.

Typical Lenox. He, Jasper, Clark, and Levi were supposed to be retired, yet they were up to date on all of our cases. They might not come into the office but each of them still accessed our reports and would make notes or send emails when they had thoughts on a certain case.

"I'm positive. It was Burma—or Myanmar it's called now."

"You said the DEA thinks Atlanta's a test bed," Echo mused. "Are they thinking general rave, club population, or actual testing?"

That was an interesting question, one we were still trying to work out.

"We're not a hundred percent sure but we think both," Jason answered. "The women who've survived were all slipped the drug at nightclubs. And before you ask, they come in clusters. After the last batch, five women visited the ER, all with the same drug in their system, all of them had at one time been to a club called Images. The time before that it was a small dive bar called Andy's. But the feds reported that overdoses are up significantly with prostitutes."

"In the last two years we've had an upswing in overdoses," Ethan admitted. "But the ones you don't hear about are the ODs with the homeless and the prostitutes. Those numbers have skyrocketed. Could Lucky be testing his drugs on hookers?"

I felt Lauren's eyes on me. Talk about an uncomfortable conversation for her to be a part of.

"Ren?"

Echo's gaze cut to Lauren and recognition dawned. He gave me a lift of his chin and quickly stood to flip the board over.

"You don't have to hide it from me," she whispered.

"Hide what?"

"Anything."

Damn.

"You don't need more shit—"

"Please don't hide it from me."

"Okay, Ren, I get you and I won't hide it from you. But how about you let me go over the information, talk it through with the team, then I'll give it to you? There's no sense in piling more on you when we're not clear what we're looking at."

"You know."

"Baby, I don't. I promise."

"But I saw his name," she rightly argued.

Guy Stevens was on the board—top dead center with lines sprouting off his name. Everything leading back to him.

But it didn't make sense.

"You did. And that's how this works. We follow all the leads, but sometimes we have to start over when we hit a dead-end or clear someone's name. I swear I won't hide anything from you but I need to know what I'm sharing with you is correct."

Lauren held my gaze and I let her. Instinct told me to shield her from the truth but if I did that and she found out she'd be pissed. It'd be outright disrespectful even if my intentions were to protect her.

"Thank you. Anyway, I didn't mean to interrupt but your mom and sister are here. Quinn and Addy are going to give them the full tour since they didn't get it yesterday." She gave me a tight smile then looked around the table. "Shiloh and Liberty are going out to the pistol range. Brady, you have an ammo delivery. UPS normally delivers right about now and you know the driver gets pissy when he has to unload by himself. Nick, you have a new client meeting at noon. If you can email me the basics I'll get a file started. Jasper, Emily called and asked me to tell you she needs you to call her before you leave TC. She texted you but knows you don't always check your phone before you leave. Levi, Blake called and asked me to remind you that the two of you have dinner reservations at six and she needs you home by four. Lenox, Lily texted me and asked me to remind you to stop and pick up the new handrail for the deck. Oh, and, Trey, Addy asked me to remind you she has a late client tonight so you're on your own for dinner."

When Lauren stopped talking there was a round of thank-yous from the men she'd delivered messages to. Ian was still standing close to her. He didn't need to follow her down the hall; she was absolutely safe in the building, but he'd done it anyway.

Ian at Lauren's back. Ian who'd spent his day yesterday helping my team. Ian who'd handled my mom gently when she was scared. Ian who made Jill and Jackie smile. Ian who made my mom laugh—really laugh, something I'd heard very rarely in my life.

They turned to leave but halted when I called Ian's name. His attention came to me and I couldn't for the life of me figure out how he didn't hate me for the way I'd treated him, or at least harbor a grudge. But like Lauren, he seemed to understand my reaction to meeting him. And much like Lauren, he was willing to forgive me for acting like a dick.

"I appreciate you staying and pitching in. Means a lot to me."

"It's what family does, Logan," he replied and held my stare. "But I suspect you already know that."

His gaze traveled through the men in the room and he ushered Lauren out the door. But before he did I didn't miss Lauren's beautiful smile.

I should be strung up and tortured for stupidly pushing her away. All this time I could've had that. But more, I could've spent this last year giving her something to smile like that about.

Damn, I was dumb.

"Jace and I have to get back to the station," Ethan announced. "We're looking for Moore and Robinson. Echo, if you can send me anything you have on either of them I'd appreciate it. Jason, I'll send you my report to give to your DEA contact."

Ethan stood. Jace followed but it looked like there was something on Jace's mind and he'd been silent through the meeting.

"Jace?" I called. "Before you leave, do you have anything to add?"

The man didn't look at me even though I'd asked him a direct question. His eyes were glued to the board.

"Four different markets," he muttered.

"Come again?" Carter asked.

"Heroin, coke, pills, and the date rape drug. Four different markets. From here to Atlanta to the neighboring states. Manufacturing, distribution, transportation all in-house. I read the report, no one's seen Lucky. He's a ghost. A name. A figurehead. He's building an empire. And it would make sense for Moore to be working with multiple dealers, providing transport for the drugs for who we think are rivals if they're not really rivals. What if the different crews are all branches? Lucky sets up different crews, gives them territory, we take down one, Lucky doesn't lose shit because he's got others. Before he feels any real loss he also sets up a new crew and it's business as usual. I'd fucking bet Moore's never even met his boss. Lucky keeps himself invisible so no one can ID him. If the empire crumbles he walks away free and clear. What's different about this date rape drug?"

Everything Jace said made sense. Everything fit together and snapped into place. But there was one piece still missing—where did Guy Stevens fit in? What was his role in Lucky's empire?

Jason's cold, hard tone disrupted my contemplation.

"Unlike what's on the street now, this drug's an upper. Think ecstasy on steroids. The woman's not stumbling out of the club, she's not passed out, she's so high she's hyper. Her body is in a drug-induced frenzy, all inhibition gone. One of the victims reported she knew what was happening but couldn't stop it. She knew she didn't want to leave with her rapist, didn't want to have sex, wanted to stop it, but she couldn't control her body's urges." Jason stopped, pulled in a shaky breath, and finished on a growl, "She said she begged him to rape her."

"Motherfucker," Jace grunted.

"When I get to work, I'll talk to my Cap, fill him in if he hasn't already been, and put some feelers out, ask some of my informants if they know where to find Moore or Robinson. Moore's a slippery fuck, so finding Robinson might be easier," Echo said.

"I'll find the connection between Guy, Moore, and Robinson," Dylan declared. "Guy's still in Nashville. I caught him on the hotel camera last night going to his room."

"Logan?" I glanced from the board to Carter.

"Yeah?"

"What's on your mind?"

Everything.

"Guy was waiting outside of Lauren's house."

"Hold your shit, Logan. He's Lauren's ex and we know he can't catch a hint Lauren's done with him," Brady interjected.

That was true but...

"So it's a coincidence? Guy's waiting, follows us, I peel off the main road, and suddenly Moore and Robinson are behind me?"

"We didn't send you in soft," Jason added, referring to our last trip to Atlanta. "We knew it was a possibility someone saw one of you."

The DEA was getting antsy; they wanted this new drug off the street and Lucky's operation shut down. It had taken longer than they thought it would. We'd made the decision to go in hard and hope someone fucked up.

"It could've been Moore himself who saw you in Atlanta," Echo surmised. "Word is if a statement needs to be made, Moore delivers it personally."

Still something nagged the back of my brain.

"I admit, everything fits but there's something that's not working for me. A gut feeling that we're missing something big, that we're not looking deep enough. And it bugs the fuck out of me that we have proof Guy's been to all the cities and he's not fucking hiding it. He travels under his real name. Except to Burma apparently. But anywhere in the US, he just waltzes around without a care."

"He's a smart fuck," Jace put in. "Guy Stevens *is* hiding, right in plain sight. Smart, actually. We're doing exactly what he wants, questioning why if he's involved with the drug would he travel using his real name. Added benefit if he gets pulled in, a defense attorney is gonna be all over that. A man traveling to different cities for work; booking flights, hotels, rental cars all in his real name. Guy's not hiding shit, but he is."

That was when it hit, a delayed reaction.

I had put Lauren in danger.

None of this was about Guy being her ex. It wasn't about Guy not wanting to let go of her, it was the case.

Which also made me wonder how Guy and Lauren met. Was it by design? Did he know he was being investigated? Did he target Lauren, date her to fuck with us?

"How'd Lauren meet Guy?" I asked no one in particular.

Luke's head tilted to the side as he took me in, then his eyes flared, and his jaw clenched. Years of friendship, count-less hours on the battlefield, made for a bond that tethered Luke, Matt, Trey, Carter, and I together. Meaning, I didn't need to voice my thoughts, Luke just knew.

"You think?" he asked.

"That would make a fuckton of sense," Trey put in.

"That shit would be whacked!" Matt added.

"You guys mind filling the rest of us in?" Brady requested.

"Logan's wondering if Guy went after Lauren to get close to us, or the investigation actually, but you catch the drift," Carter explained.

"That doesn't leave this room," Jasper growled. "I agree Lauren needs to be kept in the loop and her insight's helpful. But she doesn't need to know that shit."

"Agreed."

"One of you assholes with women need to start poking around," Matt said. "One of them knows the story."

Every phone in the room buzzed. Every man checked the notification, including me.

"Gotta roll, UPS is here." Brady stood and with a lift of his chin, he was gone.

"We're leaving, too."

"See you, E. And, Jace, thanks for your help," Nick added.

"I'm gonna go find my sister, then bounce. I'll be in touch."

Echo left and I wondered if he'd be saying goodbye to *my* sister as well.

Just because I was focused on the discussion and my woman didn't mean I missed the way the beast's eyes lit when Lauren announced my sister was in the building.

"You might have to look the other way with that, brother," Matt mumbled from beside me.

"Whole way to the airport Jill was talking about Echo and Jackie. Or I should say she was talking about how hot she and Jackie thought he was, which, I have to tell you, she's not my sister, but I still felt like I wanted to puke. But what Jill was really excited about was the way Echo looked at Jackie like he wanted to eat her. Her words, not mine."

"Christ."

"New leaf, Logan."

"What?"

"You falling in love, accepting Ian into your family. You've turned over a new leaf. Don't look back, not for a second. You keep moving forward with your woman and you're going to have to accept that your sisters are beautiful women and they deserve to be happy."

"With Echo?" I growled.

"With anyone they choose. And if Jackie chooses Echo you should be thanking the universe she picked him and not some dumbfuck we'd have to run a check on."

Matt wasn't wrong. I liked Echo, he was a good guy. So were his brothers River and Phoenix. And it went without saying, we all loved Shiloh. She was perfect for Luke.

"Maybe Lauren should get that shock collar."

"Whoa there, buddy, I don't need to know about your kinky games."

I shot him the middle finger and added, "dumbass" before I turned to leave. I needed to find Lauren and say hello to my mom and sister.

"Logan?"

I craned my neck and caught Matt's eyes.

"'Bout fucking time you're happy."

He wasn't lying.

24

I was in the bathroom putting the finishing touches on my hair when Logan appeared in the doorway and in the reflection our eyes locked.

"Damn, you're beautiful."

I unlocked my gaze and used the mirror to do a slow perusal. Crisp white button-down shirt, black slacks, and even though I couldn't see down to his feet I knew he hadn't put on his shoes. If we were home Logan was barefoot. I don't know why I liked that but I did—him in our home, relaxed, with no shoes on.

"You clean up well, Haines."

His chuckle filled the bathroom and I closed my eyes.

It had been a week since I'd moved in with him. A whole seven days and there hadn't been any drama, no more high-speed chases, no shootings, nothing. It was great. It also sucked because Moore and Robinson hadn't been found, so Logan was still being *way* over-protective. I didn't mention it. I gave him what he needed to feel comfortable and in return, he gave me everything. He laughed all the time. He smiled all the time. He was great

with Ian. He even told me that if Jackie made a move on
Echo or vice versa he'd mind his business. And he actually
muttered, "She could do worse." It wasn't a ringing endorse-
ment but it was good he felt that way because over the last
few days I caught them staring at each other when they
didn't think the other was watching and they did it
longingly.

I wasn't sure how much longer Echo was going to be
able to keep his distance. But if a move was going to be
made one of them had better light a fire under it because
last night at dinner Dee had said they were leaving in a few
days. And, yes, Echo had been at dinner—like he'd been
over a lot in the last week.

I felt Logan's hands go to my hips and his lips on my
neck and kept my eyes closed as I savored his kiss. I no
longer felt desperate to memorize them, to commit every
touch to memory. I didn't need to; I knew that before the
recollection had a chance of wearing off he'd touch or kiss
me again and it would start all over. And Logan kissed me a
lot but he touched me more. If he was close he was holding
my hand, or his arm was around me, or my head was on his
shoulder, or my feet were in his lap. It was divine. It was
perfect. He was everything I'd ever dreamed I'd have.

"What are you thinking about, baby?"

"How happy I am. Are you happy, Logan?"

"Never been happier, Ren. Believe that."

"Good."

"I'm gonna let you finish getting ready."

I opened my eyes and caught his in the mirror. My
breath caught when I saw the hunger. You'd think I would
be starting to get used to it. Logan looked at me a lot like
that but every time I saw the desire in his eyes I felt it in my
womb.

"She gets it," he mumbled and pressed his erection into my backside.

I smiled my confirmation.

"I'm gonna fuck you in that dress tonight."

"I know you are."

His gaze dropped to my cleavage and I shook my head. "Don't even think about it."

"About what?"

"I know that look. It's the same one you get when we're at work and I go into your office. You're trying to figure out a way to fuck me now without wrinkling my dress and messing up my hair." I watched his lips twitch and his eyes dance. "I admit you're good at it but if something happens to my bridesmaid dress Emily will lose her ever-loving mind."

"Emily? It's Quinn's wedding, baby."

"Quinn would laugh herself stupid and high-five me if you ripped this dress off of me before the ceremony. She wouldn't care if we all showed up in jeans and tees. But Emily wants everything perfect, so that's what Emily's going to get."

"Tonight."

"Every night," I corrected.

Logan dropped his hands like I was on fire and he took a step back.

"Christ," he growled.

"Lo—"

"Don't say another word, baby. And do not come near me or I swear to God that dress is gonna be shredded and your hair'll be a mess. Christ, nothing sweeter than you."

Logan turned and stomped out of the room.

I smiled at myself in the mirror.

Oh, yeah, tonight was going to be a good night.

But then, every night was.

"It is my pleasure to present Quinn and Brice Lancaster," the justice of the peace announced.

The sound was deafening. Cheers, whoops, clapping.

Hudson in his little-boy suit danced, jostling his baby cousin Emma as she tried to wrap her arms around him. Arianna getting into the action while her twin brother looked on. Nolan was always watching his sister. Hadley explained it was a twin thing. Her mom had told her that when she and Addy were young, Addy would watch over Hadley. Likely because Hadley was a spitfire and Addy was the good girl. Not much had changed with those two. Carson held the newest addition to the family—baby Cecile —Jason standing so close to his niece holding his daughter he was crowding her.

Walker men. Lenox men. Clark men. Levi McCoy. They were a protective bunch and they'd found men just like them to bring into the family fold.

Speaking of Walker men, I stopped looking at the kids and found Jasper and Emily in the crowd.

Jasper had the same look as when Delaney had married Carter and Hadley had married Brady. It was a cross between pain and immeasurable joy. He loved his girls, no doubt about it. And it wasn't about losing them to their husbands; he knew that would never happen. It was the look of a father who would sleep well at night knowing his beloved daughters were well cared for. I'd be remiss if I didn't mention Jason, but the look he gave his son was different. It was one of pride and satisfaction. Jason would carry on the Walker legacy. He would one day walk his daughter Cecile to her future husband with the same expression Jasper had.

Brice finally ended the kiss and stared down at his wife. Thankfully I was close, so close I could see Brice's brown eyes were glossy. I was also close enough to hear his whispered words.

"Prettiest girl I've ever seen."

Quinn beamed then returned, "I'm your wife."

"You ready?"

"Absolutely."

Brice turned them and they took off running toward the pond. Emily, Blake, Lily, and Reagan had done a beautiful job decorating the Clarks' backyard. There were even floating candles in the water and the dock had mason jars of fresh wildflowers along the edges.

"She wouldn't," Addy gasped.

"You know she would!" Hadley laughed.

"Oh, shit!" Liberty added.

Together, Mr. and Mrs. Lancaster ran hand in hand down the dock, and with their clasped hands in the air, they jumped.

More claps and cheers rang out as everyone happily stared at the couple now splashing in the water. But there was one sound that rang the loudest—Quinn's beautiful laughter.

I felt an arm slide over my shoulders and looked up to see Logan smiling down at me.

"That one's *your* daughter," Emily snapped.

"As far as I know they're all my daughters," Jasper returned.

"No, that one is you. All you, Jasper Walker. You made her that way."

"Yeah, Em, I made them all that way. When you find the one thing in this life you cannot live without you grab ahold of it, run away with it, then jump. But, baby, you taught me that lesson, so really, *you* made them that way."

Emily melted and Jasper being the smart man he was didn't waste the opportunity to kiss his wife, and he did it deep and wet.

"I'm pregnant and I quit my job to come work at TC and the foundation we started," Hadley announced.

Her parents broke apart and stared at her in shock.

"Oh, thank God, I was getting ready to throw cold water on them," Addy snapped. "No one else's parents make out like that in public. No, just ours, like they're teenagers or something."

"I don't know. Last barbeque, Drake and I were sneaking away and we caught my mom and dad on the side of the house. Let's just say my eyes were burning," Liberty groused.

Brice was carrying a soaking wet Quinn across the grass, her once stunning wedding dress full of muck.

Both smiling. Both the picture of happiness.

"What'd we miss?" Quinn chirped when they hit our huddle.

"Mom and Dad were making out so Hadley broke the news."

"Isn't that awesome!" Quinn shouted. "Hadley and Brady are gonna be parents."

Logan's body started shaking and I looked up at him.

"Did you know?"

"Nope. But it does explain why Brady's looked a little green this week."

"He's not excited?"

Surely that couldn't be true. Brady adored Hadley.

"Baby, look at Jasper." I glanced over and found Jasper and pinched my lips. "Jasper's not stupid—they're married, hell even before they were married, Jasper knew. But it's one thing to know and it's another thing to *know* your son-in-law knocked up your daughter. Brady's the son-in-law that knocked her up."

Logan was back to laughing and I went back to people watching. The whole backyard was packed full of family including Brice's parents and two brothers. It must be said, Bryan and Adam looked just like Brice. *If things don't work out with Echo, Jackie should think about one of them.*

Quinn was back on her feet passing out hugs and thank yous when a blood-chilling, painfilled whimper rent the air.

The conversation around us ceased. Silence ensued except Delaney's continuous panting.

"Oh my God! No." Quinn rushed to her sister. "I was kidding. It was all a joke. You can't have the baby here. Call nine-one-one. No, Carter, get the car. Laney, close your legs. Oh, shit. I was joking!"

"Oh. My. God," I breathed.

"Bring her in," Reagan calmly instructed. "We've got everything ready."

"No. Carter, get the damn car and take Jackson with you. Brice, you go, too; you know what to do."

"I'm fine," Delaney panted. "Everything's fine. Where's Emma?"

I scanned the yard, found Emma, and answered, "Blake's got all the kids by the bouncy house."

"Can you walk?" Carter asked.

Why was he so calm?

She nodded but whispered, "My water broke."

"Okay. Do you need me to carry you?"

"Emma came fast, Carter."

He dropped his forehead to hers and I couldn't help but admire what a perfect couple they made.

"Laney, you think we're not prepared? You Walker girls

are trouble. We planned for this. It's not ideal, your midwife thought I was crazy when I asked her to come to the wedding just in case. There's a birthing tub set up in Uncle Clark's master bathroom. Everything's ready to go. Here or at the birthing center, what's the difference?"

"I liked the tub when I had Emma."

"Then let's go have a baby."

"Let's go have a baby."

The crowd parted as Carter led his wife across the backyard to the patio. Jasper and Lenox were already there with the door open.

"Mom?" Quinn's voice trembled.

"Quinn, my beautiful daughter. It's your wedding day. Enjoy it."

"But, Laney—"

Emily looked around before she stepped closer to her daughter and softly said, "We all knew you were joking, but Delaney, she liked the idea of your niece or nephew sharing this day with you. She's been having contractions for days; she knew the risk. Carter knew what she was up to and arranged everything. Now, in a few hours when she's up there with no pain meds, she might be rethinking how important it was to share this day with you and Brice. But it's happening, and soon you'll get to meet the newest member of our family. And he or she will come into this world with a new uncle to welcome him or her."

Quinn seemed pleased with her mom's explanation and nodded.

"Oh, and tell Hadley she's not off the hook with that little announcement. And tell Addy, we have big problems if she was kissing boys like I kiss your father when she was a teenager."

"It's an expression," Quinn defended her sister.

"It's a stupid one. Trust me, your father's a man, not a teenager and he kisses—"

"Aunt Emily, my ears are bleeding," Liberty thankfully interjected.

Emily Walker smiled at the crowd and winked. Then she walked away, sheets of the shiniest black hair I'd ever seen swaying behind her.

"Well, you got what you wanted today," Brice told Quinn.

"No, honey. I had everything I wanted the day you told me to knock on your door."

Brice's gaze heated. Then Quinn was up over his shoulder and he was carrying her to the side of the house.

"We're being invaded," Logan muttered.

"Invaded?"

"They're multiplying. In a few hours, there'll be a new Lenox. In nine months, a new Walker. Quinn and Liberty will start soon, then Addy. Total invasion."

I thought it was awesome. But by the look on Logan's face, I wasn't so sure he felt the same.

"We need to even the playing field," he declared.

"What?"

"Inject fresh blood."

Fresh blood?

"I don't understand."

"You and me, we need to add some Haines into the mix. All these damn Walker women, they'll take over, populating the family. The rest of us need to pitch in, even the playing field."

Was he...

Did he...

"You want kids?"

"Yep."

"You said—"

"I didn't want them. But with you I do."

I tamped down the excitement dancing around in my belly and instead narrowed my eyes.

"Shit timing, Logan!"

"Baby—"

"Don't *baby* me. You suck. You tell me here, at the reception, that you want to have children with me when I can't cry without ruining my makeup or looking like a fool. Or maybe show you how happy I am by kissing you."

"Kiss me, Ren."

"No. I'm pissed at you."

"Kiss me, baby."

"Really mad, Logan."

"Kiss me, Lauren."

"No."

"We're naming the first one Anabella."

Bella.

I loved it.

"And the second one Jane. You can name the rest."

"The rest?" I blanched. "How many are we having?"

"Sixteen."

"Are you crazy?"

"Yep. Now kiss me."

I was not having sixteen children. I wasn't having five children. I might have four if Logan pushed it, but I wanted three.

"Three."

Logan didn't respond. He kissed me and it was a highly inappropriate kiss. Thankfully, the party-goers were too wrapped up with the bride and groom and the baby being born in the master bathroom to care.

One hour later, Carter and Delaney didn't break tradition when they welcomed their son into the family.

There wasn't a dry eye in the backyard when Carter went straight to his brother, wrapped his hand around the back of Ethan's neck, gave him a manly jerk, and asked him if he wanted to meet his namesake. Ethan Ford Lenox.

Cheers, hoots, hollers, and loud cries filled the yard. But before the brothers went back into the house they went to The Tree.

It had been years since it was planted in memory of Carter and Delaney's first child. One who didn't make it to earth but was never forgotten.

Lenox joined his sons, and like Jasper and the rest of the men who were all-men, the best men, he didn't shield his emotions. They had a lot to be grateful for, a lot to celebrate, but they'd always feel the loss of the baby who was a Lenox.

Six hours later Logan did as promised.

My dress was ripped.

My panties torn.

The sheets pulled off the mattress.

We fell asleep sweaty, with no blankets, and with Logan smearing his climax on the inside of my thigh. I should've tried to stay awake a little longer. I shouldn't have stopped memorizing all the moments. I should've cuddled a little closer. I should've told Logan everything I thought I had time to say. But I didn't know time wasn't on our side.

25

Have you ever woken up and thought to yourself, today's gonna be a shit day?

That was how I felt as soon as my eyes opened. Two seconds later with my eyes still blurry I heard Lauren moan.

"What's wrong?"

"Shh," she hissed. "My head hurts so bad."

I thought back to last night and how much Lauren had to drink and I couldn't remember her drinking anything but water.

It was three days after Quinn and Brice's wedding and my family was leaving today. They came over the night before, which was what had become the normal. Lauren had selected furniture she wanted online and the guys and I went to pick it up. Now, I had a revolving front door. Ian, my mom, and my sister had been staying at Lauren's old place but they were at our house every night. Matt, Echo, and Dylan were frequent visitors, Luke if Shiloh was working. Echo I suspected only came around to spend time with my sister. I was getting used to the idea they obviously liked each other, though neither had said anything. But the way they looked at each other had changed after Quinn's wedding. I was actively ignoring the reason behind the change. I was a man, I knew the look, and if I thought about it too much I felt my temper flare. Matt and Dylan stopped by because they knew Jackie, Lauren, or my mom was going to cook which meant not only did they get free food they got homecooked free food.

"Just your head?"

"I think so."

I glanced at the alarm clock, then carefully rolled Lauren off my chest.

"I'll go call in, be back."

"You can't call in. You have two classes today and Carter's on paternity leave."

Fucking hell.

"Ren—"

"Please stop talking, Logan," Lauren whispered, her voice full of pain. "My head hurts so bad I feel like I'm gonna puke. Shut the curtains on your way out, please."

I chanced a soft touch of my mouth to the top of her head and she groaned.

"Maybe I should take you to the doctor."

"Shh. *Honey*," she whined. "Please let me go back to sleep."

Yep, it was going to be a shitty day.

I got up, took a shower alone, got dressed, brought headache medicine and water back into the room, and made sure the windows were locked and the curtains were closed. I didn't bother making coffee or eating breakfast before I double-checked that all the doors were locked and armed the alarm.

I should've stayed home.

Ten minutes after I got to the office my family showed up to say goodbye.

There was something to be said for family—the real kind. The family you're born into and the family you choose. Jasper, Emily, Levi, Blake, Clark, Reagan, Lenox, and Lily all showed up to see my mom and Ian. The women with promises to keep in touch with my mom and the men with a consultant job for Ian. Jackie wasn't left out of the women's huddle and Shiloh, Hadley, and Liberty had stopped in to see my sister. Echo was noticeably missing during all of this. I was waiting for the right moment to pull Jackie aside and ask her what happened when Ian approached.

"May I have a minute before we leave?"

"My office," I conceded, not wanting to have whatever conversation was in store.

I had a feeling this was coming. I'd spent the last few days preparing and yet I still couldn't stop the fear from pooling in my gut.

"Sorry to hear Lauren's not feeling well," Ian began.

"Hopefully when she wakes up the headache will be gone."

Silence fell and the quiet did nothing to help the dread that was seeping in.

Totally irrational but it was there. The fear that the man standing in front of me, who had done nothing wrong, had done nothing but treat my mother like she was the most precious person in his life, had only been kind and loving to my sisters, had shown me respect, and had been great with Lauren, would somehow turn into a monster.

I knew I was censuring him for something he hadn't done. In my mind, Ian was paying for another man's abuse.

"I'd like to ask your mom to marry me again."

Fuck.

"But I'm going to wait."

Fucking shit.

"I've been told by your mom and sisters that you rarely visit Bad Axe and there's zero possibility of you ever moving back to Michigan."

Hell to the no.

"Jill is in Michigan for a while with her new position. Lucy and Dotty are moving to Alabama for Lucy's new job. Jackie has expressed interest in Georgia and your mom misses you. I'm going to suggest we move here."

Christ.

"I think this is the last piece your mother needs to heal."

"What piece?"

"Seeing you fall in love. Watching you with Lauren. Knowing you are happy and at peace. She doesn't need to hear about it on the phone, she needs to witness it. It'll be good for Jackie, too, having her big brother around."

"And you? What's in it for you?"

"I get to see my girls happy and DeeDee put the nightmare that was her life behind her. I get the opportunity to get to know you better and build a friendship like I've done with your sisters. You, Lucy, Jill, Jackie, and your mom are a unit. I cannot build a life and family with your mom if all of her children don't accept me into their lives. It would break her heart to cause discourse and I would never put her or any of you through that."

Goddamn it.

"I am not a man prone to waste time; I know how valuable it is. I'm also a man who lost a good woman and has been blessed enough to find an extraordinary woman to spend what days I have left with. Most people don't find one, true, great love. I've found two. There's no comparing DeeDee and Nicole. They are opposite in most ways. I loved Nicole in a very different way than I love your mother. One is not more than the other. One is not better. But I will tell you that your mom fulfills me in a way I have never been. I struggled with that in the beginning. Wondering how I could've loved Nicole so much but still had been missing something. But it is what it is and there's no reason to dwell or question my feelings. I have more important things to think about. I have a family to build and make happy."

Christ.

"I am not Dave Haines."

I felt every muscle in my body strain.

"I'm not, Logan. I have *not* nor would I *ever* raise a hand to a woman or a child. I am not him. I don't give a shit what was so broken inside of him that he would harm his wife and children. What I know is the man is dead but his ghost lingers. That's over. I'm claiming the family he should've cared for and loved. Your mother is not his. Your sisters are no longer his. They're mine. And one day you will be, too. I will care for and love all of you the way you all should've been. It might take years but one day you will trust me with your family."

Fuck. I needed Lauren. The panic was encroaching.

"Ask her," I croaked.

The words rolled out of my mouth and I braced for the poison to creep into my blood and the anger to surface.

But none came.

"Logan—"

"Time is valuable," I spoke over him. "Don't let my shit stop you from making her happy. What that piece of shit left might always be inside of me. His ghost doesn't linger. It haunts but that's mine to deal with, not my mom's and not yours. Ask her."

A change came over Ian. His normal, mild-mannered disposition flipped in a flash.

"Bullshit, Logan. No part of him is *inside* of you. It is not yours to deal with, that's not the way family works. You didn't have a good father so let me educate you on family. What's yours is ours. What's haunting you is ours. It's Lauren's. We move together as a family."

"I'm sorry you didn't have children," I told him honestly and his eyes filled with pain. "You would've been a great father. If you can talk my mother into moving out of that fucking town she should've left twenty-five years ago, I'll be grateful. If that's by Lucy and Dotty, I'll come visit and be grateful. If you make my mother happy I'll forever be indebted to you. You want family, welcome to ours. But warning, Jackie acts the sweet twin and she normally lets Jill be the quick-tempered, sassy one but that's because she's smart. She knows if she lets Jill take the lead, Jill will also be the one who catches Mom's wrath. But Jackie, she's not sweet, she's a handful. You lucked out with Lucy. She's chill and pretty much nothing bothers her. It's those twins that will give you an ulcer."

"And you?"

"You want the Herculean task of exercising my demons, have at it."

"Lauren's seeing to that, Logan. And by the looks of it, she doesn't need my help. But if the occasion were to arise, and she needed me, she'd have me. I was asking when you were going to start building your family."

Lauren's seeing to that.

Actually, Lauren wasn't seeing to anything, she'd already seen to it. She'd performed the miracle of pulling my head out of my ass. I wouldn't be calmly having this conversation if she hadn't. I wouldn't've told Ian to ask my mother to marry him if she hadn't healed what had been terrorizing me since childhood.

"Soon," I answered. "It's been a crazy few weeks. I figured I'd let her settle for another week or two then ask her to marry me."

"Good. Your mom and sisters love her. Lucy's talking about her and Dotty coming out to meet her soon."

"And you? Do you like her?"

I couldn't believe I asked but what's more, I couldn't believe I actually cared about Ian's answer.

"I adore her. She's smart and funny and her kindness shines through. There are a lot of things to like about her but mostly I love the way you look when she's near. Do you know how you know when the woman sitting next to you is the woman you belong to?" I shook my head and he continued, "Peace."

Before Lauren, I hadn't felt much of anything except anger. Now that I had her she certainly gave me peace. She made me a better man. She motivated me to let go of my past so I could give her what she deserved.

"Has my mom ever told you about Huron Beach?"

"No."

"Every year after Dave died she'd take us there for vacation. It was the only time in my childhood when I saw the burdens lift. There she was free. She was happy and smiling. I don't know if it was just because we were out of Bad Axe where everyone knew who she was, who we were, or if that beach meant something more to her. But she loves it there. She loves lakes, ponds, the ocean, anywhere near a body of water. Take her there and ask her, take her anywhere near the water, but please do not ask her in that Godforsaken town. The memory of your engagement shouldn't be tarnished by the past."

"Is that what you think, that you're tarnished by your past?"

"Dented, cracked, stained, and tarnished."

"Adversity paradox," Ian mumbled. "It's all about how you leverage the past. You are who you are because of what you went through and no one can argue your past shaped you into a good man. Your mother is the strongest woman I know and she became who she is today because of her past. Your sisters are smart, watchful, wise, successful, and they are those things because of the adversity they faced. The paradox. You think of it as tarnished. I see it as a family who triumphed, who overcame, who stuck together and came out the victors. Your family won, Logan. All you need to do is embrace it."

I didn't have a chance to digest Ian's statement before there was a knock at my office door.

"Come in!"

"Sorry to interrupt but we have to get going."

I took in my mom's tentative, cautious smile and that shitty feeling was back.

"It's all good, Mom," I told her as I moved toward her.

Just like all the times before, my mom didn't make me wait. She wrapped her arms around me and held on tight. Not ever had she withheld her affection, never had she failed to cuddle me or my sisters.

How difficult had my mom's life been with Dave? How much had she hidden? How much more pain had she endured that we didn't see or hear? She might not have been able to shield us from much but she always showed us how much she loved us. She was a good mom.

"I love you, Mom," I whispered to the top of her head.

"I love you, too, son."

"I'm happy for you." My mom went stiff in my arms and

I hated that I'd made the beginning of this trip so difficult for her. I hated that she worried about how I would treat Ian. But more, I hated that I'd given her reason. "I'm happy you found Ian—for all of us."

I heard my mom's breath catch and I felt her body hitch with a sob.

"Do you think he's ready for us?"

Her head nodded against my chest.

"Good. We've been waiting a long time for him, Mom. It's time for all of us to be happy."

She nodded again and asked, "And you? Are you ready to be happy?"

I didn't need to think about my response. "Yep. Gonna make it official in a few weeks. I tried to talk her into giving you sixteen grandkids, she negotiated me down to three. So Lucy, Jill, and Jackie are gonna have to pitch in and fill your house full of babies."

I didn't hear it, my mom's body didn't move, but I felt it. Her relief and joy penetrated straight through me.

"I can live with three," she mumbled. "But I bet you could talk her into four."

I smiled.

I could do four, or I could do three, or even one. As long as they were Lauren's I could do the sixteen I teased her about. The truth was, as long as Lauren loved me, I could do any-fucking-thing.

My family left for the airport right before my first class was due to start. I checked my phone as I was walking out to the range. No calls or texts from Lauren but I did have one from Jill.

Jill: What'd you say to Ian?

I quickly tapped out my reply: I've said a lot of things to Ian. You have to be more specific.

A few seconds later my sister replied.

Jill: Every day since I've been gone he's texted asking if I was alright.

Me: So?

Jill: I already have to check in with you, Mom, Jackie, and Lucy.

Me: So?

Jill: Ug. Overprotective ape.

Me: Yep. Love you, sis.

She texted me back a middle finger emoji with three hearts after it.

Maybe having another man around would work in my favor after all.

It was nearing on three and I hadn't heard from Lauren. I still couldn't shake the shitty feeling I'd woken up to. As the day had worn on I'd tried to tell myself it was because my family was going back to Bad Axe. Not only would I miss them but I despised the thought of them living there. I rarely went there and when I did it was for a day, two at most. That left them to come to me. When I was in the Navy those visits sometimes came every few years depending on what my team was doing. I hadn't spent any real time with them since I'd moved away. Having my mom close for more than two weeks reminded me how much I missed her.

I was done with my classes for the day and was planning on taking the rest of the work I had to do home with me when Nick walked into my office.

"Robinson's in custody."

Fucking finally.

"Moore?"

"MIA. Jason wants us in the conference room."

So much for going home.

I grabbed my cell and followed Nick to the conference room.

26

Dylan Welsh stared at pictures he'd printed from Finn Stevens' sportfishing website. Then his gaze went back to the abandoned Myspace page of May Lucas, Guy's sister who was now married but at one time had been hot and heavy with none other than Frank Lester the pimp. May's husband Gary wasn't a pimp but he wasn't a saint. His sheet included armed robbery, grand theft auto, and the most recent charge of possession.

What if...

Before Dylan could formulate his thoughts fully, a notification buzzed and he picked up his cell phone.

Logan's alarm system had gone down.

Gone down not breached.

What the fuck?

Seconds later Dylan had a screen full of nothing. None of the four cameras positioned around Logan's house were working. He flipped to Luke's house. The cameras were on. He randomly chose another house. Matt's cameras were functioning.

The cameras were a separate system, not connected to the alarm. Both were down.

Lauren was home sick. She was alone.

Fuck.

Dylan went back to Logan's feed, backed up five minutes, and watched. Nothing. Not from any angle. No one was lingering, no one walked past the house, not even a car had driven past.

The power.

An internet search showed a power outage. The entire neighborhood was out.

The knot in his gut started to ease until his gaze dropped back to the pictures.

Lauren was home alone.

Fuck.

Dylan scooped up the pictures, pushed out of his chair, and ran.

Lauren was alone in a house with no alarm, no cameras, in a neighborhood with no power. There wasn't a storm rolling through, there hadn't been a report of an accident taking down a pole, and that outage hadn't been scheduled maintenance, therefore, Dylan didn't waste time when he burst into the conference room.

"Have you talked to Lauren?"

The room became alert but it was Logan who went wired.

"No."

Logan already had his phone out, dialing Lauren before Dylan could explain. "Power's out on Logan's block. No Alarm. No cameras."

"Did you—"

Nick didn't get the rest of his question out. "No one was near the house before the blackout. Something else." Dylan tossed the pictures on the table. "Lucky's not a person. Jace was right, Guy Stevens is building an empire."

All eyes went to the pictures.

Finn and Guy Stevens in front of one of Finn's fishing boats—the *Lucky 7*. Another image of Finn in the *Lucky 6*. A picture from May's old Myspace page—she and her brothers in identical Lucky Brand tees, all pointing to the name with huge smiles on their faces.

A family affair.

An empire.

"What do you do when you have no muscle or street cred?" Brady muttered.

"You make up rumors, tell stories about a fictitious man, and spread that shit far and wide until you can recruit," Jason answered.

"No one's fucking seen Lucky because there's no Lucky to see," Trey put in and jogged out of the room.

Logan didn't utter a word before he was gone.

"Fuck," Matt snarled and followed.

27

I felt like I was floating, or rocking. My headache was gone but my body itched like I had ants crawling over me.

I wanted to scratch. I really, really needed to scratch but I was too tired. The air was cool and the sheets were soft, so soft they felt like silk or satin.

Oh, maybe velvet.

Velvet sheets would be spectacular. I wondered if I could talk Logan into buying a set.

Did they make velvet sheets?

I stretched and groaned when my legs rubbed against the silky coolness.

The ants were gone.

God, that felt so good.

I moved again and felt goose bumps rise. It felt like someone was using a feather to tickle my legs all over, not just a trail, and the feel of it consumed me. I wanted to feel it again and again. I wanted to roll around and see if I could make the rest of my body feel so good.

I felt fingertips travel up my back. The sensation was out

of this world, so good I curved my back in an attempt to get closer.

"Logan," I panted. "More."

His fingertips continued to dance up my spine, and as they moved the pleasure started to build. I felt it between my legs—even though I wasn't being touched there. My nipples tingled—even though they weren't being touched. It was like my flesh was sensitized. Every inch of it tingled.

"Logan." My groan sounded unnatural but I didn't care.

I just needed *more*. More touching, more sensations, more tingling, more of everything.

His hand went into my hair and my scalp electrified. His fist wrapped around my ponytail and pain exploded. Top to toe. In an instant, everything hurt.

"Good, you're awake."

There was another vicious tug. More pain, more agony.

And that was when I knew something was very wrong.

Life-changing, soul-splintering *wrong*.

My mind was fuzzy but I knew Logan would never hurt me.

My hair was yanked again and the worst pain I ever felt in my life radiated.

"Please stop."

Seconds later my hair was released. The relief was overwhelming. Then I felt a gentle glide of fingertips travel down my arm and like a switch pleasure bloomed.

"Do you like that, Lauren?"

"Guy?" I groaned even though I didn't want to. I wanted to shout instead.

I was paralyzed but I wasn't. I could feel everything but everything felt heavy. I wanted to move but couldn't.

His hand continued to move up and down my arm. Whisper-soft but disturbingly good.

Yes, everything about this was disturbing.

"Feels good, doesn't it? The slightest touch leaves you begging for more. But the slightest pain..." he trailed off and pinched the inside of my bicep and my back came off the bed as a scream tore from my throat. "Hurts like a sonofabitch, doesn't it?"

He released my skin and I felt his lips touch my skin.

Wrong. All wrong. So, very wrong.

"Please don't."

"Soon, Lauren, as soon as the sedative I gave you wears off you'll be pleading for me to take what you should've given me."

Then nothing.

No more touching. No more pinching. No more noise.

I didn't know how long I lay on those soft sheets falling in and out of consciousness. What I did know was when I came fully alert I would beg and plead.

Not for Guy to touch me.

I'd beg for him to kill me.

Unfortunately, my brain and body were completely disconnected.

28

I knew she was gone before I pulled down my street. I didn't need to see my front door kicked in to know. I didn't need to walk through the house or see our empty bed.

I fucking *knew* this morning.

I never should've left her at home alone.

"Logan!" Matt yelled from the living room but I couldn't move.

I couldn't stop staring at the unmade bed. The new comforter Lauren had picked out but my mother had bought, half off the bed. Same with the top sheet. I gazed around the room—nothing else disturbed. No signs of struggle, no blood. Just the sheets ripped off of her and taken right from her own goddamn bed. From her home.

"We need to roll," Matt said from inside the room.

I still didn't move.

I continued to look around. Lauren's lotion and perfume were on the dresser along with a hairband. That was it. I knew if I were in the living room and looked around there'd be no pictures on the wall. No decoration. Not even a framed photo of the two of us together.

Why the fuck hadn't we done that?

"You need to—"

"I know what I need to do," I snapped. "I just can't."

"For Lauren, you'll find a way."

Fucking, fuck.

Think.

"Where would Guy take her?"

"We don't—"

"We damn well do know. He's got her, Matt. Where would he take her?"

"First thing he'd do is get her out of town."

He sure as hell would. He'd snatch her and run. No way would he stay close.

"Florida, to Finn? Texas, to his sister?"

"Too risky driving all the way to Texas. Florida's a better choice. Less than a three-hour drive."

"We never found his office," I muttered. "Did Dylan run his brother's name?"

Think. Where would he take her?

"Yeah. None of his family owns or rents property in Georgia other than Guy's house. Trey and Brady are on their way there now."

I inhaled and Lauren's scent assaulted me. How the hell could I have been so stupid? So goddamn careless.

"I didn't even tell her I loved her this morning."

"Don't fucking do that," Matt warned.

"She had a headache. I left and didn't tell her I loved her."

"You can tell her when we find her."

I would tell her, but the question was, would she hear me?

Matt's phone rang and I sucked in another breath.

Think, asshole.

"Is that Dylan?"

Matt answered me with a nod and answered Dylan on the phone, "Yeah, I'll tell him."

"Before you hang up ask Dylan to check the security cams from the gas station on the corner."

Matt disconnected and shoved his phone in his back pocket.

"He's already on that. Jason called his contacts at the DEA and filled them in. They're headed to Finn Stevens' place in Florida and to his sister's in Texas. The locals in Atlanta will grab Frank. Luke called Echo, he's activating who he needs to get on the search. Shiloh's team is on standby in case we need them."

We wouldn't need Shiloh's SWAT team. No way in fuck was I waiting for a hostage rescue team and their red tape to get my woman.

"How the hell did we miss Guy coming back to town?"

"We didn't. His car is still in Nashville. No flights in his name have been booked. No rentals. You know Dylan's been monitoring him."

I did know that. It was the only reason I'd left a sick Lauren in our bed. I thought she was safe.

I was wrong.

Everything was right there all along. Right under our noses and we missed it. Fisherman Finn, fuck, we checked him out. No priors, his business was clean. But we missed it.

It was right fucking there.

Lucky 7.

"The boat. She's on the boat."

"Logan—"

"She's on the goddamn boat. He wouldn't chance driving her. We'd catch him easy; too many traffic cams on 95. Guy doesn't have an office, he has a warehouse, and it'd be by the seaport terminal. Access to the water. That whole section is industrial, no one would question traffic in and out of there all hours of the night. Hell, no one would question rough trade hanging around; day workers don't wear a suit and tie to work. Easy to move product from Georgia to Florida using a fishing charter or personal watercraft."

"I'll call Clark, tell him to get in touch with the Port Authority. Lenox has contacts with the Coast Guard."

"I want a boat."

"We'll get you a boat, Logan, but you need to stay cool."

Fuck cool.

Lauren was where she was because of me. From start to finish my fault. If I hadn't been such a dumbass Lauren wouldn't have been available to Guy. He wouldn't have been able to target her and use her for intel.

I pulled my phone out, found the number I needed, and hit send.

It rang once before it connected.

"Drake called me. I'm on my way."

"You sure you want to get involved?"

"Don't be stupid!"

"Meet us at the Seaport Terminal."

"Copy."

"I owe you, Liberty."

"Now you're talking stupid again. You saved my life. Now I'm gonna return the favor. We'll get her home safe, Logan."

I walked out of my empty bedroom and made one more call.

Again it rang once.

"We're on our way."

"Don't call in the Coast Guard."

"He has a head start."

"Then get me a fast boat but don't call in the Guard. They'll fuck it up and you know it."

"They won't. I know the—"

"Tell me, Lenox, would you trust Lily to anyone but your team? Not trying to be a dick but you know any one of us has more training than a whole crew of them. We're goddamn SEALs, we don't need interference, and we don't need to be slowed down."

"I won't call," Lenox said and I blew out a breath. "One condition."

Fuck me.

"What's that?"

"You leave him breathing."

"No."

"Logan—"

"He snatched my woman out of our bed," I hissed. "He uses that drug on her..."

I trailed off even though I had more to say but the words literally wouldn't come out. If he drugged her there was no telling what Guy was doing to her. No telling the nightmare my woman was living. I'd read the victim statements. I knew what that drug did. I knew what he could do to Lauren. Her mind would say no, but her body would say yes. She'd be confused and scared and violated.

That's a fuck no. I'm not letting him live.

"Make it self-defense."

With that Lenox hung up.

"Let's roll!" I shouted and walked out the front not bothering to right my broken door.

29

I'd figured out what the rocking was—I was on a boat.

I could smell the briny saltwater air. And now that I wasn't so groggy I could open my eyes and focus on my surroundings. I was under the deck in a sleeper cabin. It wasn't very big—maybe big enough to sleep four with a small kitchenette.

I could move minutely but I couldn't get my arms to lift or my legs to swing over the side of the bed so that I could get the hell away from Guy. I didn't care if I had to jump overboard. I didn't care if I drown in the middle of whatever body of water I was in. I knew what Guy was going to do to me. I knew what drug he'd given me. Logically, I knew I had to fight it but I couldn't control what was happening.

Panic clawed my insides and a sheen of sweat coated my body. I squeezed my thighs together needing something to quench the need that was building. It was gross—disgustingly gross. I didn't want to feel the way I did.

I shouldn't want this.

Terror pounded in my skull, making my head hurt worse

than it did when I woke up this morning. Sweat trickled down my neck. Even that felt good.

I shifted my restless legs and the horrible thought pierced my brain: was I trying to wake them up so I could run or was I attempting to get myself off?

"Paralytics are fun, aren't they?" Guy asked from the doorway. "A little goes a long way. I don't need to tie you to the bed but I unfortunately have to wait. I don't fuck dead fish."

Oh. God.

Guy moved closer, holding a bottle of water.

"Here, drink this."

He leaned over me bringing the bottle to my face. The bastard knew I couldn't lift my arms to fight him off or poke his eyeballs out with my fingernails.

"No."

"Yes, Lauren. Drink."

I pinched my lips and turned my head away from him.

"Fuckin' drink."

Pain once again exploded when his fingers dug into my cheeks to force my head in his direction. I gasped and cried out.

Why did that hurt so freaking bad?

Guy took advantage and poured the water into my mouth until I was choking and sputtering. I thrashed my head but couldn't stop swallowing. Logan's t-shirt I'd worn to bed was soaked. Freezing cold water dripped off my chin and down my cheeks, cooling my overheated skin.

Why am I so hot?

I felt like I was in the middle of Death Valley in the dead of summer. I'd never been so hot in all my life and I grew up in the desert.

"You always were a difficult bitch," Guy spat. "If I didn't

need you to get close to those assholes I never would've put up with your shit."

What?

"Yeah, I see you're starting to understand." Guy smiled.

But he was wrong, I didn't understand. I couldn't think clearly enough to comprehend much of anything. The need I felt before was nothing compared to now. A wave of desire washed over me. The kind that only Logan could create. The kind that only Logan could tease out of me.

So wrong.

All wrong.

Lust shot through me and a moan slipped past my lips even though I begged it not to.

"Works fast, doesn't it?"

Shit. The water was drugged.

Drugged with more of his date rape drug. The one that women had overdosed on. The one that would make me beg for relief.

"I hate you."

"But your body's gonna love me."

Guy lifted my useless arm and handcuffed my wrist to what looked like a metal cupholder.

"Can't have you getting away before the fun starts. I'm gonna weigh anchor." Guy straightened and started for the door but stopped and looked back at me. "This isn't gonna be fast, Lauren. I'm taking everything I'm owed for all those months you held out."

I closed my eyes so tight tiny bursts of light bloomed behind my lids.

Logan.

I would think of Logan. Only him. Guy could take me but I'd only ever want Logan.

A long time passed before Guy came back into the cabin.

Long enough for the paralytic to wear off and for me to be able to move. One moment I was mostly paralyzed, the next I was jittery. My pulse pounded in my neck, my sex throbbed, my nipples tingled, and my skin was electrified.

I needed to move, run a marathon, jump, do something.

My mind raced so fast I couldn't keep a rational thought. The confusion made me growl. The desire made me moan. The fear made me wish for death.

Through it all, I kept chanting one person's name —Logan.

Just Logan.

"Playtime," Guy announced.

I bit my lip until I tasted blood.

I would not beg. I would not plead.

Logan.

30

"That's him," Drake confirmed and lowered his binoculars.

The *Lucky 1* bobbed a thousand yards away from our boat. Three-thousand feet. If I had my McMillian Tac-50 I could place a bullet between Guy's eyes. From trigger pull to impact it would be one second, then lights out and it'd all be over.

But I didn't have my McMillian, and besides, a bullet was painless; the motherfucker would never know I had a lock on him. He wouldn't feel fear and he wouldn't feel the pain of his death.

"He dropped anchor," Luke unnecessarily announced.

Through my field glasses, I watched Guy go below deck and I felt the burn of violence blossom in my chest.

"Take us five hundred yards off the port side," Drake ordered his wife. "We need a slow crawl."

"Copy."

Liberty pulled back the throttle and slowed the boat.

"Ready?" Trey asked, zipping up his wetsuit.

Wordlessly I dropped my binos and did the same.

Trey, Drake, Luke, and Matt moved into place, getting

ready to roll overboard as soon as we were close enough. We could, of course, have swum from a thousand yards but it would be faster to cut the distance in half, getting us to the *Lucky 1* in seven minutes instead of fifteen.

I felt the boat slow even more. Drake jerked his chin at his wife. Liberty swung her AR around and clutched it to her chest.

"I got your back. Enjoy your swim."

As a unit, we rolled into the water.

"Go time."

Seeing as Drake was our team leader when we were in the teams it was natural for him to take the lead. Something I didn't mind and actually needed. I was intent on getting Lauren and couldn't be bothered with logistics. If I had my way, Liberty would've pulled up beside the *Lucky 1* and I would've simply shot Guy in the face. Unfortunately, there were laws that prohibited me from doing so. Laws that I would ignore depending on Lauren's state.

I inhaled fully, exhaled, then filled my lungs with as much oxygen as I could. As if we were one, we disappeared under the water, diving down four feet where we wouldn't have to fight the current. Muscle memory took over, my heart rate lowered, and the tranquil, quiet of sea belayed my tumultuous thoughts.

A few minutes later I felt a tap on my ankle. Time to rise. I tapped Drake and as one we slowly ascended. We surfaced just enough to fill our lungs to capacity then we dove back under. Like the well-trained SEALs we were we sliced through the ocean.

Freediving was an art. You had to be comfortable in the water, find peace in the murky silence, keep your mind clear and pulse steady. There was no room for error when you were pushing yourself until you heard the buzzing in your ears reminding you that you were not a fish and needed air to breathe.

We resurfaced and descended several times before I finally saw the chain of *Lucky 1*'s anchor. Drake made an exaggerated hand signal indicating he was changing directions, leading us to the stern. Then he held out two fingers and motioned up. I was his second in command, Drake was telling me to exit the water first.

Thank fuck.

The swim ladder came into view and I waited for Matt to come up beside me. Once he sabotaged the two outboard motors, cutting any lines he could find, uncaring what he cut, only needing to render the boat inoperable, he flashed the "okay" sign. I popped my head out of the water and slowly climbed far enough to see over the transom to confirm Guy wasn't at the helm.

Then I heard a guttural groan. All of the emotions I'd crammed aside during the swim sprang to life.

All of the fury.

All of the malice.

I shot over the side.

"*Logan!*" Lauren growled.

The sound of her voice cut me to the quick.

"Say my fucking name!" Guy roared.

I hit the cabin door with my shoulder. The flimsy door gave way and my blood instantly boiled.

Lauren on the bed wearing her panties and my t-shirt, twisting and moaning loudly. Guy only in a pair of boxers. My gaze zipped around the room, praying I found a weapon —a knife, a gun, a plastic fucking fork would do. Anything to justify killing this motherfucker in self-defense.

"Logan," Lauren whined and thrashed around.

I was shoved from behind, propelling me toward the

bed, and Matt rushed by me. Guy slammed into the wall, taking the full impact of Matt's power punch to the jaw.

I pushed aside my need for vengeance and rushed to Lauren.

"Ren, stop twisting for a minute."

Drake tapped me on the shoulder before a handcuff key appeared.

Always prepared.

"I can't," she panted.

"I know, baby, just let me get this off you."

The moment I did she launched herself at me and attacked. I went back on one foot before I regained my balance, then I twisted so I was sitting on the edge of the bed with Lauren's limbs wrapped around me.

Fucking hell.

"You've gotta control it."

"Can't," she moaned.

Jesus Christ.

"Grab that motherfucker and clear the cabin."

Matt unceremoniously yanked an unconscious Guy off the floor and dragged his ass up the three steps without care or concern of causing bodily harm.

"I'll call Liberty in. We'll get off the boat."

Thank God, Drake understood without me having to tell him.

There was zero chance I would give in to Lauren's pleas, but her body would do things she didn't want it to do, and I'd be damned if anyone heard.

The cabin cleared and the door slammed shut. Lauren hadn't stopped rubbing herself against me.

"You're safe now, baby."

"Logan!" she mewed.

"I know, Ren. I got you."

"I can't stop it." Her breath was coming out in short choppy breaths.

"I know you can't."

She shoved her face in my neck, tightened her legs around me, and sobbed while she lost control.

"I love you, Lauren. So damn much, baby."

Her breath hitched and she moaned while clawing at my back.

My vision blurred and my anger soared.

I was utterly helpless. There wasn't a fucking thing I could do but hold her until the drugs cleared her system.

"I...love...you...only...you."

Her teeth sank into my skin and I relished the pain. Needed it to keep me grounded. Needed it to prove to me she was in my arms and alive.

31

"Explain to me again why Matt wants us to meet him on a Wednesday night to play pool."

I waited for Logan to answer but he didn't. I looked up from zipping up my boot to find him staring at the new bookshelf he'd put together last night for me. He hadn't seen it adorned with frames and knickknacks yet since I'd gotten home from work before him and gotten busy.

A lot had changed in the two months since Guy kidnapped and drugged me.

Everyone had rallied around me. Once the girls ascertained I was good and wasn't burying any trauma they backed off. The men—that was all the men I worked with, the Uncles, but mostly Logan didn't back off. They'd pushed protective to such an extreme I lost my mind. They were freaking me out and making it worse by hovering. Jasper had words with the men and they slowly eased back, even Logan. But I suspected that was because for the first two weeks after he'd saved me, Logan didn't sleep. He watched over me waiting for me to wake up in the middle of the night in the throes of a nightmare. When that never happened and each day he saw me going happily about my business he realized I was telling the truth and I was okay.

I had him, the best friends anyone could ever ask for, a great job, great bosses who were more family than employers. I also had Logan's family and they were awesome. After talking to Emily I decided to call my parents and give them a modified version of what happened. She explained that no matter how distant the relationship they loved me and should be told. That conversation led to my mom sobbing but quickly pulling herself together. It also led to my dad speaking with Logan. I didn't hear the conversation but it lasted awhile. Whatever Logan said to my dad put him at ease and they decided to come out to Georgia during the next down-season. That didn't make me feel bad, or unloved, or anyway at all really. That was just how it was with my parents.

And the house had been completely transformed. It was no longer empty. I'd been on a mission to make Logan's house our home.

I had to admit at first this was in an effort to keep my mind occupied so I wouldn't think about what happened. It was also my way of wiping away the bad memories—not mine, Logan's. I couldn't remember how I got on the boat. I wasn't sure if I heard Guy break in, or if I was scared or tried to get away. Guy had admitted he gave me a sedative and when I was checked out at the hospital that was confirmed. The doctor had explained that memory loss was normal and most likely I'd never get back those hours before I woke up on the boat. I was almost thankful, I couldn't remember. What I struggled with was, Logan feeling the terror of walking into our bedroom seeing what he saw, knowing I'd been taken and I didn't. My first clear memory was waking up on the boat and being terrified.

I also knew that Logan had rescued me before Guy could violate me. And I remembered Logan holding me while the drugs took over my body. Through it all he told me he loved me, he whispered that I was safe, he told me it was okay to give in to what was happening. It was that permission, the reminder that no matter what, I was safe with Logan, that allowed me to not feel shame. I had no control over what was happening. And the harder I tried to stop it the more painful it was.

It had taken longer than I'd thought for Logan to snap. And it happened in the weirdest of ways. Me, Chelsea, Liberty, Quinn, Hadley, Shiloh, and Addy were in the conference room at TC talking about our plans for Inspire —that was the name of our new business venture. Liberty had given up the ghost of naming it Women, Inc when she realized Hadley would never budge. We'd finished going over the plans for our first fundraiser when Quinn was scrolling through Facebook looking for non-profits we could partner with when she stumbled upon a meme. She got out the first sentence, "Did you know a woman can have twenty orgasms in one go?" when in an unfortunate stroke of bad timing Logan stepped into the room. His face turned a shade of red that was close to the color of a strawberry. His jaw locked, his eyes turned glittery in a scary way, and his fists clenched.

Then he was gone.

He'd spent two hours in the gym with the men. I didn't interrupt and I didn't question his response. I was just happy to see he'd wrapped his knuckles seeing as the heavy bag was no longer hanging when he was done.

The one positive from the whole experience was Logan and I grew closer. For me, it was knowing he'd been there for me during the worst moments of my life. From the time the power was cut to when Logan had found me it had been a little over three hours and it had taken another thirty minutes for the drug to wear off. Apparently, that was the 'downside' of Guy's date rape drug—the short lifespan of the drug meant the woman or man had to drink more and more and that was when the overdose happened. None of the other women interviewed remembered drinking more. But they reported their ordeals had lasted hours and I could understand that. If Logan hadn't told me it had only been half an hour I would've said the same thing.

Not being in control of my body was terrifying and perplexing. There were contradicting thoughts battling in my head. But I had Logan to hold me through it. I tried to talk to him about it once, help him understand that I was okay. After a few minutes, he shut down the talk explaining that he would have to see it to believe it. So, every day I showed him I was coping.

I was dizzily happy.

I had Logan.

"You know after you were taken I was in our room thinking about how bare the walls were. There wasn't even a picture of us together."

Uh-oh.

His gaze came to mine and his eyes pinned me on the couch.

"Thank you, baby."

I didn't know what he was thanking me for.

I glanced at the shelf and looked at the picture of him and me that I'd had printed. It was from Quinn's wedding. My dress was beautiful and Logan looked totally hot in his suit. Then I took in the one next to that. It was a group shot from a barbeque at Lenox and Lily's house to celebrate Hadley's pregnancy and the birth of baby Ford. Shiloh had been taking a picture of Matt, Logan, and Luke when I jumped on Logan's back and photobombed the picture. Logan had a look of shock on his handsome face but the rest of us were caught mid-laugh. I had all sorts of family pictures around the house. We also now had guest bedrooms and artwork up on the walls.

It was our home.

"Why are you thanking me?"

Now that my boots were on and I was ready to go I stood up. As soon as I was on my feet Logan hooked me around the waist and pulled me close.

"Babe."

"Babe, what?"

Logan dipped his head and kissed my shoulder. "I love this shirt."

"You do?"

"You were wearing it the night of our first kiss. But you had on jeans instead of a skirt."

I couldn't believe he remembered that. I didn't even remember what I was wearing that night.

"Replay?" I asked.

Logan's eyes lit with humor and he smiled. "New rules."

"Same game?"

"Oh, yeah, but this time that skirt's gonna be around your waist, and your panties will be dangling from your ankle while I fuck you against that wall."

"Scandalous," I teased.

We arrived at Balls and I only saw familiar cars and trucks in the lot. Logan parked his new 4Runner and I jumped out. That was another part of the "a lot had changed." I was surprised when Logan took us to the Toyota dealership and he got an SUV instead of a sports car like he'd had. His explanation was "You can't put kids in a 'Stang, baby." My belly had done a flip-flop and I followed him home, me driving his new vehicle and him in the company Suburban.

"The door's locked," Trey said as we approached.

Over the last month, Matt had been behaving so secretively I was beginning to think he was hiding a girlfriend and he was using tonight to introduce us. What other reason could there be to invite all of us out for pool in the middle of the week?

It was odd.

"Are you sure?" Addy asked.

Trey stepped aside and motioned for his fiancée to try.

The door opened and Addy beamed a bright smile.

It was Matt's appearance standing in the doorway that told me he'd unlocked it from the inside at just the right moment, but Addy wasn't going to let an opportunity to bust Trey's chops pass by with something as pesky as the truth.

"Just needed a woman's touch."

"I could use a woman's touch," Echo muttered, and Logan stiffened beside me.

There had been no word from Jackie or Echo about what had happened between them. I'd tried to gently coax it out of her but she blew me off. I asked Jill if Jackie had said something to her and Jill said Jackie wasn't talking. And Logan refused to ask Echo straight out so I had to go to Shiloh. She reported that Echo was behaving like a bear with a thorn in his ass and anytime she brought up Jackie's name he acted like he didn't know who she was talking about.

But I hadn't seen Echo with a woman since Jackie had

left. Not that I'd *ever* seen Echo with a woman but it was good news he didn't have a girlfriend.

"Come in," Matt invited and opened the door farther.

Trey caught the edge and motioned everyone to enter before him.

The first thing I noticed was the pool hall no longer smelled of stale beer. The second was the inside was completely remodeled.

"Welcome to Balls Deep Billiards and Bar." Matt excitedly pointed to the new signage above the bar.

"Holy shit, you did it!" Logan laughed.

Matt shrugged and smiled.

"Drinks are on the house," Matt offered. "But don't get used to it. I'm in the business to make money, not supply you animals with free booze."

"Right, because you're in danger of running out of money."

"A rich man spends money. A smart man saves it."

"And you just happen to be lucky enough to be both," Trey put in.

The crowd dispersed to take in the newly remodeled space. Despite the raunchy play on words, Balls Deep was pure class.

"Holy crap, this place is awesome."

Everywhere I looked my eyes landed on something new. The walls were a matte Navy blue. New faux wood flooring had been laid. The bar was completely redone in dark wood. A mirror was mounted behind the bar with glass shelves to display all the booze, with cool as hell up-lighting. The ceiling no longer had the dingy whiteish-yellow dropdown tiles; those had been replaced with distressed corrugated tin. The back wall was accented with horizontal planks of wood, *Balls Deep* stenciled over the wood. New billiard tables and high-top bar tables completed the room.

The remodel alone must've cost a fortune.

"You ready to check out the bathrooms?" Logan whispered.

I tilted my head back and to the side so I could see his face.

"I think we better. It would suck if Matt put so much work into the remodel and forgot to spruce up the restroom."

"Yeah, that would suck, baby."

Logan grabbed my hand and marched me through the space. We were at the mouth of the hall and I thought we'd gotten away with our bathroom rendezvous when out of the corner of my eye I caught Quinn smiling. With a quick wink, she went back to her conversation with Liberty and Chelsea.

Then I was in the bathroom. Logan flipped the lock and backed me up against the wall.

He went down to his knee but then nothing.

He just stared up at me.

"Marry me?"

Say what?

"What?" I whispered.

"The first time I saw you I knew. It took me a year to find the courage to kiss you. It took you by my side to realize what happiness is. It took me loving you to understand how beautiful it is. But it took you loving me to understand peace. Marry me, Lauren."

"You've got the shittiest timing."

Logan smiled.

"Marry me, Ren."

"Yes."

One could say my man liked my answer. He surged to

his feet, shoved his hand in his pocket, and pulled out a beautiful ring. The diamond was so large I had to blink twice to make sure I wasn't seeing things. Though I didn't have time to comment after he slipped it on my finger.

His mouth came over mine and just like the first kiss we shared in this bathroom he didn't start slow and tease—he raided. He didn't coax—he demanded. And just like every kiss since then, it was aggressive, insistent, commanding. And like always I willfully followed every glide, every stroke, every brush until I was lost in sensation.

I was so enthralled with our kiss I missed him pulling up my skirt and his hand going into my panties.

"Wet," he mumbled against my lips. "Hop up, baby."

I did as I was told and felt the tip of his erection nudging my entrance. I guess I missed him unbuckling his pants, too. What could I say, Logan was good with his mouth. I tended to lose track when he was kissing me.

"Push your panties to the side for me."

My hand was still between my legs when he drove his hips forward and filled me.

"Logan," I whispered.

"I never thought it possible," he returned my whisper.

"Thought what was possible?"

"To love someone so much you'd give up oxygen to keep them."

I smiled against his lips and said, "You've got super shitty timing, honey. When you say sweet stuff like that it puts me in the mood to give you my mouth. But there's zero chance of my knees ever touching a bathroom floor."

"Later."

"We'll see."

"Yeah, Ren, we will see what you look like sucking me off in our bed."

"Whatever."

"Baby?"

"Yeah?"

"Love you."

After that Logan kissed me.

And all rational thought fled.

32

Matthew Kessler

"We need more champagne."

If it had been anyone but Quinn I would've said no but I had a soft spot for the spitfire. Quinn Lancaster amused me. She was bold and said whatever popped into her head even if she knew it was going to piss her brother, cousins, dad, or husband off. She didn't back down from anyone. I admired that. But she also knew when to admit she was wrong.

Brice was one lucky sonofabitch.

"I think you need water," I teased, already slipping off my bar stool.

"Brice is driving," she slurred. "And this is my last hurray, or is it hoorah?"

"Why is this your last hoorah?"

"Because starting next week we're trying for a baby. And Brice has bionic swimmers." She wagged her eyebrows, nodded her head, and smiled.

The girl was crazy.

"I wish you the best of luck with your endeavors."

"I don't need luck. I have super sperm."

"Right. Please don't ever talk about your husband's sperm to me again."

"Why are men so touchy about their penises?"

"Girl, we're not touchy about *our* penises, we're touchy about discussing other men's penises. Specifically other men's sperm."

Quinn busted out laughing and threw her hand out to balance herself on the bar.

"We have a lot to celebrate." Quinn changed topics, thank God.

"Yup."

"Will you have something to celebrate soon?"

"Um. You're sittin' in my brand new bar, drinking my booze. I thought we were already celebrating me."

Her nose crinkled and she leaned in close. "We are celebrating the bar. The bar is awesome. I love the bar. But I was talking about you celebrating a woman."

I felt my lips twitch and I returned her conversational stage whisper. "Fear not, Quinn, I celebrate women all the time."

Her eyes narrowed and she shook her head.

What? She brought it up.

"Thought you wanted more champagne," I prompted.

"Oh. Right. Yes, please."

Yep, Brice was lucky. So were Brady, Trey, Drake, Luke, and the newly engaged Logan. I never thought I'd see my friend date a woman, let alone fall in love and get married. If any of us deserved to be happy, it was Logan. He and Brady both had shitty childhoods. Scratch that—horror-filled childhoods. A nightmare's nightmare of fathers.

I made my way to the back room when I heard a muffled cry. I turned back and looked around the bar, tallying the couples to make sure I didn't walk into something that would lead to years of awkwardness. Everyone was accounted for but Addy's friend Chelsea. I hadn't opened to the public yet and double-checked the front door was locked after Trey had let everyone in.

What the hell?

I walked deeper down the hall and heard it again. When I rounded the corner I saw her. Pretty, long brown hair curtained around her equally pretty dipped-down face. Both hands up covering her mouth. Ass against the wall but she was bent slightly at the waist and her shoulders were shaking.

Fuck. This was the only time I didn't know what to do with a woman. When the tears started I bailed. Not because I was an ass, but crying women scared the hell out of me.

Chelsea's head came up, I saw her suck in a breath, and she straightened. Red-rimmed startled eyes came to me and I stopped breathing.

Many times I contemplated asking Chelsea out but she was Addy's friend. Actually, she was close to all of the women. If things went bad, it would be awkward so I'd steered clear. Though right then with her flushed face and wounded eyes I couldn't remember why.

"Should I get Addy for you?"

"No. Please don't bother her."

"Doubt Addy would think it's a bother seeing as you're cryin'."

Chelsea's back snapped straight and her shoulders stiffened.

"I'm not cryin'."

"All right."

"I'm *not*," she snapped.

Whatever you say, sweetheart.

"Do you wanna use the bathroom in my office to wash up?"

Wounded turned to cynical in one-point-two seconds.

"Why are you being nice to me?"

"Come again?"

"You normally avoid me. Why are you being nice?"

What the hell?

"Are you sure you're not mixin' me up with someone else?"

"No, Matthew, I'm not mixing anything up. Anytime I'm around you avoid me."

"Are you drunk?"

Those chocolatey brown eyes I'd thought way too much about got squinty and one hand went to her hip. Maybe she'd spent too much time with the women of TC; she had their signature pissed-off pose down pat.

"No, I'm not drunk. But I wanna know what I did to make you walk out of a room every time I enter it."

Because you make me forget all the reasons why I can't touch you.

"Alright. You first; tell me why you're crying."

"So you admit it," she pushed.

"Sure, I'll play along and admit I avoid you if you tell me why you're standing in the back room of my bar by yourself, cryin'."

Her hand came off her hip and in an unfortunate twist, she crossed her arms in front of her which only exaggerated her cleavage.

"My sponsor called to inform me they're pulling their money for the next season. And right after that, I got a call from my ex telling me I have two days to move my horses off his property because his new woman doesn't like the smell of horse shit. Forget that I have a lease and rent his property.

So now I've gotta find a new place to board my babies that doesn't cost a fortune because the only thing Todd was ever good for was the discount on the use of his barn." Chelsea sucked in a breath and said, "Your turn."

I'd heard Chelsea was some sort of rodeo princess. She'd hooked up with Addy when she needed physical therapy after an injury but I didn't know anything beyond that.

"I'll sponsor you."

"No."

"Let me rephrase—the bar will sponsor you."

"Let me repeat, no. Pony up, Matt; I told you now you tell me."

I'd rather play 'you show me and I'll show you.' But that offer wasn't on the table. Nor would it be.

"I avoid you because I think you're a beautiful woman."

Those insanely pretty eyes narrowed again and she shook her head. "I didn't take you for the type."

"What type?"

"The lying kind."

Was she crazy?

"Woman, have you looked in a mirror? You're gorgeous."

"So, what, you have a phobia of pretty women?"

"Gorgeous," I corrected. "And no, not all of them. Just the ones I have filthy thoughts about. Correction—the ones I have filthy thoughts about when I can't act on 'em."

Chelsea's mouth fell open, then she clamped it closed and stared at me like I'd lost my mind.

"Don't look at me like that. You asked."

"Why can't you act on them?"

Yup, Chelsea Sullens was crazy.

"Because you're close to my friends' women."

"And that matters because?"

Maybe it was the attitude she was throwing my way.

Maybe it was the months of lusting after a woman I'd deemed untouchable, yet I couldn't turn off my attraction even though I had done what she accused me of and avoided being alone with her. But there was something in the way she was staring at me that made me step closer.

"Because if something goes bad it might be uncomfortable."

"So you don't think I'm mature enough to act like a woman and not a hissy-fit-throwing girl?"

"That's the problem, Chelsea. I know you're a woman."

"Why's that a problem?"

I was close enough she had no other option but to lean against the wall or stand nose to nose with me.

She didn't lean back. Instead, she held her ground. Not only that, she smiled.

"Dare you?" she whispered.

Accepted.

My mouth slammed over hers and she tasted like a dream. The kind you wake up from and immediately wanted to roll over and go back to sleep to find it again.

Unfortunately, the next morning when I woke up my life turned into a nightmare.

Up next Matthew and Chelsea in Tainted.

Click here to order your copy.

BE A REBEL

Riley Edwards is a USA Today and WSJ bestselling author, wife, and military mom. Riley was born and raised in Los Angeles but now resides on the east coast with her fantastic husband and children.

Riley writes heart-stopping romance with sexy alpha heroes and even stronger heroines. Riley's favorite genres to write are romantic suspense and military romance.

Don't forget to sign up for Riley's newsletter and never miss another release, sale, or exclusive bonus material.

Rebels Newsletter

Facebook Fan Group

www.rileyedwardsromance.com

facebook.com/Novelist.Riley.Edwards
instagram.com/rileyedwardsromance
bookbub.com/authors/riley-edwards
amazon.com/author/rileyedwards

ALSO BY RILEY EDWARDS

Riley Edwards

www.RileyEdwardsRomance.com

Takeback

Dangerous Love

Dangerous Rescue

Gemini Group

Nixon's Promise

Jameson's Salvation

Weston's Treasure

Alec's Dream

Chasin's Surrender

Holden's Resurrection

Jonny's Redemption

Red Team - Susan Stoker Universe

Nightstalker

Protecting Olivia

Redeeming Violet

Recovering Ivy

Rescuing Erin

The Gold Team - Susan Stoker Universe

Brooks

Thaddeus

Kyle

Maximus

Declan

Blue Team - Susan Stoker Universe

Owen

Gabe

Myles

The 707 Freedom Series

Free

Freeing Jasper

Finally Free

Freedom

The Next Generation (707 spinoff)

Saving Meadow

Chasing Honor

Finding Mercy

Claiming Tuesday

Adoring Delaney

Keeping Quinn

Taking Liberty

Triple Canopy

Damaged

Flawed

Imperfect

Tarnished

The Collective

Unbroken

Trust

Standalone

Romancing Rayne

Falling for the Delta Co-written with Susan Stoker

ACKNOWLEDGMENTS

To all of you – the readers: Thank you for picking up this book and giving me a few hours of your time. Whether this is the first book of mine you've read or you've been with me from the beginning, thank you for your support. It is because of you I have the coolest job in the world.

Made in the USA
Middletown, DE
21 January 2024

48196974R00179